Shooting Sdax

V. Jolene Miller

FIRST EDITION

www.authorsinkalaska.com

ISBN: 978-1-7335552-0-3

DEDICATION

To Anji Audley, for a childhood of best friend memories and asking for Starr's story. This book is for you.

In honor of those who devote their lives to the helping field. In memory of those who have lost the battle.

CONTENTS

ACKNOWLEDGMENTS

I owe a great deal of thanks to several people. Celeste Ryane, thanks for the great discussion about the wounded child concept and helping me discover the word to use when identifying Sdax and Oscar. Jen Morrisett, you always make time to be my first reader and give critical feedback. My books would be garbage without you. When I asked Laura Karr if I could take pictures of her house because "it reminded me of Starr and Geoff's place" she didn't laugh. Laura is awesome like that. Thanks Trevor for gifting me books about Oscar Wilde to help me develop Morris' character. Minnie Simon, thank you for introducing me to Hooper Bay and giving me an incredible tour of your hometown. Not only were you kind enough to connect me to people who proved valuable resources for this book and the next one, you make amazing pork chops too! You are a dear friend and I'm grateful to have you and your boys in my life. Ellen Wuerffel and Patricia Fick, thank you for taking the time to share your stories and experiences with me. May God bless the work you do in the mission field. Travis Burks, thanks for the unexpected but always appreciated support. Congratulations...you're immortal now. I'm excited to see where your character goes in book 3. Shooting Sdax wouldn't be complete without incredible beta readers like Berntina Sankwich, who finds all my spelling and typographical flaws and Tara Bertone, a fellow 10Minute Novelist with a background in mental health. Cathy Walker, thank you for another stunning book cover. Many thanks to Michele Mathews for her editing services. A great big thank you to Wassilene Pleasant for helping me with Yup'ik spelling and reading parts of this book to make sure it is culturally appropriate. Jonathan, my fabulous husband, I'm so thankful you took me to San Francisco and treated me to the San Francisco Writers Conference in 2014, giving me the perfect city to tell Starr's story. Your unwavering support of this most expensive hobby of mine makes me so glad I married you.

CALRICARAQ

Healthy living.
Never lance it.
Splay the wound, Wider still.
Scoop the poison, thick like pulp.
Weep and mourn.
Grieve.
Wail.
Caress it.
Lovingly, Bid goodbye.
Wash with tenderness.
Wrap.
Rest.
Begin to heal.
Calricaraq.

WAR OF THE WISPS

Wisps are everywhere. Little no-grows housed inside and alongside their respective carapace. Petulant, scatterbrained, and full of their own childish, irrational ideas. Some helpful, some not. Traumatized or idealized, wisps are the miniature versions of adults. Seen only by one another and their respective adults, wisps round out the population to double what the census man marks on his forms. The census man's wisp uses crayon when he decides to help his adult finish his job.

Though strong and capable of resilience, many wisps suffer stunted emotional health. Their attitudes are built on unresolved pain and trauma. Fuel their fear and anxiety, you might find yourself in the center of a temper tantrum or plunged into the deep end of the pool in an irrational game of holding your breath. In those instances, if you give them what they want, you might regret it. Tread carefully. Wisps are everywhere, and they're watching.

The single easiest way to find out how you feel about someone? Say goodbye.

~Phil Knight

CHAPTER ONE

Evening was on its way. Starr Randel stood on Steiner Street examining the houses like they were a row of hookers, and she was trying to decide which one to bed down for the night. Each house was three stories tall, and they reached into the clouds where they mingled with mythical creatures who danced until the rain came. Starr checked the note on her iPhone: 1368 Steiner Street. She was right where she was supposed to be, yet her boyfriend, Geoff Stone, was nowhere in sight.

"Now what?" Starr muttered. She rummaged through her oversized purse and dug out a compact. Flipping the lid, she examined her face closely in the round mirror. "I should be glad he's not here. I look awful."

Starr slouched her shoulders belying her five-foot nine-inch height. Her dark brown hair was ratty. Between the flight, the layover, and the cab ride, the look she'd started her day with was gone. Her long bangs had been held back with a barrette that disappeared hours ago, lost somewhere on her cross-country commute. The quiet smile she infrequently shared replaced by a frown and an occasional nervous tic in her cheek from the stress. Trying not to cry, she held the compact between her teeth and struggled to finger comb her hair into a more becoming look before checking her reflection again.

"How is it possible I look worse now?" she moaned.

Her precocious wisp, the eternal six-year-old wounded version of Starr, pirouetted for the empty sidewalk. Clad in a plaid jumper and black patent leather shoes, Sdax grinned. She liked showing off her missing front tooth. Her dark eyes matched Starr's exactly but held a sparkle that faded with Starr's age. After a stretch and a wiggle, Sdax took a bow. The hazy blue wisp was a combination of timid and rambunctious. Her single determination in life was to wear a fancy party dress at Starr's celebration of life. All she had to do was convince Starr to die.

"This house is giant, giant, giant," Sdax said, rising up on her toes.

All the rectangular windows were empty except the one next door to Geoff's where a lone cat perched. Starr, surrounded by two large suitcases, a carry-on satchel, and her gigantic purse, fidgeted beneath the cat's watchful eyes. Her purse was filled to the brim and so heavy, her shoulder ached from carrying it. Starr stretched her neck and rolled her head from side to side. She looked at the highest windows trying valiantly not to look like a peeping Jane. Still, only the cat watched her. It reminded Starr of her old cat Stanlie, an aging tuxedo cat she'd gifted to her former client, Rachel James. The decision had been spontaneous, brought on by Rachel's report of her young son who couldn't stop talking about cats. Rehoming Stanlie had seemed appropriate following Geoff's invitation to move to San Francisco. A pang of loneliness and regret sucker punched her.

Starr tried not to cry. "You're easily amused," she said. Starr let her purse slide off her shoulder and land on the sidewalk. It pitched forward but stopped before her belongings shifted and fell out. "Thank God."

"So cool." Sdax twirled, trying to get the cat to notice her.

Starr snickered and scanned the area that was her new neighborhood. Steiner Street was a one-way. At the end of the block on the right was a corner deli. Next to it, a small walk-in coffee shop. It's neon "Open" sign was dark. There were matching row houses from where Starr stood to the stop sign, and across the intersection were more row houses. Only a few young trees populated the area, planted neatly in holes dug into the sidewalk. Starr looked the other way. There was more of the same—row houses and trees. Across the street and catty-corner to where she stood was a large empty lot. It looked like a park without equipment. A tall, thin sign had writing on it that Starr couldn't read from the distance.

Not a soul walked past, so she plopped down on the biggest suitcase right in the middle of the sidewalk and looked back at Geoff's house. "Cool? He better not expect me to clean that place by myself."

Starr met Geoff over a year before during what turned out to be the biggest mental health case she had ever worked. Her client, Rachel James, had discovered she was kidnapped at birth and had to make tough decisions about what family meant to her. Through it all, Geoff was kind. He helped her manage stress. They took long walks together with his dog Bridgette. Starr balked at first. She wasn't one for dating or traditional relationships. She preferred a life of introverted solitude. Once she agreed to that first walk, things progressed quickly. Movie dates, dinners out, weekend brunch, and invitations from Geoff to stay the night at his place. Though Starr repeatedly affirmed her disbelief in couplehood as well as marriage, she continued to accept Geoff's invitations. By the time the James' case began to wind down, the media fallout from it ramped up, and Geoff took a job in San Francisco. They continued their long-distance relationship though Starr expected whatever flame Geoff had for her would eventually diminish and snuff out completely. But he upped the ante and suggested a cross country move from her home in nowhere Indiana to San Francisco, California.

Maybe it was the fact Geoff hadn't been traditional that tipped the scales for Starr. It was nice to think he loved her, and since he wasn't down on one knee, she figured it was possible to continue growing their relationship in a non-traditional sense. A spiritual joining of lives, perhaps. If marriage presented itself, she would keep her last name. Separate finances, no kids. There was potential in a plan like that. So Starr accepted Geoff's offer. A few flights and a taxi later, she was deposited on his front door step.

Starr rubbed the heel of her shoe against the sidewalk in frustration. "Maybe it's things like this that make women demand a ring and a date before they say, 'I do.' At least then they're guaranteed to have a house key," Starr said. She shook her phone as if doing so would cause Geoff to respond to the three texts she'd sent since the plane landed hours ago.

Sdax's infatuation with the cat grew, and she called to him, ignoring Starr's mood. "Here kitty, kitty. Here, kitty."

Pressing the Bohemian style skirt against her legs, Starr was thankful the weather was comfortable. It was her anxiety making her sweat. She twirled the layered ring on her left finger reserved for a wedding band—a symbol of the question that was haphazardly mentioned but never formally asked. The ring and her bracelets doubled as Starr's coping mechanisms. For the most part, she practiced what she preached to her clients. Besides, it was better to look stylish than crazy when resisting the pull of self-mutilation.

She found most of her jewelry at antique malls on her days off, choosing the ones that called to her. Bracelets were her favorite. Thick, thin, metal, wood, or beaded, it didn't matter. What mattered was the sense of calm they gave her. The others she'd found in an old cigar box she received shortly after her aunt Cecilia's death. With them was a stash of yellowed letters tied with a faded purple ribbon. Starr tucked them away, never giving them another thought until she cleaned out her small one bedroom back home and made the trek to San Francisco. She shipped ahead all but the luggage at her feet and the letters sat waiting to be unpacked somewhere in the gargantuan row house in front of her.

"There are worse things, right?" Starr asked her wisp. "Worse than being out here on a nice day?" But she couldn't think of anything other than her craving for a cigar, the kind her aunt used to smoke. She inhaled deeply, pretending to suck in the sweet tar, and put her head in her hands, covering her eyes against the dread she felt.

"Peek-a-boo," Sdax said, giggling. She crouched in front of Starr, dropped her head in her hands, and pulled them away in glee.

A smile tugged at the corners of Starr's mouth. It'd been the two of them against the world for so long. "Ha ha. I hope your shenanigans keep you entertained when we're living in a cardboard box."

"Peek-a-boo."

"You realize that's going to happen, don't you?"

"I said, peek-a-boo."

"Fine. Peek-a-boo right back at you."

The little wisp put her hands on her hips. "No, like this," she insisted and demonstrated a proper stance.

"Rascal," Starr said lovingly and followed directions only to shriek and jump to her feet when she opened her eyes. "Shit, Sdax!" Starr sidestepped the line of ants making their way under the hem of her skirt. A few feet away, she smacked her hips, legs, and backside twisting and turning until she was satisfied they weren't crawling on her. "You could have told me I was sitting in a pile of bugs," she growled.

Her little wisp sat stone still, crouching above the ants. It scared her when Starr swore and yelled, reminding her of when they were little and frequently banished to Starr's bedroom for being too loud, too annoying, or too childlike. Sdax opened her mouth to apologize, but before she could, she shimmered brightly and faded into the color of air. Someone was coming.

"Is that some newfangled video call you're on?" The question came from a woman, age undetermined. She was well endowed with curly brown hair that poked out from her head in various directions. Her belly sagged some, and she carried the cat from the window. It purred and stared down in Sdax's direction as if he could intuit her presence.

"What?" Starr asked.

"Your phone." The lady tapped an ornate cane against the ground. "You on video with someone? I didn't even hear it ring."

Puzzled, Starr pulled the phone away from her forehead to inspect it. Was she on a video call? The black screen looked back at her. She tapped the home button only to be rewarded with a picture of her and Geoff's smiling faces. They took the picture six months ago, the last time he'd been in Indiana. Starr frowned and wondered again why he insisted on her moving when it was clear by his lack of presence that he didn't want her here. "No. I'm just waiting," Starr told the lady.

"Hmmmph. I guess your shouting is for the rest of our listening pleasure then? You interrupted my piano playing, you know." Her cane bent under her weight as she inspected Starr from head to toe. She pointed her cane at Starr's luggage. "From the looks of it, you're the one he told me about."

"Okay," Starr replied.

"Now, I'm no holy roller like your friend, but you can keep your language to yourself."

"My language?"

The woman snorted. "I've said my fair share of curse words back in my day, but 'shit Sdax' is a new one."

At the sound of her name, Sdax fizzled back into her blue aura and sidled up to Starr, hiding in the folds of her skirt. She knew the woman couldn't see her, but she was still scared.

"Excuse me?" Starr asked.

"You're excused," the lady said. She rubbed the cat against her nose like a tissue. "I'm Mossie Caulton. Ms. Caulton to you. And most people." She held out an arthritic hand.

Ms. Caulton looked down her nose at Starr though she was only a few inches taller. There was something about the way the old woman wore irritability like most people wore clothes. She pulled it over her head and lived in it like her favorite sweatshirt, bulky and warm. At first glance, the material looked inviting only to find it molded to the person wearing it. Mrs. Caulton's irritability was hers alone. She shared it only with those she deemed worthy. Around her mouth were deep laugh lines that looked as if someone held her oval face in one hand while wielding a blade in the other. Though if asked, no one could recall the last time a smile had graced her puss. Was she pushing seventy or only creeping toward her early sixties? It was hard to tell.

"I'm Starr. Randel." Starr was surprised by Ms. Caulton's firm grip. "Sorry if I bothered you."

"I'm used to it. Not that my constant battle with spitfire young people means I want to hear that kind of talk or anything.

You get old, and people forget you still have ears to hear. Keep it to yourself. I know I'm old. I've got no patience for that kind of talk anymore." She glared at Starr. "Shit Sdax. That some kind of new age swearing?"

Sdax peeked around Starr's leg and examined the stranger. All big people were nothing more than carapaces with an inner wisp. Some wisps were wounded and emotionally stunted. Others, happy and healthy. She wanted to know which kind Ms. Caulton had, and she wanted to pet the furry cat so badly. She reached out her hand only to snap it back when she heard someone burst out laughing.

"Pet him already. She can't see you." Two feet away was Ms. Caulton's wisp. She was older than Sdax but younger than Starr and much younger than her adult with the cane. The wisp wore her hair in a ponytail and was clothed in jeans, a button-down shirt, and loafers, surrounded by a slate blue haze, just like the one that surrounded Sdax.

The little wisp bristled. "I know that."

"If you knew that, you wouldn't hide like a baby."

She had a point. "Well, I didn't know then, but now I do."

"Whatever," the wisp said with a shrug.

The words 'shut up' were on the top of Sdax's hazy blue tongue. She was ready to engage in an all-out wisp war, but the cat meowed and Sdax remembered her goal. Pet the cat. Her hand was in motion, reaching slowly for him. Her aura shimmered with excitement. Sdax loved animals, and they her. Wisp fact: Animals are more likely to sense a wisp's presence than the wisp's own adult version. That was why Sdax hesitated. Once she made contact, the cat would respond. With a mewl, a purr, or a hiss even, if he was taken by surprise or if Sdax, in her excitement, pet him too roughly. And then what?

"You're such a baby. Pet him. You know you want to," the older wisp taunted.

Sdax scrunched her nose at Ms. Caulton's inner child. "You're not my mom. I don't have to listen to you."

The older wisp yawned. "Gawd. You sound like her. Like them." She pointed across the street where a group of teenagers shuffled down the sidewalk, sullen and quiet. Mixed in between the four boys and lone girl were smaller versions of them, trailing blankets and teddy bears, trying in vain to keep up. "And like them. And those guys. And that one, too." The wisp jabbed her finger in the direction of the others—all walking alongside their matching adults. A car drove slowly by. The driver's wisp sat on his lap, one hand on the wheel and a thumb in his mouth.

The cat was nearly forgotten as Sdax swiveled around, looking everywhere this older, wiser wisp pointed. "There's so many of them," Sdax said. "So many of us." She rubbed her nose. "I always seed them in ones." She pointed her finger, then bent and straightened it.

"Saw them," the other wisp corrected. "You always saw them in ones. By themselves or alone." She tossed her ponytail. "Have you ever been to the mall? The mall is full of wisps."

Sdax shook her head, and her mop of hair swung in response, kicking up her blue energy. The only time the mall ever came up in conversation was when Starr complained about going to crowded places and how she preferred to find everything she needed and then some online. "We usually just go to Starr's work and home. What's your name?"

"Jomi," the wisp said. "But what about on the plane? I bet you saw tons there and in the airport."

Sdax grimaced. "I closed my eyes."

"Well, they're everywhere here."

"Are they nice?" Sdax asked.

"I guess. Ms. Caulton and I don't get out as much as we used to. She's got a bum knee. But we used to go to lots of places. Now it's church and home, church and the VFW, church and the store. I make her take a vacation every year, though." Jomi jerked her thumb at Starr. "Just tell her you want out more. We're in charge, remember? The more wounded we are, the stronger our pull."

Jomi knew she was right about this and waited for Sdax to acknowledge her superiority. Sdax fidgeted. All she wanted to do was pet the cat. She missed Bridgette, and now being so close to her big, furry dog friend, yet unable to cuddle her, had Sdax on edge. "I guess," Sdax murmured, deciding that Jomi was a truly wounded wisp. Mean and bossy to boot.

"Look," Jomi said, frustrated. "You're stronger than you think. I heard her yell at you. Right here in broad daylight. How did you think I knew you were here in the first place?"

Sdax teared up. "I hate it when she yells."

"Then tell her. Make it clear that you're the wounded one. You're the one she failed to protect, remember? You call the shots. If you want to pet the damn cat, pet it," Jomi demanded.

Sdax trembled.

"What? I suppose you don't like it when people cuss?"

"Huh-uh."

"Alright then. What do you want?"

Sdax spoke so quietly that Jomi couldn't hear. "What?"

"I want a party," Sdax said, surprising even herself. She'd been holding in her wish for ages.

"For real?" Jomi's eyes lit up, and she traced a finger along the cat's spine. It arched its back in response.

In the wisps' world, a party was code for funeral. It was the demonstration of the wounded child's ultimate power and strength. At a party, it meant the wisp had convinced his or her person that the only solution to all of life's problems was solved by being laid to rest. Not an easy task at all considering the human species' vicious will to live.

Sdax giggled and clapped her hands, tickled by the awe she inspired in Jomi. "Uh-huh." As if buoyed by the respect she'd earned, Sdax rubbed her small hand across the cat's nose. Annoyed, the feline yowled and wiggled out of Ms. Caulton's arms. Sdax bounced in delight. Maybe Jomi was right. Maybe Sdax was strong enough to get the party Starr had been hinting at for years.

The wisps laughed and shimmered at Ms. Caulton who hollered at the cat. The old woman waved her cane in anger. As she hobbled after him, she threw a parting jab at Starr. "See what you did? Shit Sdax to you, little lady. Now my Clarence is gone, and I have to chase him."

"See you around, kid," Jomi said as she trotted after Ms.

Caulton. "Be careful what you wish for."

"Bye! Bye," Sdax said excitedly and waved at her new friend.

Starr watched Ms. Caulton go. The entire episode with the woman took less than ten minutes but left her exhausted. Starr wore a bracelet that matched the brown hue in her skirt. She twisted the beads round and round. The motion caught Sdax's eye. She was transfixed. That was the kind of emotion she craved. Sdax faded into Starr until the two became one. Tentatively, she put her hands out like Starr's and helped her human twist the bracelet harder and faster. They stared at the rowhouse together. By the time the yellow taxi pulled up behind them and Geoff jumped out, frantic and apologetic, the streetlights glowed, and the moon had started its ascent. Tears streamed down Starr's face. The skin beneath her bracelet was raw.

Sdax licked Starr's salty tears as they fell and shrunk smaller and smaller as Starr and Geoff shouted at one another. He tried dragging Starr's suitcase to the door while he dug for his keys, but Starr swore and pushed against his chest. She pulled the suitcase by the handle, an instant tug-of-war, as she edged toward the sidewalk to hail another cab, determined to leave.

"You don't even want me here. If you did, you wouldn't have left me standing on the doorstep," Starr shouted.

Geoff's temper flared. "Starr, stop it. I said I'm sorry. You need to calm down. People are staring."

On the other side of the street, a man hurried by. At the sound of their yelling, he paused. He looked across the expanse of Steiner Street and glared at the couple. A rueful shake of his head, and he waved a hand, dismissing them.

Sdax saw the man's wisp, a teenager with earbuds around his neck and Converse on his feet. She waved fiercely, childishly, excited she'd spotted one of her own. But the young man ignored her. He gestured with his hands in an attempt to convey something to his person. She remembered Jomi's words. "I'm stronger than I think," she whispered.

"I'm going home," Starr said. "I won't stay here if I'm not wanted."

"Don't be ridiculous. I was late. That's it. Do we have to start this part of our lives with you nagging me?" Geoff matched Starr's volume. Maybe it was the fact that he raised his voice—something he hadn't planned on doing—that stopped Starr in her tracks. She appeared stunned, and her tirade was cut short. He felt a physical shift in the atmosphere.

Fast as lightning, Sdax folded herself into Starr's angry stance and using Starr's voice blurted, "If you hate me so much, I should kill myself."

Starr's face went blank, and Geoff's crumpled. He choked up. "Hey, no, Starr, honey. Please don't say that. I'm sorry. Really. I'm a jerk." He touched her hand, cautiously coming closer to her, afraid she'd bolt if he moved too fast.

Shocked by her outburst, Starr slumped into his arms. She was exhausted. "I don't know why I said that."

Geoff led Starr inside, and Sdax trailed behind them. She pictured the coffin and beckoned Starr to see it, too. Behind the trio, Geoff's wisp, Ian, followed them in. He repeatedly tapped Geoff on the shoulder, desperate to tell him that the threat was Sdax's idea. But Geoff paid him no mind.

CHAPTER TWO

Starr surveyed her office at Cloverleaf Counseling Center for anything that didn't belong. A previous patient's forgotten hat or glove. A left behind homework assignment, an earring back unknowingly separated from its front. The intern, Julle (pronounced Julie) Sherman, watched her with a curious look.

"It's a trick I learned from my graduate school mentor. 'Never let the current client think you have others.' You should write that down," Starr suggested and handed Julle a notebook and pen.

Starr had mixed feelings about Julle. The spelling of her first name gave a millennial flare to the young graduate student's collegiate aura. Her plaid skirt that fell just above the girl's tanned and shapely legs seemed expertly crafted, like a sexy school girl. Dishwater blonde hair hung down her back with just the right amount of curls. A waterfall of scented locks that Starr wanted to stand beneath. The kind of curls crafted by a large, heated barrel that could also be flat ironed into strands of straw. The make-up, button-down blouse, and tortoise shell glasses pulled the outfit together. Julle was the sexy nerd type, and Starr waited for the intern to realize she'd taken a wrong turn in the career department—social worker instead of a swimsuit model.

She wanted to believe Julle was an excellent protégé. As the veteran therapist in the office, Starr had eagerly agreed to take the young woman under her wing and guide her into Starr's paying position that she'd soon vacate. Starr had been practicing for a decade, and she'd been hired at Cloverleaf Counseling Center after moving to San Francisco. It frustrated her that the Rachel James case helped seal the deal at the interview, but Starr decided it was better to take the job and work toward opening her own private practice.

"The person in your office should believe he or she is the only person who exists in your world," Starr said. A year under her mentor's tutelage, mimicking everything he'd said and did in an effort to be the best therapist she could be, and the office once over had become rote. "I've gotten to the point that I can prevent stray items from lingering based on whichever client I usher out the door. The kids leave the important stuff—the homework. The adults leave the less important things—hats, gloves, reading classes, half empty coffee cups—their own and the Styrofoam ones Cloverleaf provides."

Julle popped her gum and doodled in the notebook. "Seems easy enough."

Frustration gnawed at Starr. How dare this overprivileged scholar belittle her efforts? It was as if she found therapy beneath her. Juvenile even. "Well, it's not. Especially after an emotional session. Once, I held this grieving woman's baby while she processed the death of her husband. Afterward, she walked out without her baby."

"She left her own kid?"

"In her defense, we were both rather stunned by the breakthrough she'd experienced. It didn't even occur to me that she'd forgotten her precious cargo until a couple minutes later. By then I'd steadied myself and was ready to tidy up for my next session."

"It took you that long to realize you were holding a baby?" Julle's disdain for Starr's oversight was apparent in the girl's arched eyebrows.

"I know, right? I freaked out. Thankfully, the woman had opened the sliding door to her minivan when she realized she didn't have her child to put in the car seat."

"What did she do? Run back inside and demand her baby?"

Starr struggled with the fact that Julle focused on the concrete details instead of the meaning behind them. She wanted to teach her about the dangers of triggers and behaviors. But all the girl wanted to know was the who and not the why. "No. I met her in the parking lot. The poor woman's face was flaming red. She was so embarrassed. And I mean, so was I. As a therapist, you're supposed to be calm and rational the whole time, not let someone's sad story get to you. You know? Yet there I'd been, totally overwhelmed by what she was going through that I didn't notice a sleeping baby against my chest."

Julle laughed. "Maybe you should write that down before it happens again, huh?" She held out the notebook.

"Not funny."

"Did she blame you? Or accuse you or anything?"

Starr blushed. Maybe she'd engaged in too much self-disclosure with this girl, who was not her friend. "No. She was upset. Afraid I'd call social services or something." She didn't add that she'd been afraid the woman would call her out. Tell her supervisor or worse, call the licensing board to tell them about her state of duress.

"Does that happen a lot in your field?"

Starr waited for Julle to realize what she'd just said. The seconds ticked by while Julle stared at her waiting for an answer. Starr prompted her. "You mean our field?"

"Hey, look!" Julle squealed. She showed Starr the doodle she'd been working on. "Good, huh?"

"Does what happen in our field?" Starr asked, pushing aside the sketch of a hanged man with a raven circling overhead. "And shred that after. You can't be giving people ideas. It's morbid."

"I'm only joking," Julle ripped the page out and folded it in half inside the notebook's cover. "Therapists, though. Does that happen a lot—where they get in the way? So overwhelmed they can't see what's right there in front of them?" Julle frowned. "I don't think that would happen to me. I wouldn't let someone else's mood control me."

"Aha. See that? A wad of tissue. If I'd overlooked this, my next patient would know I have others." Starr tapped her head. "Always have to stay a step ahead."

Her protégé wrinkled her nose. "Do you feel like a maid

sometimes?"

"The kid who left this is kind of a drama queen. Pretty normal for kids her age. Grace Wu. She'll be one of yours soon. She doesn't get along with her drill sergeant father. He's worried she'll end up like her mother."

Julle stretched and leaned back in the corner chair. She had yet to participate in any of Starr's sessions, and Starr wasn't ready for a set of eyes and ears watching her work. Besides, Julle had yet to ask permission to do so. As of yet, she was content to read case notes and participate in staffing sessions. Even in staffing, Julle's interest for clinical work waxed and waned. Starr wouldn't be able to make a graceful exit, ensuring her clients were well taken care of if Julle didn't develop a love for patient care. Soon.

"Her mother's no good?" Julle asked.

Starr reached into her supply cabinet and pulled latex free gloves out of the box marked '100 small' and shoved the box back inside. "Eh. I don't know about 'no good' but definitely different from the girl's father. She's a free-spirited type. The mother, not the girl. The mom allegedly left the family during a routine grocery store run. I guess she lives in a commune somewhere in Montana and writes heartfelt postcards to her daughter about life on the range."

Julle spit laughter. "Life? On the range?"

"True story." Starr raised her gloved hand in solemn oath. "I've seen the postcards. Occasionally, the girl cries about the whole situation and other times she doesn't. Hard to read her. That's what the gloves are for. No sense in assuming she didn't cry when she did and end up with tears and snot on my hands."

Julle nodded and asked, "Has she seen the cards?"

"The girl? God, no. Her father doesn't want her influenced in any way. He's strict." She ticked his rules off on her gloved hand. "No parties. No boys. No sleepovers. He even has all the passwords to her social media accounts as a preventative measure." She stood ramrod straight and raised a hand in oath. "'There will be no communication between my daughter and that flake.' His words, not mine. He reminds me of the rule every single week."

"Sounds extreme."

"Well, you don't know the whole story," Starr said. She felt a sense of camaraderie and checked to be sure the office door was shut. If Julle asked for details, she'd share them.

"No, the gloves. It seems extreme you'd wear gloves to pick up one possibly soiled tissue."

Starr's hopes flickered and died. She'd missed the cue, and her confidence, already shaky, wobbled hard to one side. She laughed it off. A mild delay in the punchline reaching her. "Might as well give the place a thorough once over since we've got about four minutes before the next one." She started with the Lysol wipes that were in a container in the supply cabinet. She wiped down every hard surface—the end table that sat between two chairs, her keyboard, monitor, door knob (inside and out), the arms of the chairs—and finally ended up at the window where she slowed down and began wiping the blind rod. It had been a long day, and the motion soothed her.

"The girl spent part of our session standing here with her back to me as she twisted and untwisted the rod. It's kind of her 'thing' as she put it." Starr rubbed the rod and noticed the dust caked on the blinds. "Here at Cloverleaf, therapists do it all."

"Really?"

"Most of it. Brandy, receptionist number twelve since I've been here, does the scheduling, and there's someone who takes out the trash. The rest is up to us." She wondered if this was one of the reasons Julle was apathetic to the idea of taking on her caseload.

"What's the rest?"

Starr turned and smiled, desperate to make a connection. Julle didn't reciprocate. Her eyes were locked on her phone. Starr looked away before Julle could be privy to her feelings. "We make our own reminder calls and submit our own billing. Service authorizations when a client needs more sessions. We vacuum, clean, and dust." She heard the words tumble from her lips and backpedaled. "I suppose I should be glad for what I have, considering where I started in life. Silver lining, right?"

"I guess. You've obviously paid your dues, or you wouldn't be heading out the door for the private practice life," Julle said with a smirk.

A flare of anger took root in Starr's belly. She doused the feather duster with Lemon Pledge and jammed it between the blinds. One swipe to the right, one to the left, and then on to the next row until all of them were clean. Cleaner than when she'd started at least. She sneezed as the dust settled down around her shoulders. She closed her eyes. Her decision was final. She would leave this place and open her own practice. No matter how hard or isolating it was. No matter if Julle took on her Cloverleaf clients. Julle was the least of her worries. What mattered, in the moment, was that Starr became self-sufficient. Independent. No longer reliant on Cloverleaf, Julle, her exhaustive list of clients. Geoff. She would fend for herself or die trying.

"You like it here, don't you? You're going to miss this place?" Julle asked.

But it was too late. Starr was done connecting. Done mentoring. Done encouraging. "Cloverleaf rents the bottom suite of this building and a few offices on the top floor. There are a handful of designated parking spaces on the side of the building. And this fantastic view." In one swift motion Starr yanked the cord on her left, and the slats smacked together like dominoes as they rose, revealing the window. She grabbed the bottle of window cleaner and attacked the smudge along the bottom right corner. "We also do our own windows." She sprayed and wiped, sprayed and wiped. Then she used her gloved fingernail to scratch at a particularly stubborn spot. The view cleared as the spray evaporated.

Across the back, a strip of grass separated Cloverleaf, a short, squat building, from another building and its lot. The latter, painted Granny Smith apple green, towered above Cloverleaf. Even the windows and doors were green with a repetitive pattern of squares that covered the surface. To the right was Cloverleaf's dumpster.

"What's with that building?" Julle inquired.

"No one really knows. If you aren't familiar with it, you can't even find the entrances and exits. There's no indication of them anywhere. No signs or directional arrows. Only the street number in black along two of the walls. 1046. Cloverleaf is 1044."

Julle was intrigued. "Any guesses about what's inside?"

Starr kept her eyes on 1046. "Not really. The addresses, theirs and ours, remind me of time. 10:44 and 10:46. I don't know why. Maybe because time seems to stand still when you spend all day in an office listening to people talk about their problems. It's weird." She pulled the cord again and slowly let the blind stretch itself out, an accordion elongated to its full length. Then, like the girl, Starr twisted the rod and watched the blind close. She twisted them again and watched them open. Back and forth, back and forth. The third time she did it, there was movement.

"See?" Starr said. "There's the girl."

Julle arched her neck until she caught a sliver of a girl who walked to the dumpster and lifted the lid. She struggled with its weight, and the lid fell shut.

Starr explained. "After every session, she's rewarded with a bottle of flavored water and a bag of chips from the vending machine. It's the only junk food her father allows."

"That he knows of," Julle said.

"Yes, right?" Starr momentarily forgot her disdain for Julle and leaped across the invisible chasm between them. "That he knows of. Who knows what else the girl is eating and drinking all day at school. Or what she sneaks into the house if he ever leaves her home alone. Anyway, he's anal about their car, so she has to have her snack standing next to it while he drills her about her session. Then she has to put the garbage into the dumpster before they leave. Same routine every week. Sometimes I think she keeps up the sessions for the sake of the snack." By the time she finished talking, Starr was spent and out of breath.

Outside, Grace wiped her hands on the butt of her jeans.

"I think they're called jeggings. Like leggings, only jeans. You know, tight like leggings, but made out of blue jean material. I don't really know. They seem like clothes for young people. I'm more a fan of my style," Starr babbled. The last sentence faltered, lacking the confidence she yearned.

"What's your style?"

21

"Hipster maybe? I guess. Bohemian?" Starr lifted the hem of her skirt and released it.

They watched as Grace tipped her head back and shook chip crumbs into her mouth. She stuck her finger in the bag and licked the salt off her fingers before balling up the sack and tossing it toward the mouth of the receptacle.

"Ope. Wind caught it," Starr said.

Grace floundered for a minute as she yelled at someone—probably her father—behind her. She scurried around the back of the dumpster. The two women lost sight of her. Then, just as quickly, Grace bounced back to their side of the dumpster, trash in hand, and dunked it.

"She got it. Nothing to worr—Did you see that?" Starr jabbed at the clean windowpane.

"See what? She lost her trash in the wind, chased it, found it, and threw it away. Big deal," Julle returned to her chair, bored.

"No, see? She still has something in her hand. Paper or something." Starr tapped the pane again.

Grace did have a piece of paper in her hand. She played it off like it was nothing and loped back to her father's vehicle, tucking the paper in her pocket.

"Maybe it's a tissue or something. I didn't give her any homework today. She was too skittish and had a hard time concentrating. She kept messing with the damn blinds." Starr was puzzled, and she put her hand to her mouth. When she was puzzled, she chewed her nails. She stopped, realizing she still wore the gloves.

"Shoot. We're out of time. I barely have a second to run to the restroom before the next patient. Moses or something. Be right back."

"But what about—" Julle asked.

"Two seconds." Starr removed the gloves and dropped them in the trash can by the door. The hem of her skirt swished around her ankles. Her bangle bracelets rattled against each other as she hurried out.

"Whatever," Julle said and took a final peek out the window.

The guy appeared to be in his late twenties. Too old to be an intern, too young to be a partner in a firm. He wore a pink paisley tie that hung loosely around his neck. His suit was tight, like he wanted to be noticed. His hair was short, but not too short, and curled on the top in boy band fashion. He looked like an average business guy or a dot com type of entrepreneur. He came out from behind the dumpster and headed toward the green building. He didn't carry an office trash can or wear gloves like a pretty boy type would if he was taking out the trash.

"Weird," Julle said and dismissed him.

CHAPTER THREE

At four o'clock in the morning, Starr woke with a jolt. Another bad dream. She tearfully reached for Geoff when she remembered he slept in the guest room and had been for the last three months. She stewed another hour, angry at Geoff and at herself for letting him get to her. When she extricated herself from the queen-sized bed, already in pajamas, she pulled on a pair of fuzzy socks. There was no sense in looking sexy if he didn't want to be with her.

"At least Bridgette doesn't mind spending the morning with me," she muttered, grateful for the large Saint Bernard. As if it wasn't enough she'd been sleeping alone, by evening, she'd be living alone too. She sensed many weepy days ahead.

When Geoff Stone had asked her to take their relationship to the next stage and move to California to be with him, she hadn't wasted any time deliberating. She was emotionally drained from her work as a therapist and the media debacle that occurred following her care and treatment of Rachel James, the last client she had in Indiana. Though Rachel had faced the demons of her past and Starr was happy for her, she'd been left feeling empty and drained from the ordeal. California was supposed to be Starr's fresh start. Hers and Geoff's.

Though still somewhat hesitant about the idea of marriage, Starr had slowly warmed up to it. He was going to give her a beautiful chocolate gold band with a ring of tiny diamonds encircling a gorgeous teardrop centerpiece. The image and all it symbolized made her happy. Starr saw the band as her commitment to Geoff. The center was her whole self, whether in pain or not, and the ring of diamonds were her fiancé's strong arms wrapped around her, always protecting her, always loving her. With her parents, grandparents, and Aunt Cecilia long gone, Starr believed they watched over her and had brought Geoff and Bridgette into her life somehow. Yet things changed between them. A little bit here and some more over there. Geoff took Bridgette for long walks and didn't invite Starr. He worked long hours at the church. The phantom pain in his long-ago amputated leg led him down the hall to the guest bedroom to sleep alone. Talking about the strain in their relationship was a button she didn't want to push for fear that Geoff would decide they were better with many states between them.

Starr watched the coffee maker gurgle to life. She gave Bridgette a scratch on her rump and set up her therapy supplies on the table: laptop, notebook, pen, highlighter, and a couple of therapy reference books. She didn't want to think about her own problems or the fact that Geoff was leaving. She had clients with issues she was intent on resolving and her own therapy practice to open. When the coffee finished percolating, Starr filled her favorite mug and added a shot of hazelnut creamer. She settled in at the dining room table, her feet resting comfortably on Bridgette.

"They say you shouldn't blame your parents, Bridgette, but I've got a host of clients intent on doing just that."

Bridgette snored and rolled over.

"You blame your parents, buddy?" Starr sipped her coffee, gathering the motivation to type. "I don't suppose you can. You were what? Nine weeks old when Geoff adopted you? Scientifically speaking, you wouldn't have memories of your parents at that age."

Bridgette raised her head and emitted a low growl. She stared into the corner of the living room where the fireplace sat dormant.

"Alright, I guess you can have memories at that age. It probably wasn't easy to be separated from them. Painful and confusing even. Though if my parents had left me at that age—

with someone responsible and loving, of course—maybe I'd be different. Wholesome or healed somehow and not this walking wounded version of myself. No history, no answers…" she trailed off. There was no sense in depressing herself before the day even got started.

Bridgette stretched and gave a cavernous yawn. She growled again, though less ferociously, before hoisting herself up. She padded to the fireplace where she nosed around, yapped, and then stepped back again before lunging at the corner of the room.

"What is it, girl?" Starr asked. Unable to see past the dog's hind end, she got up to investigate, coffee mug in hand.

There on the floor, Sdax burrowed herself into the corner. Her knees were drawn up to her chest, and she wrapped her spindly arms around them, her blue tinted hands gripped one another tightly. She wore a dingy pink nightgown that reached her ankles. A faded picture of Rainbow Brite covered the front of the gown. Sdax's doll rested across her knees, and the little wisp rested her head on the doll's torso.

"It's not like you don't know her," Starr told the dog. The last thing she needed today was her wounded wisp stirring up trouble. Wasn't it enough Starr was emotional and about to be abandoned for Geoff's higher calling? "She's nothing to worry about, Bridgette. Nada. You know if we ignore her, she'll go away. And believe me, we're better off without her."

Sdax brushed her messy hair out of her face. "Are you better off without Geoff?" Sdax asked the doll.

Starr pretended not to hear her. "You, me, and coffee is all we need," Starr said to Bridgette. "And my coffee is getting cold."

Being alone made her anxious and jumpy, two feelings she did not handle well. But she despised the thought of being alone with Sdax. The girl had a pull on her that Starr had been trying to shrug off for years. Geoff's absence for the next two months sounded less empty and scary if Sdax wasn't hanging around.

A chill ran the length of Starr's spine as Bridgette poked her nose in the corner and whined again. Starr recalled her grandmother Betty's tales of spirits watching over her. Little people capable of performing magic and transforming themselves into the shapes of willow trees or animals. It was the only thing about her grandmother that had ever frightened her. Starr teased Grandma Betty when she mentioned the spirited little people tramping through the tundra wilderness ready to snatch up unsuspecting children. Starr loved her grandmother dearly and thought her uniquely beautiful despite the scar that took up one side of her face. Betty was self-conscious about the flaw and Starr's only way to combat the scary stories.

"Look at you getting me all worked up over nothing," Starr muttered. She raised her mug halfway to her mouth, ready to turn back to her morning work and get on with her day when Bridgette whirled around and barked with excitement.

"Cheez-its, Bridgette! You scared me to death," Starr yelped as Geoff walked down the stairs. He fastened his belt around his waist.

"Hey," Geoff said.

"Hay is for horses," Sdax said. She was on her feet, bouncing on her tiptoes. She loved Geoff and was always trying to get his attention. Unless he was grumpy, and then she hated him.

"I didn't—You scared me." Starr wanted to cry her eyes out and hug Geoff while begging him not to leave. "I didn't mean to wake you."

She was often taken aback at how much Geoff meant to her. He had a way of making her feel beautiful and safe. He found her thick hair, the color of milk chocolate, attractive. He liked holding her close and breathing in her scent. He took an interest in the fact she loved hazelnut and often joked she wore it like a perfume. She'd even tucked a small can of hazelnut coffee into Geoff's duffel bag for his trip, hoping it would hurry him back home.

Determined to handle his departure like a supportive girlfriend, Starr went to him and wrapped her arms around his middle. He responded, tentatively at first, and then with the deep, crushing kind of hug she would miss terribly. She blinked back tears and breathed deeply as she sunk into his embrace.

"Do you remember when we met?" she asked, her voice

husky with emotion.

Geoff never talked much about how he'd ended up as the receptionist at the agency back in Indiana, but she knew he'd enjoyed his work there. They had both made good friends with their colleagues who often teased Geoff about his constant pursuit of Starr. Everyone said they were a unique match. Starr was a Bohemian hippie while Geoff was a slacks and button-down kind of guy. He was traditional and kept to a schedule. While Starr kept to a schedule for her clients' sake, she had a creative streak spurred by her spontaneous zest for life. A devout altruist, Starr volunteered at soup kitchens on holidays and worked long hours and extra days at the clinic. She was quirky, and they grew together as a couple. They complemented one another.

"I remember," Geoff said, kissing the top of her head. "Best thing that ever happened to me." He stroked her hair lost in the memory.

If it hadn't been for Rachel James, Geoff might have been able to continue his life with Starr in Indiana. Rachel's case garnered national attention and cost Starr more than she would ever make in salary. Starr, who'd given him a reprieve from his old life, became anxious and worried. She hardly slept and smiled even less. He convinced her to take walks with him and Bridgette. He tried talking to her and reassured her often that he was there for her. Nothing seemed to help. Starr was stuck. Geoff was out of ideas, worried that her downward spiral would spread like a virus and cause the same kind of deterioration to him. He convinced himself that a new place and a fresh start would change things for the better and add another layer of forgiveness to the bandage on his soul. It had been a cowardly move, and he knew it.

"I'm lucky, you know. I'm really lucky that fate brought you into my life," she whispered as she squeezed him again.

Geoff's past and luck were not a combination he liked to consider. "You sleep well?" He disentangled himself from her hold.

It was a stupid question considering the lines around her eyes that had been there for weeks. Many nights he'd heard Starr shuffle through the house as if searching for something she couldn't find. She blamed it on her work, but he had a feeling he was somewhat responsible. Their conversation about sleeping arrangements haunted them both—he because of the lie and she because of the distance the lie created. He'd spent the last two weeks thinking of ways to take her with him to Alaska and found nothing. That morning he woke up feeling like a heel.

"Enough," she said, miffed and confused by the change in his tone. "Coffee?"

"I can get it." He was an ass, and he knew it. No matter his love for her, he couldn't bring himself to feel lucky about the events that led up to him meeting Starr. How could he call the deaths of his parents and his role in their demise luck?

Bridgette scooted across the floor on her belly until her nose was between them. She wagged her tail with fervor. She was Geoff's dog but had taken to Starr immediately. Geoff hadn't minded. He preferred Starr over himself. Her kind heart and deep sense of compassion for others had a way of making an average guy like Geoff want to be a better person. Her curves and wit made him want her for his own.

Starr looked into her cup, searching for an answer to a question she hadn't been asked. "I don't mind," she said finally with a weak smile and padded back to her seat at the table.

His plane left at eleven. There was plenty of time for coffee, breakfast, and even a walk to their favorite coffee shop, where Geoff could soak up her presence and stare into her eyes for a while. But that kind of morning required an honesty he couldn't muster. "Okay," he replied.

Bridgette tried to get their attention with a lunge and a yelp. Lately, they were too busy having stilted conversations to notice her or Sdax.

"I'll pet you, Bridgette," Sdax reassured the dog.

Bridgette gave Geoff a mournful look, very aware he hadn't petted her this morning. She waited to see if Starr would call her back and invite her to be a footstool again. But Starr put her feet on the chair opposite herself instead. Bridgette returned to the corner.

Sdax had moved in when Starr did. The two looked alike though the wisp was small and spent most of her time in the corner of whichever room Starr was in, coloring or playing with her doll. Bridgette nuzzled Sdax who rubbed her face into the dog's fur. It was a good feeling. Even though Bridgette couldn't chew on the crayons or the doll, she felt the wisp's kisses on her nose. She circled Sdax a few times and hunkered down beside her. Bridgette groaned but allowed Sdax to rest her doll on her back. Together, they watched the humans.

Starr opened her mouth and began what had become their daily conversation. "How's the pain?"

With his back against the kitchen sink, Geoff sipped his coffee. Unless he advertised it, most didn't know that his right leg was missing, amputated just above the knee following a car accident when he was in high school. Physical therapy, the kind words of a stranger, and a couple of relocations later, he was still outrunning the pain and memories.

"It comes and goes."

Starr wished he'd be more specific. She wanted to know what helped the pain subside. What made it worse? How was he coping? Was it time to see a doctor? She wanted to know if she could help. Would a massage help? More exercise? Less? A cold pack or a heating pad? Yet these were questions she'd asked in the past, and his answers had been as vague as they were this morning. Now when he said the pain came and went, she translated that to mean his feelings for her waxed and waned as well.

"Oh."

"You okay?" Geoff asked.

"Why wouldn't I be?" The question sounded aggressive though she was going for nonchalant. "Just working on some research and my business plan. Busy, you know? A lot on my mind."

Geoff knew. He carried the same burdens. His belief that Starr could break out of Cloverleaf and make it with her own practice clashed with Starr's lackluster belief in herself. He was sure she could make a go of it on her own. But Starr's enthusiasm for this new venture came and went like his phantom pain. She was two months away from hanging her shingle, and he'd chosen those same two months to go on his own adventure.

"You know, you can be successful without the structure and comfort of an agency. There's no sense in leaning on a corporation."

"You keep saying that," Starr replied. She blushed at his praise.

"Anything I can help with?" he asked.

Starr's sidelong glance at his luggage answered his questions. The bags sat in the entryway, a mountain of clothes and gear packed neatly in a large duffel bag and a carry-on backpack. The guilt he felt for leaving slugged him in the stomach and left a bitter taste in his mouth. "Right," he said. "I just meant…" Sorry Charlie. You're the worst.

"I'll manage," Starr said. "You have a lot going on yourself."

When Life Spring Church announced the mission trip to Alaska, Geoff had been intrigued. Who wouldn't be? Two months of village hopping in remote southwest Alaska, teaching Vacation Bible School, and doing construction jobs for the various churches sounded like a challenge and an adventure. The missionaries, members of Life Spring, had spent the previous two years raising funds. Teenagers staged car washes, babysat, and cleaned houses for anyone willing to hire them. The adults dipped into their savings and poured their money into the offering plates that were passed among the pews during each of the three Sunday services. When the money was tallied, the church pastor announced from the pulpit that Life Spring was doubling the money raised, and the congregation leapt to their feet in praise.

Geoff had been envious of those scheduled to participate. It hadn't occurred to him to be part of the trip until one of the group member's had become ill at the last minute, and Geoff's name had come up. The day Starr arrived on his doorstep, the missionary leader cornered Geoff at work and begged him to go. That conversation made him late getting home, and Geoff's dream of a romantic reunion with Starr was a total flop. Telling her he was leaving a few months after she'd come to live with him in San Francisco hadn't gone any better.

Geoff winced. Her pain was a knife in his gut.

In the corner, Sdax sang to Bridgette. "Twinkle, twinkle, little Sdax. How I wonder what you are."

Starr's mother had first taught her daughter the nursery rhyme when Starr was three. She'd been hiding under her bed, certain one of her grandmother's legendary spiritual creatures was trying to catch her and take her away. Though Starr and her mother were as ordinary as any Hoosier, her mother felt a connection to something she called Aleut spirits. Starr was resistant to embracing the strange, Aleut world her mother occasionally spoke about. She didn't understand it and felt it kept her mother strangely disconnected.

"Up above the world so high. Like a diamond in the sky."

That was the other thing Starr didn't understand. Stars lived in the sky, far away from people, yet her mother had named her Sdax, the Aleut word for star. There had been no explanation, no link to her reason behind the decision. When Starr turned eighteen, she changed her name to the English version and added an 'R.' It made more sense than explaining what little she knew about the origin of her name every time she spelled out Sdax.

No, I'm not Aleutian. No, I'm not familiar with that tribe. No, I don't know where they come from. No, no, no. Twinkle, twinkle, little Sdax.

"You seem upset," Geoff said.

Starr didn't look up. "I don't know what you mean."

"Starr."

"Mmmhmm?" She continued reading the text in front of her.

Geoff put his hand on Starr's. She wore three bracelets on her right wrist, and he pressed them lightly against her skin. "I said you seem upset."

Starr wrenched her hand free knocking over her water glass. The notebook and book were spared. She grabbed her laptop by the keyboard and held it above her head, shaking it back and forth to get every last drop of water out from behind the keys. Her bracelets collided with one another as she moved.

Sdax leapt to her feet. "Now look what you did!"

"God, Geoff. Look what you did!" Starr exclaimed.

He sidestepped her accusation and tried to help. "Honey, let me." He was determined to bring Starr back to a state of semi-calm. What he'd hoped would be a quiet morning had turned to chaos.

"You've done enough," Sdax shouted, holding her doll by the hair.

"You've done enough," Starr snapped.

Geoff pressed the palms of his hands against his face, digging them into his closed eyes until he saw floaters. When he took in the scene again, he knew he was defeated. In front of him was Ian, the angst filled teenage version of himself. Ian was seventeen, the same age Geoff had been when his life upended on a slick road in his hometown. One minute he'd been arrogant and determined, a bully even. The next, he was pinned beneath a vehicle facing death and potential criminal charges. He never really grew up after that and opted to turn his life into a one-legged race for forgiveness. When Ian was around, Geoff was in for a real fight.

Now he was up against Starr and Ian. Geoff considered his options.

I could challenge Starr and insist she tell me how she really feels.

"And risk a bigger fight before we leave?" Ian asked.

Or I can coax her into talking to me. I can remind her that I know what it's like to feel sad and lonely.

"Right," Ian said. "She'd nag you into telling her the whole truth about that accident, and you don't want to go there."

I could pry the lid off her bottle of antidepressants and beg her to take a pill.

"What good would it do? You know she hasn't taken one in months," Ian reminded him.

Geoff knew his wisp was right. The first and last options had worked in the past, but he suffered some scathing. He still carried the emotional battle wounds from nearly losing her right after she'd arrived on his doorstep. The best option would be to sit and talk. However, Starr was known for burying her feelings deep, and he didn't have time to unearth them. He opened his mouth to speak, uncertain which path he'd take or if a new path would miraculously present itself. "I'm sorry," Geoff said.

Sdax approached and took Ian's hand. They were an unlikely pair. She wore her hair in pigtails and had a slightly upturned button nose while Ian was tall and lanky. His hair hung long over his forehead. A smattering of acne freckled his cheeks and the bridge of his nose. He slouched down on the floor with Sdax, who settled on his knee. She shared her crayons with him as the adults continued their discussion.

"I said I'm fine, Geoff. You need to trust me."

"We have a deal, you know." Starr hesitated. *She* was the mental health expert. Not him. *She* knew when she reached her threshold and needed assistance. Not him. "That's fine. But the deal is that I'll tell you if I'm having problems. And I'm not. I'm awake at this hour because I had a bad dream. That's all." Starr wanted to tell him that he'd know about her dream if he hadn't abandoned their shared bedroom. She wanted him to hurt like she was, but she also wanted him to love her so hard that he stopped the pain.

"You said you would let me know if you had suicidal thoughts. Not just problems," Geoff corrected her.

"See? Even more reason not to ask about it or grab my wrist like I'm bleeding out. It was a dream. Not a problem."

Geoff tried to control himself. "I didn't grab you." He wondered if the neighbors could hear them.

"Would you care if I did? I mean, you asked me to live with you and marry you, and look at us. You've literally packed up your life, and you're leaving me."

He raised his hands in surrender. "Leaving you? Starr, I'm leaving. Then I'm coming back. Those are two different things. You know that."

Starr let her gaze travel away from Geoff's terse look to the corner by the fireplace. Sdax was there, huddled near Bridgette and keeping out of the fray. Sdax wouldn't leave her. Maybe she was better off with the little wisp. Let Geoff run off to save the world. She didn't care.

She shook off her frustration the way Bridgette shook herself after a bath. "This is nonsense. What am I so angry about? It's spilled water, not the end of the world." Starr pushed her book away and faced Geoff. "Let me at least make you breakfast before you go." She hurried to the kitchen and pulled a skillet from the cabinet.

Geoff watched her locate eggs, portabella mushrooms, and cheese from the depths of the refrigerator. He loved her and hated that he couldn't fix her. Her mood swings worried him. "Come with me, Starr. Please."

"We've had this conversation. Remember?"

He remembered it well. That night had been the last time they'd made love. They'd stayed up late into the night drinking wine and reminiscing over old pictures of their first months together as a couple. He was thick with emotion, enamored that a woman like Starr loved a one-legged man like him. He pushed aside the memories of his past and took her, right there on the plush rug in the living room. She wept against his shoulder when it was over. He wept the next morning, alone in the shower, his head and heart full of guilt for all of his sins, knowing he didn't deserve to have a life of happiness after what he'd done. Geoff didn't know Starr heard him crying when she walked into the bathroom for a Q-tip or that she'd mistaken his tears as regret for having made love to her.

"What you need is a good, hearty breakfast before your big trip," Starr said and kissed him sloppily on the cheek.

"I need you. I need us. We can get married in Alaska."

Starr trembled at the thought. There were so many reasons she couldn't go with him. Her clients, the new practice. She didn't like flying. Geoff was a member of the church that she had stepped foot inside only once. During a jarring two-hour service with drums and singing, people had danced around and shouted what sounded like unintelligible gibberish. Geoff had hung back, and ushered her to the balcony where latecomers sat. When she'd mentioned getting together with some of the other staff for lunch after the service, he'd balked and said something about traffic and their needing to grocery shop for the week ahead. After the last song, he'd hurried her out of a side exit, avoiding the customary handshaking and visiting.

Starr stopped chopping the mushrooms. "Don't be silly. You know they hate me."

"Honey, they don't. No one hates you."

They squared off, another argument on the brink. Starr wielded the vegetable knife when Sdax materialized in a shimmery blue haze at her side. Ian rolled his head from side to side, a boxer in the ring, ready to defend himself, his actions, and his God. Sdax reached up on tiptoe, determined to remain unnoticed until just the right moment. The knife shone in the kitchen light, sharp and inviting.

Bridgette barked and rushed for Starr's legs, a furry tidal wave that couldn't be ignored. The spell was broken, and Starr dropped the knife, narrowly missing her foot. She yelped and put her hands out to catch the charging dog's face in a squeeze.

"Heel," Geoff instructed, and Bridgette stopped in her tracks. Geoff picked up the fallen utensil. "You didn't cut yourself, did you? Come sit down. Let me check."

"I don't think so," Starr said but followed his instructions. She put her leg out, and Bridgette rested her head on Starr's knee.

"No bleeding. No puncture wounds." Geoff winked at her. "You look pretty good to me." He held her foot between his hands and conveyed his love for her with his eyes. "You're beautiful."

Starr patted Bridgette and blushed. "Thanks. I feel crazy sometimes. Possessed almost." The alarm in Geoff's eyes was vivid, and she noticed his muscles tense. "Not like that. No. I swear. Really. I'm not even thinking about hurting myself. I promise. I just..." She looked away.

"Just what? Tell me."

"I feel like a kid. Like there are all these decisions that have to be made. I'm drowning under the weight of them. I worry so much, you know? About my clients. About my practice. About us."

He could tell her. He could own up to his guilt and shame. Put it all on the table. Starr was an amazing therapist. She would see him through it. All he had to do was open his mouth and form the words. He licked his lips and hesitated. "We're fine."

Ian brushed against Geoff's side. "You can't tell her. She'll never forgive you."

Starr squirmed. "I know. Yet I can't help feeling like you're about to abandon me. I mean, I get why you need to go. It's work. I know that, and we need the money."

They didn't need the money, but Geoff nodded along. He couldn't explain his finances without telling her everything. "So you're not mad?" he asked.

Starr shook her head. "No, I'm not. I'm being a pain."

He pulled her out of the chair and held her close. They swayed to imaginary music until the doorbell rang. His ride. It was time to go.

"Lock the door behind me and before you go to bed. This dog is more bark than bite," Geoff said. He patted Bridgette's head with one hand and held Starr's hand with the other. "I will." She didn't want to let go.

Geoff said, "I'll be back. I'm already counting down the days."

"Me, too."

He kissed her hard on the lips and hoisted his bags on his shoulder, a Christian soldier marching off to a war his girl didn't understand. She thought he'd be emotional or be tempted not to go. But he wasn't, and he didn't seem to be.

"Love you," he said.

"See you, little buddy," Ian said to Sdax. He tousled her hair and gave her a hazy blue wave before he followed Geoff out the door.

"Love you, too," Starr whispered. She didn't follow him out but twisted the lock into place and leaned against the door. Bridgette settled under the table for a nap. Sdax nervously petted the furry animal.

"Twinkle, twinkle, little Sdax. How I wonder what you are," the wisp sang to her doll.

Starr twisted the ring around her finger in full circles. She'd started the habit a couple of months ago. Living in Geoff's world was confusing. From the outside, since the day she'd arrived in San Francisco, she'd learned her role quickly. She was his girlfriend turned live-in girlfriend. His almost fiancé. Their relationship in an odd stage of regress. The need to throw something was intense. "Don't do it," she chastised. "Focus. Ground yourself."

Grounding was one of her favorite therapeutic techniques. There was much reward in quieting the mind and truly seeing one's surroundings. She closed her eyes, breathed deeply, and opened her eyes again.

"Focus. You've been lonely before. It's not the end of the world. Look around you. Get some perspective."

With the front door behind her, Starr straightened her spine and reached for the ceiling. She stretched her calves, luxuriating in the tingling sensation that came with it. The ceiling was nine feet tall, and she forced herself to pretend she could touch it if she tried hard enough. When her arms began to burn with the effort, she allowed herself to return to a relaxed state. Then she inhaled like a cocaine addict before exhaling slowly.

"You are safe in your home that you share with a man who loves you. He adores you. He's going to make you his wife."

She grimaced at the thought of being someone's something. It was as if she'd agreed to be his property, and her nagging desire to be a devout feminist caused her shaky determination to crumble. *How did others so easily tether themselves to someone for life?* She shook her head. The uneasy thoughts were mere debris, ready to be swept up and tossed into a waste basket.

Her eyes traveled to the corner of the living area that doubled as an office space. Geoff had presented her with a roll top desk to help her feel more at home, but Starr preferred the kitchen table for her work. She could spread out at the table without feeling like she had to be neat and tidy. Beneath the desk was a wire wastebasket the color of deep bronze. Starr took in the desk's long legs from the other side of the room and hurried to it. She would ground herself, damn it. She would not succumb to her fears or her demons.

"I love this desk. Do you feel that? The rows of wood? Each

one feels like a long, smooth piano key. They even sound musical when you raise the top. See?" She grasped the handle and lifted the lid slowly, letting each bar of wood rub and click into place until she saw the desktop. An untouched yellow stack of sticky notes. Next to it, a thick spiral notebook she'd deemed too pretty to use. In the corner was a ceramic cup with ink pens and a pencil standing inside it. Another item, long and sharp, stood sentry and beckoned her.

"Ignore it, Starr. Think about the man who bought the desk for you." She clenched her eyes shut to conjure up his image. Anything to deter her from seeing the long, pointed letter opener with the gleaming tip sharp enough to slice through the thickest envelope. Sharp enough to prick the skin. But the only image of Geoff that came to mind was of him leaving her all alone.

"A dust covered penny. Two paper clips. An overstretched rubber band," Starr rattled off the other items on the desk.

"The kind of rubber band you use to snap against your wrists when you want to— Sdax shouted.

"Shut up, Sdax. Shut up. Shut up!" Starr blinked her eyes and flexed her hands. She would not pick up that letter opener. She would not move her hand to the cup that read "Blame your mother." Because she knew if she did, she wouldn't be able to trust herself. Instead, she slammed the desktop shut again and pushed herself out of the corner.

"Brown leather couch. Short windows. Squat windows that need new curtains." She stopped her frantic rush through the room and flexed her toes against the carpet desperate for words. "Thick. Soft, like worn cashmere. Plush. Creamy white polar bears."

A large polar bear loped into her mind's eyes. His fur was dingy, the color of dirty snow. He sat on his beefy haunches, and Starr was taken aback by the size of his paws. She recalled a television commercial of playful polar bears sipping Coke from glass bottles against the backdrop of a wintry slope.

Sdax walked into the scene, a shy child in awe of a real live teddy bear. She wore a thick hand sewn parka that hung almost to her knees. The hood and waist were edged in fox fur. Her feet were clad in matching mukluks, her hands cloaked in thick seal skin mittens. The sensation of a chilly night, a sky filled with winking stars grew vivid, and Starr breathed in the crisp air. She clasped her arms across her chest, a sudden need to warm herself. The thick living room carpet gave way to a snowy expanse of endless tundra.

"Hey, pretty bear." Sdax's breath was a cloudy white puff. "Pretty bear." Palm down, Sdax extended her thin arm. *Sniff me. We can be friends.* She licked her lips, struck by the bear's calm demeanor. Other than a slight bow of his massive head, the bear didn't move. Sdax inched her way forward captivated by the creature. In the distance the sound of Native drumming sashayed across the wind.

In her chest, Starr felt the tightness release. This was better. She could breathe again. She felt safe. Safer, at least. Less alone, less lonely. There was nothing to fear now. She settled into the daydream, a doting caretaker pleased to see her young charge make friends with an unusual creature. Sdax glanced back, and Starr waved her on. "You can do this," she whispered to the little girl. To herself. She locked eyes with Sdax and luxuriated in their connection. The usual emotional charge she felt toward this younger version of herself gave way to kindness. Resistant to physical touch, Starr urged her wisp toward the bear. He would be her arms, her embrace.

Sdax accepted the gift, giddy about it. A childlike wave to Starr and she turned back to the bear. "We can be——."

The bear smacked its massive paw against Sdax's head. She fell to the ground. He pummeled her cheek and her stomach and batted her around like a rag doll. Starr cried out and covered her mouth with her hand. The wisp went limp, but Starr was rooted to the ground. She couldn't rescue her. Doing so would risk her own life.

When Sdax moaned, Starr's knees quaked with relief. Maybe she'd be okay. Probably she wouldn't. It was a daymare and Starr couldn't blink it away. A pink stain oozed out from Sdax's ear. Starr shook her head, determined to wish it away. She had to save her wisp.

As she took a step toward the scene, the bear looked at Starr. He raised a paw and hit Sdax's limp body. Again and again, a wintry puff of snowy air rose each time he made contact with her hazy body. He pounded her into dust, and the sound grew louder and louder. Starr couldn't look away.

Bridgette barked and shoved her wet nose into Starr's palm, trying to get her attention. It worked. Starr was ripped away from the violent image in her head. Her breathing was ragged and heavy. "What is it, girl? What?" She pet Bridgette and tugged gently at the dog's ears. The beating from the vision took up residence behind her eyes.

The dog wiggled and nudged Starr again. She whined and barked, insisting Starr go with her to the front door. The image of the bear towering over Sdax froze in place. Someone was at the door.

Coming," Starr called. She straightened her clothes and checked the time. "Who is it?" Maybe Geoff came back. When she opened the door, her hope vanished. "Oh, hello, Ms. Caulton. Geoff isn't here."

Sdax sulked in the corner. She hated Ms. Caulton for coming. She hated Starr for letting the bear attack her.

"Starr takes care of everyone but me," Sdax whispered to her doll. She clutched the discarded letter opener and gouged a hole into the carpet. "Nobody cares about me. So close, little doll. We were so close to having a party," Sdax whispered and hugged the rag   doll   to   her   chest.

CHAPTER FOUR

Morris Oscar Wilde met Larimore Inez Destin in the San Francisco Public Library on a day filled with rain. It was the kind of rain that drizzled from the sky, punctuating the aches and pains of the elderly and arthritic while arousing the creativity of artists. The kind of rain that encouraged readers to settle in with a hot beverage and captivating plot. Morris liked to think himself an artist though the canvases he'd once slathered with paint sat gathering dust in a locked closet in his basement apartment. There was something about his type. The loner, single male, living off his savings. He chose to live life as a minimalist. Simple. Quiet. Introverted. Rarely bringing attention to himself.

Though the rain that day enticed Morris to twist the lid from an oil paint or pick up a charcoal piece and stare between the drops, he couldn't bring himself to comply. A large blank canvas sat atop his favorite adjustable easel, puffed out its chest and beat against its wooden frame, demanding Morris' attention. He hushed the sound and focused on the joy he often felt when he considered an introspective day filled with people watching—a book in his hand while he sat in an empty, perfectly situated library carrel. That was the best—portraying an image or a persona without showing people his real self.

Dressed in tattered jeans and a t-shirt, Morris zipped a lightweight black jacket over his angular frame. He preferred an old-fashioned cardigan. Grey or brown with faux suede patches sewn on the elbows. The kind professors and intellectuals wore. The glasses were fake but indicated intelligence and a well-read worldview. His shoulder length hair was the color of fire, and he brushed it back into a ponytail, perfecting his cynical, edgy look. He looked in the mirror. Something was missing. Shoes, but he'd put those on at the door—low rise Converse. Black to match the jacket. Wallet? Morris felt his back pocket. No. It was there. Tucked neatly against his left cheek, one ATM card and twenty-six dollars made up of one-ten dollar bill, two fives, and six George Washingtons. The ones were on top of the fives that were on top of the ten. All the bills faced the same way. He'd checked the night before. In the clear photograph holder was an ancient picture, creased and worn from years of viewing. The image was that of a cabin facing the mountains. There was a faint line of fog that crossed the mountain range. Whoever had taken the picture had captured what Morris considered a breathtaking view of peace and tranquility that he yearned to achieve. The mountains were a magnificent precipice from which one could stand and see everything below him. Morris often imagined he could sit there and ponder, never once to be interrupted by anything other than nature like the rain that fell outside. In that kind of environment, Morris knew his wisp would find solace and finally let him rest.

His headphones. That's what he was missing. A quick search of his room and there they were. Standard, white headphones of the non-Bluetooth variety. Morris didn't care for Bluetooth. Having tried them before, Morris was not impressed with the quality of battery life. So quickly the juice drained, leaving him mid-song or mid-audio book only to be left with piercing silence. He disliked being jarred from a mood induced by eloquent lyrics or story lines.

Like most people, Morris had a certain self-cognizance. Wary of his wounded child self, he visualized his wisp as an independent person with whom he spent a great deal of time. He called his wisp Oscar after his own middle name. It was Morris' single acknowledgment that they were one and the same. Morris hesitated when it came to an intimate relationship with Oscar because the teenage boy had a Jekyll and Hyde personality—volatile one minute and plaintive the next. Morris found Oscar unsettling to be around for long.

Like Morris, Oscar wore the same tattered jeans and t-shirt. His jacket matched Morris' and his wallet contained the same monetary denominations. His feet would soon be shod in the same black Converse. The difference? At fifteen, Oscar did not match Morris' height and weight. Nor would he ever. Oscar's personality was also different. He vacillated between an impish, wimpy persona and a sullen, dark mood. His inconsistency bothered Morris more than the whining. He believed Oscar needed to develop a radical acceptance to life. Nothing could be solved by moping and complaining. Even less could be solved by covert violence and maniacal control. Morris wanted Oscar to find his center, the kind of peace that cabin in the mountains produced. He was desperate for Oscar to find this at whatever cost necessary.

Morris scowled at his reflection and inspected his skin. There was a minuscule line of blood under his chin. A dull razor had one upped him.

Oscar patted his hair into place. "Nice," he said, ignoring the flawed chin.

"I know," Morris replied. He squinted into the mirror and wiped angrily at his left eyebrow. It was pertinent he look complete and comfortable. Oscar had a tendency to leave Morris feeling rattled as if he'd been mildly electrocuted.

"Here. Let me." Oscar honed in on the unruly eyebrow hair. When it refused to be tamed, the wisp licked his pointer finger. He slicked and poked the stray hair into place. "That's better."

Morris nodded his approval and plugged in the earbuds. "Now I'm ready."

"You have no intention of listening to anything. You do know that."

"Not now."

"Then why the charade?"

"Maybe later," Morris snarled. "What do you care?"

"Suit yourself."

"I do suit myself. I'm in control here. You have nothing to worry about."

"Suit yourself." Oscar brushed a thread from his jacket, turned, and followed Morris out the door.

Morris knew the wisp spoke truth. He had no intention of listening to anything at the library, save the muffled conversations that were sure to go on around him, but Morris paid Oscar no mind. He connected the dangling end of the headphones into his phone, slipped the phone into his front left jacket pocket, and gave the buds a reassuring pat. After all, he had an image to depict.

The Golden Gate Valley branch of the San Francisco Public Library system wasn't Morris' favorite. He'd been up since seven and had been ready to start his day since 8:05. The facility was nearer his home than the others—it's only saving grace since Morris was not a fan of public transportation. There were simply too many sweaty bodies with bad breath crushed up against one another on the transit. The one problem with this particular library branch: the odd hours of operation. Who waited until ten o'clock or later to go to the library? Ten a.m. was not conducive to Morris' early riser routine. Sunrises were lovely, and he enjoyed the morning dawn much more than the sunsets. He was clearheaded and productive in the morning. The early hours were his opportunity to wake up before the San Francisco masses. Morris liked it better that way. He pushed aside his frustration and decided to make the best of the dreary day.

Choosing the right book was important. Both for ease on the eyes, he did like to read, and for deterring people from inviting him to talk. He had a system and employed it strategically.

Crime fiction and true crime were stern no-nos. Holding one of those in front of his face brought on sideways glances from distrusting people. Mothers held their children closer and put themselves between him and the little ones, certain Morris was looking for clues on how to implement the perfect murder or a foolproof kidnapping plan. This didn't bother him if the mothers were unattractive with stringy hair and plump bodies stretching out Lululemon tights or wide hips sporting muffin tops whose blouses didn't cover their expanse of skin. Or if the woman had unruly children in tow—howling babies covered in crusty snot and juice stains or toddlers going limp requiring the mother to drag them past his perfectly chosen place. Let those women and children think he was searching for prey. He didn't care.

Romance novels were also left on the shelves. Women weren't attracted to a man who held a book covered with a half-naked male on the cover. Though he'd experimented once before, Morris wasn't interested in men. Not that he was judgmental or homophobic, he was merely attracted to beautiful women. Strong yet docile, stern yet capable of acquiescing when the situation called for submission.

Science fiction, coming of age, and YA/NA books meant young adults eager to talk to him—book lovers and social butterflies with an itch to explore and discuss the latest riveting life stage or make-believe world. They craved answers to questions like: Who's your favorite character? Have you read the *Eragon* series? Don't you wish there was a really good book about cats that created their own language while fighting off the characters in *Harry Potter*? Morris had no interest in answering those questions. He had questions of his own. Why are we here? Who are we trying to impress? Why must we label people? When did coffee become an accessory at seven dollars a cup? And why? What was the real reason behind the image of the Beatles crossing the street? Besides, cats who talked and fought with fictional characters gave Morris the creeps.

Self-help books annoyed Morris. He didn't feel it necessary to have someone tell him how to help himself. He'd figure that out on his own. Nor did he want to attract those who wanted to talk about how they used yoga and meditation to ease their anxious minds. History books were too heavy and encouraged historians to explore the past with him. Add to it that the librarians had a tendency to look him over, silently judging whether he was capable of understanding Egyptian history. Morris had to fight the urge to open their primers and carefully rip out random pages, the sound of the sheet breaking free from the binding giving him chills.

Morris chose the only kind of book that prompted curious looks while keeping verbal interaction at bay: books with interesting yet vague titles. That day's choice was a memoir, *Shoe Dog*. Morris touched his fingertips to the cover and selected a seat in the far corner of the nonfiction section. The seat was heavy and comfortable against his body. He settled in for the afternoon, headphones in his ears, and eyes downcast.

An hour later Morris was genuinely invested in the author's story, mesmerized by the novel-like quality this businessman used to tell of success. In many ways, it was a business book cloaked in personal confession and anecdotes. Morris turned another page. The sounds of the library fell further away with each word he consumed. He couldn't recall the last time he had looked up from the text. That's when she arrived. And Morris berated himself for missing her approach.

"He writes beautifully, doesn't he?" she asked.

She was impeccable. Her open-toed sandals touched the toe of his Converse. He was struck by her soft, spring-like outfit. The white blouse with a ruched fit and floral skirt that stopped just below her knees. Her long legs were tan and emulated strength. Morris couldn't stop himself from responding honestly.

"Yes, he does. It's as if he wrote you into my life," he said. She smiled. He smiled.

Morris found that words came readily to him during their first interaction while Oscar stood idly by, hands in his pocket. The wisp's mouth hung was ajar, a squinted look of irritation furrowed his brow.

"I'd offer you a seat if there was one," Morris said.

"Such a gentleman."

When she didn't leave, Morris stood and introduced himself. "I'm Morris. Wilde." He added his last name so as not to make the exquisite creature think he was a fly-by-night kind of fellow.

"Larimore Destin."

The feel of her skin against his when they shook hands was notable. Morris, who didn't care for physical touch found himself craving more while sensing a willingness to be patient. He didn't want to frighten her away. She was a delicate butterfly and he was the luckiest flower in the field to have her light upon him.

"Would you like to go somewhere? Talk more, perhaps?"

Morris asked. He reminded himself to release her hand and was surprised when his body complied.

"That sounds nice, Morris. Perhaps you can tell me—"

"Shhhh." A young man surrounded by several thick books and notebooks in a nearby carrel glared at them. "This is a library," he whispered loudly and returned to his studies.

Larimore leaned close to Morris and spoke softly. "There's a quaint little coffee shop nearby. Saki Brothers. It's my favorite."

Morris accepted Larimore's invitation. He left Shoe Dog on the arm of the chair he vacated, still open to the page he'd been reading, and cautiously put his hand on the small of her back. She edged in close to him. Outside, Morris forgot about the rain. Nor did he notice the rain on the day he moved his wardrobe into her upscale condominium. Later, when Morris tried to pinpoint the exact moment when things went awry, he'd remember the day they met and blamed himself. If only he'd introduced himself by his full name, including the sulky Oscar, maybe things would have turned out differently.

Occasionally it bothered Morris that he didn't have her move into his apartment, but Larimore was classy. A basement with musty smelling carpet was rather insufficient for a woman of such style and taste. So Morris locked up his closet filled with paintings and rented the unit to a recently widowed woman who explained she was not ready to face the insufferable reality of moving in with her cantankerous adult daughter.

A year later, Morris was ready. He'd made up his mind. All he had to do was create the perfect environment and ask the question in the most eloquent of ways. Then Larimore would most certainly say yes, and she would be his. Forever. Until death parted them. It was perfect.

It was the start of a new week. He and Larimore would celebrate their one-year anniversary soon. Morris was determined to have dinner ready and his mind made up about the proposal. Larimore was at work with no plans to return until six. Dinner would be served in the dining alcove near the wine rack. She expected her alcohol to match her mood and would select a nice white or a rich red with no regard to the meal. On tonight's menu: liver. It would be thinly sliced and cooked well done. Morris had it marinating. Grilled asparagus and onions would require his attention thirty minutes prior to Larimore's arrival. She was always punctual. A sweet potato mash scooped in quarter cup amounts would round out the evening meal. He checked his watch. At five he would set the table with Larimore's exotic china pattern, shower (Larimore had standards of cleanliness she expected him to adhere to.), cook, and shower again (to remove the lingering odor that cooking liver wrought). He would be ready when she arrived. Morris had seven and a half hours to research the perfect way to ask his love to join him at the altar.

For weeks he had agonized over how to ask her to be his bride. Subtle hints were dropped with no response from Larimore. To ensure he made a decision and not let his anxiety about the situation convince him otherwise, Morris took a do-or-die approach. He linked his hands, stretched, and cracked his knuckles. The sound satisfied him. His laptop in front of him, he opened a Google Chrome window. Clicking his mouse in the search bar, Morris began with the first thought he'd scratched onto his pad: Romantic ways to propose to your live-in girlfriend. Results: 106,000,000 in 0.54 seconds. Without reviewing the list, he chose the first link titled "Top 50 Romantic Ways to Propose – The Aisle." The first idea on the list said to "choose a favorite place," and Morris guffawed. "What else would I do? That's not even a real idea." He kept reading. Number two suggested having "a choir, brass band, or drum line show up for a surprise performance."

Before Morris could move on to the next idea, Oscar drummed his hands against the desk. "Da, da, da-da, da-da, da," Oscar said loudly. He marched around the room pantomiming a part in a marching band line-up. When Morris didn't pay him any mind, Oscar slapped his hand against the laptop screen.

"Are you seriously considering this shit? Larimore despises noise." He tucked a strand of strawberry red hair behind his ear and somehow managed to look cool as opposed to shaggy and awkward. His freckles were stark against his pale skin.

"Don't you think I know that? She's my girlfriend. I know her." Morris rolled his eyes and returned to the screen. He scrolled to the third idea on the list. "How idiotic," he said before Oscar had a chance to say anything. "The theater is a good idea but proposing after the curtain call? Larimore deserves to come first in all things. Not last after the crowd has dispersed and the actors are wearily getting their accolades."

Number four: "surprise your fiancé with a street proposal and caricaturist." Oscar snickered from where he sat in the corner, and Morris slammed the laptop shut.

"Who asked you anyway?" Morris fumed.

Fifteen minutes later, Oscar spoke tentatively. "Isn't criticism hard? No one likes my ideas. I might as well never try anything."

Morris pulled out a pencil and sharpened it to a point. He preferred pencils over pens. The former never leaked on his clothes. "Okay," Morris said and pulled out a blank sheet of paper. He divided the sheet into quarters and titled three sections: sure-fire ways to propose, unique ways to propose, daring ways to propose. In the fourth quarter, he hesitated before writing 'Other' because he couldn't settle on a new category. He feverishly jotted an original draft of proposal ideas on a separate sheet of paper and set about organizing them.

'Over dinner' went into the other category. Morris knew he could make Larimore's favorite meal, a delicate chicken Marsala, to her liking.

"You could light candles, too. Make it really special," Oscar suggested.

Morris added 'candles' next to his entry. "I could." Morris' hand hovered above the paper, debating whether this idea was unique. He started to add it to the unique section, stopped, and crossed out the letters. "I'll think about it," he said and moved on to the next one.

'At home' was equivalent to proposing over dinner because Larimore rarely wanted to dine out. "Why should I when I have you to prepare fine meals for me," she'd asked him once when he'd suggested a new restaurant in town. Oscar told Morris it was because she was ashamed of him, embarrassed to be seen with a man like him when she was of such high caliber. Morris had been tempted to believe him, but Larimore's sly wink and tilt of the head persuaded him otherwise. He decided then he'd cook any meal she ever wanted. To hell with dining out.

Under 'unique ways' Morris scribbled Space Needle—Seattle.

"That's not a bad idea. High over the city. The skyline in front of you. A gentle breeze. City lights twinkling as she sips her drink. What could go wrong?" Oscar asked.

Morris tapped the pencil against his lip. "Yes. It would be unique and romantic. We could spend the weekend together in a fancy hotel, making love and admiring the new ring. It'll be a time for planning our future." He flipped open the laptop and googled the Space Needle.

Oscar read over his shoulder. "Twenty-four dollars a ticket. Reasonable." Morris remembered the twenty-six dollars he'd had the day they met. He'd used seven of them to buy her coffee at a stand on the way to her apartment. The man who served them had seemed offended when Morris asked for a receipt, but he held his ground. The receipt was in a shoe box in his old apartment. "I don't know about this," he said as he reviewed the FAQ page. "'...due to the volume of people and limited space...' sounds crowded." The description reminded him of an odorous bus filled with commuters on their way to modest paying jobs.

He scrolled up and down the website. "A crowd might be good. People watching and celebrating when I get down on one knee." Morris got out of his chair and knelt, imagining the crowd of strangers approving of his choice in women.

"I don't know. They'd all be looking," Oscar reminded him as he pointed out the website picture. Groups of people stared at him from the screen.

"Exactly," Morris replied. He held out his hand, cupped an imaginary engagement ring, and looked up at the woman he loved.

Instead of Larimore's graceful image, Oscar stood in front of him. "But what if they tease me? They'll stare at me with their fat, buggy eyes." His eyes watered as if he was on the verge of tears.

Morris wavered. "Judgmental pricks. Maybe you're right. Shouldn't give them the satisfaction."

"They wouldn't approve of a woman like her with someone like you." Oscar said and flinched, but Morris didn't strike.

Morris' self-doubt flared. Maybe his wisp had a point. Morris pictured himself in creased trousers black as pavement and a gray pin-striped button-down shirt. His shoes would be shined to gleaming. Larimore materialized in his mind's eye—long hair pinned loosely back at her slender neck, curls like a waterfall. She wore a bodycon dress and pointed kitten heels, her skin free of jewelry just the way he liked. He went to her, whispered her name, and knelt before her. She was regal, and Morris was mesmerized by the scene.

"Darling, will you marry me?" Morris asked.

She cocked her head to the side. She licked her delicate lips before speaking. "I will," Larimore said and leaned down to kiss him.

Around them people murmured their approval and appreciation of the elegant couple, the romantic sight.

Then Oscar appeared. His voice was nasal, and he was sloppily dressed. Clumsy from champagne he'd pilfered at the bar, he warbled, "Raise a glass, everyone. Toast the new couple. Isn't she exquisite?"

Morris stood, still holding Larimore's hand with the shining diamond on her ring finger. He was horrified when Oscar stumbled and fell against them. Oscar's elbow caught Larimore in the collar bone. She shrieked in pain and disgust.

"Stop it! You're ruining everything," Larimore screamed.

"Oh, man, I'm sorry. So sorry. Here. Let me make it better," Oscar said. He leaned in with puckered lips, his neck jutting out like a chicken on a chopping block.

"No, no. This is awful. It's awful. Stop." Morris clapped his hands repeatedly until the scene faded to black.

"She hates me. I was just trying to help," Oscar whined, shamefaced. He picked anxiously at his hair until Morris worried he'd develop a bald spot.

Morris glared at the wisp and returned to his list. The beach went under 'Other' (ordinary, cliché). Ferris wheel—daring. They could get stuck up there. It might be romantic, but the thought of a burly mechanic sent to their rescue turned him off. Hot air balloon. Morris considered this, the sound of fire whooshing up the balloon's esophagus as they soared into the sky. She might frighten and cling to him. Morris would hold her and promise to be her constant protector. This went under daring and unique.

"What about the zoo?" Oscar asked. "That's interesting. Besides, she'd be surrounded by her kind." He jumped around and made monkey sounds.

"Don't be silly. With all those people and animals watching from behind bars? It's not daring or anything. It's inhumane."

"You're right. It's a dumb idea. As dumb as proposing at...at...Alcatraz."

Morris disagreed. "That would be unique. A prison for a venue. It's not an operating prison." He did a quick search of wedding venues and discovered a problem he hadn't considered. A wedding required guests, and though Morris brightened at the thought of sober strangers applauding their union, he knew Larimore might not find a large ceremony appealing. Neither of them cared for crowds nor socializing. He fretted over how to handle the actual nuptials when he scolded himself. "You're getting ahead of yourself. Master the proposal. You can worry about the wedding later."

The clock read four. He was running out of time. There had to be something that met his criteria. The words romantic, daring, unique, and foolproof were a broken record in his head. Morris disregarded a phone or video proposal for logical reasons. If she wasn't there with him, how would he put the ring on her finger? The boat idea, though romantic, was eliminated, too. Bulky life jackets made null the romantic water view.

Oscar paced, frantic at what little time they had left. "We'll never think of anything. Nothing defies all notion of ordinary. Isn't there a place at all that would be unexpected?"

"Someplace not known for proposals. That's all we have to find." Morris tapped his pencil against his teeth.

"What about the library? That's where you met," Oscar suggested.

"I suppose you think we're some kind of bibliophiles? Destined to create a romantic engagement patterned after fictional characters?" Morris was not impressed.

"But it's where you met. I don't know."

The realization of the perfect place dropped into Morris' mind like a single raindrop hitting the surface of a pond. It gave him goosebumps. In some way, the wisp had helped by drawing Morris' thoughts right back to San Francisco where he and Larimore had met and lived happily together. As his mental fog cleared, Morris envisioned a layer of thick clouds breaking slowly to reveal the majestic arches of the Golden Gate Bridge. It was as if Eros, the Greek god of erotic love, nodded in solemn approval. The justification for selecting such an unusual location practically made itself.

Morris whispered, "Yes. At the Golden Gate Bridge. It's perfect."

"What if I fall? What if she falls? It's scary with all the talk of death and dying there. Isn't it like tempting fate?" Oscar babbled.

"You're worrying about nothing," Morris snapped.

His wisp's mood flipped from nervous to nasty. He clenched his fists at his side. "If she declines your proposal, you can shove her off the bridge. Right? An eye for an eye?"

Normally, Morris would have been rattled by Oscar's moaning-turned-murderous talk, but he was so smitten with his decision and the plan that rapidly formed in his thoughts. Morris quietly replied, "I will invite Larimore to marry me at the Golden Gate Bridge. The contrast is vivid. With so many deaths there, what better place for me to propose? What better place to ask her to be mine? To start a family with me. It is truly the most sincere and reasonable place in which to share with her my desire to create a life together."

The alarm sounded. It was five o'clock. The wisp went back to his marching band role. He couldn't think of anything to say. When Oscar reached the desk's edge, he placed a finger in Larimore's framed and smiling face. He shoved the photo. It fell but didn't break. "Just remember," Oscar said. "If she refuses, there's always plan B."

CHAPTER FIVE

The week after their disastrous date at the Golden Gate Bridge, Larimore was still among the living thanks to the length of fence that prevented her from being pushed to her death. Oscar vacillated between hating her and pressuring Morris to beg her to take the ring. It was Oscar's juvenile belief that if Larimore wore the ring, she'd eventually rethink the idea of marriage. Morris had to admit the thought had crossed his mind. Meanwhile, the ring, a hearty square cut diamond, rested in its little black box underneath a layer of V-neck t-shirts in Morris' bureau. At night when he was alone in his room and Larimore slept peacefully down the hall, Morris replayed the wedding they weren't going to have in his mind. The mental picture always ended with her in his arms as they slow danced across the ballroom floor.

The dance was something Morris and Larimore had done many times in the year they'd been together. Morris moved two steps ahead of Larimore waiting patiently and expectantly for her to arrive and join him. Like the ritual of the cicadas that penetrated the Midwest every thirteen to seventeen years like clockwork, dependent on the brood of course, Morris woke first and prepared the way for his love.

He rose without an alarm at precisely six o'clock each morning. Asleep one minute, awake the next. He slipped soundlessly from the bed in his boxers to the hall bathroom where he dressed in faded jeans, a V-neck sweater and pulled socks over his feet. He plunged a round hairbrush into his thick hair and pulled it back with a hair tie. After washing his face,

Morris positioned his plastic-rimmed glasses on his face. He was ready to face the day.

Larimore woke at seven, and by then Morris had the coffee brewed and both of her breakfast options prepared to her liking. A soft-boiled egg sat primly in a ceramic egg cup, and whole wheat toast was mere seconds from being released from the toaster's grip. Next to the plate rested a small jar of orange marmalade. Whichever dish Larimore preferred, Morris ate the other. Food was merely fuel for his body, not something he labored over for himself. Only for Larimore. For a year it had been this way. But this Tuesday was different.

Using statistics that he taught himself, Morris determined that on this particular morning in early spring, Larimore would select the egg. Steam rose from the soft-boiled egg. As his love descended from the stairs of their shared loft apartment, Morris bit back the eager smile that tried devilishly to overtake his face as he presented the egg cup with a flourish.

"No toast?" Larimore asked. A hint of a frown gathered between her eyes.

Morris leaned in close to her as he typically did in the morning when handing her a full coffee mug. He pressed his lips against her forehead. "Hmm?"

"There's no toast, darling," she said in a voice just above a whisper. "As I walked into the kitchen, I had a desire for toast, yet it isn't here."

Morris was flummoxed. His spreadsheet's betrayal threatened to choke him. He refused to be deterred. Larimore's utmost happiness was his only concern. "Of course. My mistake," he said and hurriedly prepared the toast. He dropped the bread into the toaster and pressed the lever until it clicked. Almost immediately Morris tapped the sides, begging it to release the pieces. His ears pricked up at the sound of Larimore pacing behind him.

"Don't forget the marmalade," she admonished him as she left the room, coffee untouched.

As Morris set out the marmalade with the small spoon Larimore had purchased just for this reason, he reflected on his spreadsheet. He had obviously missed a day or a mood or a measure somewhere to have made such a mistake. There was no alternate explanation. At least not one he could fathom. Their relationship, their love was so calculatingly perfect, it was nearly liturgical in nature. Larimore gave Morris purpose and meaning in this coupled world. Meanwhile, Morris was the protector, the man servant who ensured every graceful move she embarked on was captured with his eyes and his heart. He was there to relish her and make her feel like a queen. The toast, the spreadsheet, a single misstep. It was something he could recover from and would recover from, if he had his way. If only it hadn't followed so closely on the heels of his failed proposal.

"Larimore. Darling," Morris called from the bottom of the stairs. "Larimore." His voice was endearing without being patronizing. Gentle without begging or whining—two features she despised in any human being. His restitution worked. She was coming. Morris positioned himself beside the kitchen island, his head bowed slightly in remorse.

Larimore wore an old cotton robe and satin negligee she reserved for their weekend mornings of love making. The sash of the robe was tied loosely and showed off her legs. "You want me to eat that now?" she asked as she raked her hand through her glossy curls.

He looked up. "It's what you asked for," Morris said. "Orange marmalade on the side." He pointed to the topping and the silver spoon that stuck out of the jar. "With fresh coffee, of course."

She narrowed her eyes until they were slits and stared over his shoulder as if dismissing him altogether. One might think his attempt to guess her anticipated dish was such wrongful behavior, she could remove him from her presence through the sheer act of ignoring him.

"Your egg is here as well. In case you've changed your mind," he said. His patience wore thin, and he thought he heard the edge of a whine in his words. *In caassee you've changed your mind.*

"Cold egg, you mean."

Morris didn't care for the scolding. "Larimore, what do you want? Another egg? More toast? Something else?" His mind spun uncontrollably. "You behave as if you want me to be with you always. Yet I propose, and you turn me down."

As he spoke, Morris found himself bewildered. What exactly had he done wrong? Cooked for her? Loved her? Asked her to be his? After all, had she simply put on a playful pout or asked for toast, he would have toasted the damn bread with a smile and a kiss. They were playing house. Pretending to be married when they were simply lovers—two people who'd found one another in time and space. No malice was intended by his snafu, yet he felt compelled to beg her forgiveness just the same. His faults tumbled around in his head and he couldn't keep track of which was real, and which was imagined.

"Is it so wrong to want our morning ritual to be the same?" she asked.

There it was. Her need to have things remain the same. Morris felt his heart lighten at her romantic notions. "Larimore, my darling, of course not." He nuzzled her clavicle. "All you had to do was ask."

She pushed him away. "Why must I ask? Is it not the same thing I've always said each morning since you came to live here? Toast with orange marmalade or a soft egg." She paced the length of the kitchen island as she spoke, and her robe swished vehemently along the curve of her thighs. She was hysterical. "Nothing has changed, Morris."

He worried the delicate champagne glasses that hung from the cabinet's underside would crack from the growing strength of her shrieks. Because he could think of nothing to say, no action with which to rectify what Larimore felt was their near undoing, he said, "We can start again, my love. We can start again."

With that she flounced on her heel and returned to her room, no doubt to count down the minutes until she would return to find fresh toast, coffee, and a new soft-boiled egg awaiting her breakfast decision.

Oscar hopped off the counter where he'd watched their morning scene unfold. He steepled his hands beneath his chin. Oscar the professor. "So the egg and toast are to Larimore what you are to…"

"They are nothing to Larimore. They just…are."

"They simply exist? Inanimate objects in a human world?" Oscar crossed his arms, his back against the refrigerator. When Morris passed by to clear the unwanted breakfast items, Oscar stuck one foot out and refused to move, forcing Morris to step over him.

"Inanimate objects in an inhumane world, you mean."

"Ah."

Morris attempted to school the wisp. "You don't get it. They're things. They're symbols. It's not that hard to comprehend."

"Tell me what they represent then. Please," Oscar instructed.

"They're symbols of our love. Of our connection. We are rather connected, Larimore and I." Morris continued the task of recreating breakfast. He checked his watch against the condition of the egg, which sat submersed in a pan of boiling water.

"How do the egg and toast represent the love of two people?"

"Isn't it obvious? I cook them, demonstrating my love for her." Morris pushed the lever down on the toaster and hovered above the pan of water.

"And her eating them?"

Morris paused before answering. "A sign of her love for me, of course."

"Of course."

Sixty-seven seconds later, the bread, now lightly toasted on both sides, and the egg were removed from their respective cooking devices. Morris gingerly spooned the egg into a fresh ceramic cup that he'd taken from the open-faced cupboard. In his haste to erase his blunder, he'd tossed the old egg and cup into the garbage can. He would retrieve the cup later. Perhaps even the egg since he doubted it was truly bad. The can and liner inside were clean. He'd taken the trash out the night before. On a matching ceramic saucer he laid the toast down and set the jar of orange marmalade beside it, the spoon, now washed and dried, rested on top. She would enter any second now, and the ignorant observer, this wounded wisp, would see and perhaps finally understand what he was trying to explain about love.

Morris stood poised. His hair and clothes were as fresh as

they were during their earlier dance. His smile was appropriate— not too big, not too small. Not a hint of a frown or frustration about their earlier spat. He willed himself to exude love and to feign uncertainty of how she'd receive his gift, and then when she chose, he'd smile bigger and wait for her to thank him. To embrace him for his kindness—for his demonstration of unconditional love.

"Good morning, darling," Morris said as Larimore entered the room.

Morris rarely saw Larimore in anything other than soft things. Flowing, knee length skirts. Dresses with plunging necklines that exposed her elegant skin. High heeled sandals that exposed her toenails painted in neat French tips. Her hair, a soft blonde color made up of voluptuous curls, always lay down her back, showing just enough of her swan-like neck. He liked to kiss her neckline until he reached her ears where soft pearls or chunky diamonds often rested. Larimore was graceful, lithe, and exquisite in her demeanor as well as her actions. Seeing her now infuriated him.

The navy-on-white collared, button-down blouse, fresh from the dry cleaners (he'd picked it up himself), had been starched and ironed. Her hair was pulled back into a severe bun at the nape of her neck, and the pin-striped collar of her blouse rested against her shoulders. The sharp edges were angular points reaching for her armpits. The blank, stony look on her face reminded him of a store mannequin. He searched her bottom half for the rose petal look she normally wore for him. The blouse was tucked into straight-legged trousers, a crease ironed the length of her hip bones to her feet, which were encased in four-inch heels with severely pointed toes. If someone attacked her, the heels would gouge out an eye.

"I'll have coffee," Larimore said.

Even her voice was harsh, a sharp rock cutting against a windowpane. Morris felt something inside him split open when her voice made contact with his ears. He looked down at his hands, open and splayed toward the food he'd prepared. He was certain if he looked hard enough, he'd see the cut from her tone. The blood seeping out.

"She's mad," Oscar whispered.

Moving past him, she reached for a silver travel mug and poured coffee from the pot. Morris felt the first stirrings of anger at her behavior. The coffee he'd prepared for Larimore was in her favorite mug, doctored the way she preferred with sugar, the real cane sugar, nothing artificial or chemical-laden, and liquid cream. He drank his black.

Oscar studied Larimore's movements. "She's livid. Look at how she's treating you. And why? Because you cooked? You took on the role of servant for her, and this is her thanks. She doesn't deserve you. She doesn't deserve to live."

Morris twitched at the sound of Oscar's voice. It was so cold, so empty. He wanted to ask Larimore if she heard it. He wanted to feel her in his arms, to feel safe.

"Go ahead and have dinner without me. I've got a full day and a late-night business meeting. There's no need to wait up." She took a swig of her coffee. Her lipstick, a bold red he'd never seen her wear before, stuck firmly to her lips. Not a smear on the cup's rim. "Morris, are you listening to me?" Her cheekbones pulled taut, and her eyes bulged a little from the tightness of the bun she'd pulled her hair into. Her peaceful, sensual stare that Morris was used to gazing at had been replaced with a look of disdain.

"What will she eat?" Oscar inquired.

Morris echoed Oscar's concern. "What will you eat?"

"Better yet, ask where. Then we'll know where to go to poison her," Oscar shouted in Larimore's face.

"I'll think of something," she said. "Harold will drive me if I've had too much to drink. Goodbye, Morris."

The front door closed with a delicate click that pierced the silence more than if she'd taken the liberty to slam it.

"Harlot. Tramp! You don't deserve him," Oscar shouted. When that didn't rile Morris, he turned around and inquired, "Remind me how it works. If she eats the food, she loves you. If she doesn't eat the food, what does that mean?"

Morris didn't answer.

"Does it mean she's mad?"

Morris snorted, feeling a sensation along his spine that both intrigued and frightened him.

"Or that she loves Harold?"

"It means the song to our dance has changed. That's all. It means the dance has changed. It's not that unusual," Morris replied. He combed his hands through his hair, roots to ends. Roots to ends until he felt a mild sense of calm. He scooped up Larimore's breakfast eager to deposit the whole mess into the trash can. He stepped on the pedal, opened the lid, and peered inside. The first egg was clean, just as he'd expected. With his right hand, Morris stuffed it into his mouth and chewed. With his left, he dropped the second egg and then the toast into the can.

"New song, new dance. It sounds good. In theory," Oscar said.

"You have a better explanation?" Morris asked around a mouthful of egg. Larimore would be appalled at his manners.

"Maybe I'm wrong, but to me, it has nothing to do with music or dancing."

Morris picked up the marmalade from the island. He took the spoon from its neck and washed the egg taste away with a spoonful of the sweet topping. "Enlighten me."

"It has to do with what she sees." Oscar snapped his fingers, and an old-fashioned chalkboard appeared. He stood in front of it in a tweed coat and wrinkled trousers. "Have a seat, Morris. Let me educate you on what just happened here."

Morris eased into a stool at the island at his wisp's command. His stomach churned, and he knew it wasn't because of the marmalade he continued to spoon into his mouth though the sweet fruity taste didn't sit well with him. He preferred honey.

On the board Oscar drew a detailed sketch of Larimore in the center. He gave a hearty guffaw at the hefty bosom he added to her thin frame. "This is the catalyst to everything." He raised his hand to silence his student. "Before you tell me she's a person and you love her, just listen. To her, you're nothing. You're not good at making breakfast. You don't know her enough. You're a non-person, a mere man-servant." He drew Morris in chalk, hunched over in a butler's costume with a tray in his hand. The caricature had a subservient manner about him and was drawn two inches shorter than Larimore.

"She's not like that," Morris insisted.

"Let me finish," Oscar instructed. "As I said, this is you. Here is your competition." Harold appeared tall and handsome. His chalky image smirked at Morris before taking Larimore's arm and escorting her out of sight. "You are nothing like him. You'll never be anything like him, not with Larimore running the show."

Morris tried to rebut. "You can't say that. She loves me. I told you about the dance." His words fell on deaf ears as Oscar redrew Larimore's image and decorated her body parts with the kind of nasty, hateful words Morris would never dream of calling her.

While Oscar read the descriptions aloud, Morris' lips moved in silent repetition. Dirty, cunt, whore, bitch, trash, unfaithful, ugly. Morris' heart raced, and Oscar's voice filled the crevices in and around his brain until the blood vessels were full and felt as if they'd burst against the inside of his skull. He plugged his ears in an effort to quiet his hateful wisp.

"She has to go. You have to silence her. Obliterate her. Dispose of her." Oscar smacked his pointer stick against the image he'd drawn and zeroed in on his prey. "Do it, Morris. You must."

"No! No!" Morris shrieked and hurled the marmalade at his tormentor.

The jar smashed against the white wall and with it, the marmalade. Morris retreated upstairs as he smoothed his hair with his hands. The sticky, sweet fruit created an abstract painting as it dripped onto the white baseboard.

Efficiently, despite the ragged breathing and the rage that simmered beneath his breastbone, Morris started his morning bathing routine. As he groomed, Morris muttered repetitiously his love for Larimore. The words soothed him, albeit minimally, as he scrubbed himself with hot water and Larimore's stiff loofah. He reminded himself of their love for one another and covered himself with her scent. He returned to the kitchen to remove what he'd referred to as the "marmalade mess."

Downstairs, Oscar greeted him.

"You've changed."

"I'm dressed for the day if that's what you mean."

"More than that. The tie is new."

"A working man's noose, I suppose." Morris reached under the kitchen sink where he kept scouring pads, rubber gloves, and scented cleaning supplies. His chores included daily housekeeping. On weekends, hired help arrived with buckets and mops for the regular deep cleaning. Larimore refrained from getting involved regardless of the day. Morris didn't begrudge her. She was delicate. A beautiful blossom for viewing and caressing, not for menial labor. Her work self was intelligent and brisk—no time for household chores that could be outsourced or handled by Morris who felt they were benevolent tasks used to further demonstrate his feelings of goodwill.

"Death in your thoughts?" Oscar inquired. He spoke quietly. It was his way of apologizing, of reestablishing their alliance. "Something sinister must be on your mind with as violently as you're scrubbing."

Morris paused. The wisp was right. His attempt at ministering to Larimore by removing the unpleasant remnants of their disagreement had turned forceful. The scouring pad was smashed tightly in his clenched fist, and the rubber glove was the only barrier preventing the pad's rough surface from digging into his palm. Morris loosened his grip and gently wiped the remaining spots. He sprayed the lavender scented cleaner and gave the wall a final swipe as he breathed in Larimore's favorite odor. "It calms me," she was fond of saying.

"Does it calm you?" Oscar asked.

"Some. I guess."

"Too bad you didn't have it upstairs."

"Why? I didn't throw anything up there."

"To breathe. You know and to calm yourself. Before you went through with it." The wisp sniffled. His feelings were hurt as they often were when Morris took control.

"I don't know what you're talking about." Morris really didn't.

He'd gone upstairs readied himself, and now he was here again. He hadn't nicked himself shaving or punished himself by hitting his forehead against the mirror. He'd learned his lesson the last time he did that. When Larimore noticed the new mirror, square and plain, unlike the gilt-edged monstrosity that he'd cracked with his own skull, he'd had to think fast. A story about how it'd slipped off the wall and cracked because the neighbors shared their bathroom wall and had gotten rowdy was his cover. Then he'd promised to find a suitable replacement. And he had. Morris had dipped into his savings to afford it but replace it he had. Afterward, he'd basked in the glow of Larimore's appreciation. What she didn't know couldn't hurt her. He knew that for certain.

"Your hair. Not a bad job for doing it yourself."

"My hair?"

"You act like you don't even know."

Morris removed the rubber gloves and stowed the cleaning supplies haphazardly under the sink. A stray piece of glass pricked his left ring finger. "Damn it. Look what you did." He admired the black wedding band and brought the wound to his mouth and sucked.

"Missed a piece, I see."

Morris painstakingly searched the floor for any leftover shards. He found two and carefully picked them up and threw them away. "Done." He took two steps out of the kitchen and turned back. "Precautionary measures," he said and snatched the miniature vacuum that hung on the wall beside the trash can. He ran the handheld device over the floor, carefully sticking it into the groove between the floor and baseboard. "Just in case."

CHAPTER SIX

Morris left the condo and wandered somewhat aimlessly through the streets of San Francisco. In Chinatown he kept a wide berth around the crowded stores with sale signs advertising in chalk outside their front doors. Morris did not care for shopping or kitschy items, especially in Chinatown. The excessive amount of discount items that lined the dusty glass shelves disgusted him. Tea pots with matching cups and saucers wedged into Styrofoam boxes. Tall rows with hooks that held personalized keychains. Ann, Anne, Annie, Barbara, Beatrice, Claire, Deborah, Debbie…Arthur, Bob, Carl. Ten postcards for a dollar or one for twenty-five cents. Chopsticks, barrettes, fake leather wallets, hanging ornaments, and I love San Francisco stickers, magnets, bumper stickers, and picture frames. Every item an unnecessary necessity for tourists who juggled their plastic shopping bags, jumbo purses, children, and cheap umbrellas made to look like silk Asian parasols.

On the corner a college kid waved a large cardboard arrow to drive potential customers through the glass doors of a tax preparation company. Morris walked faster and tugged at the knot in his tie. He was angry at Larimore. Oscar's attitude was no help, and now the walls of Chinatown threatened to collapse on Morris.

"She likes Harold. *Really* likes him. Isn't it obvious?" Oscar needled.

"Shut up," Morris said.

"But she does. How do you know she's going to work every

day? She could be like those people," Oscar insisted. He pointed to a man and woman meandering along the opposite sidewalk.

The woman wore a professionally cut business suit with matching gray heels. She looked like she was ready for a day at the office with a short, stylish bob. Her briefcase hung over one arm. In contrast, the woman allowed her male friend to stroke her hair and hold her hand. He slowed his step and pulled her close to him. They kissed. The man reached for her waistband and slid a finger into the fabric while she playfully batted his hand away. The man motioned to a nearby alley, and they ducked inside. Morris heard the woman shriek in delight.

"How do you know Larimore isn't conducting *that kind* of business?" Oscar asked with disgust.

Morris wasn't sure. He decided to do whatever was necessary to win back his love. The only logical plan he conceived was to get a job. Perhaps if he spent some of his attention elsewhere, she would miss him and realize her mistake in declining his proposal. Up ahead was her favorite coffee shop. What better place to find a job than at a place she liked? Wouldn't she be pleasantly surprised to find him there? It was a good thing he'd put on a tie.

The manager's office at Saki Brothers Cafe & Coffee Shop was small and cluttered with barely enough room for a desk, a matching yard sale quality chair, and a metal folding chair for potential new hires. Morris sat on the edge of the folding chair. He was too close to the Saki brother for his own comfort. The brother's breath smelled like stale coffee with a hint of something unidentifiable yet sweet.

"Can I get an emergency contact number? A friend, a brother, a girlfriend, anyone really," Mr. Saki said.

"What for?" Morris asked. His finger pulsed through the too tight nylon bandage.

The brother frowned. "Just in case."

The workers went about their business beyond the partially open office. Morris heard them shout orders at one another, sniping at customers to "speak louder" and "speak slower."

Customers shouted at the workers, irritable and pressed for time. "Hurry up." "Can you move?" At one point, Morris heard someone snap their fingers and imagined a harsh business woman. He had to refrain from craning his neck to see if it was Larimore, snapping her fingers and pointing at her watch with the other, signaling how little time she had to wait on an incompetent barista. Correction. She would be pointing at her cell phone. Almost no one wore watches anymore.

"Do you have one?" Mr. Saki asked.

"A girlfriend?" Morris licked his lips, anticipating the rush he knew would come when he berated the man for asking such a personal question. He was capable of having a girlfriend. After all, wasn't he in an exclusive relationship with Larimore? They were cohabiting. What would the brother think of that?

"An emergency contact number. It doesn't matter whose," the brother explained with a wayward glance toward the line of customers in the café.

Morris hesitated.

"What a hoot. This is your grand idea? You think this will make her forget about Harold?" Oscar taunted. "Man, you have to be powerful. Manly. You have to own her."

"What should I say?" Morris asked the brother.

"You can tell them it's a formality. I doubt we'll ever need to use it." The brother looked around the cramped room. "Probably the worst thing that could happen here is some of this junk could fall on you." He laughed and nudged the stacks of paper that rose from the desk and flirted with the power cord that hung from an open tile in the ceiling.

Morris chuckled along with him. "Or I could burn myself pouring coffee, right?"

The brother smiled. "Sure. That's happened once or twice. But nothing that required us to call anyone. Most people order iced coffee. They have to be different than their parents' generation, you know?"

"Right," Morris said though he really didn't know. He took the application and looked at the form where the brother pointed. EMERGENCY CONTCT: _____. He was on the verge of pointing out the error when someone banged on the office door and walked in.

"Amigo. They're killing us out here. You hire somebody yet?"

Alfonso was twenty-one. Latino. His parents crossed the border into Texas illegally when Alfonso's mother was eight months pregnant with him, swollen and cross, ready to take down anyone who dared to prevent her from giving her son the American life. When he turned sixteen, Alfonso dropped out of high school. By twenty, he was tired of working under the glare of the California sun at whatever construction site he'd managed to find work. He fathered two daughters by two different teenage girls. He had a son on the way whose mother, also twenty-one and Latina, had made it clear: Alfonso would have no rights to him unless he stepped up and handed over a weekly paycheck. He had no sooner been given the ultimatum when he traipsed into Saki Brothers where an old-fashioned and sun bleached "Help Wanted" sign stood in the window. He was hired on the spot and proved his worth by working any shift the brothers asked of him. Thankfully, they paid him under the table. Immigrants themselves, the brothers weren't interested in bringing any INS attention to their little corner of San Francisco.

The Saki brother sighed. "Calm down, Alonzo. Geez. Does it look like I'm on a date? Hell, no. I'm interviewing this guy."

"It's Alfonso. And what's the point of an interview? He's breathing, ja? He wants to work, right?" He took a step closer to Morris who shrank back. "You want to work, amigo? Su trabaja?" Alfonso shouted. He pantomimed pouring coffee.

"I want to work. Can I start now?" Morris asked the brother.

"See? The guy wants to work. Let him work," Alfonso said as if the interview process was completely overrated.

"He finishes the paperwork, and then he can work, Alonzo." The brother reached for the application. "You done?"

"Here you go." Morris avoided the brother's gaze and handed the application and clipboard back to him.

"All you need is this apron and a hairnet. Ándele. Let's go." Alfonso shucked his apron and handed it to Morris as he started out the door.

The apron was light brown with dark brown stains covering it. Morris grimaced and put his head through the hole. A second noose around his neck. He imagined his esophagus being crushed by them in a combined effort to stifle his breathing. Morris wrapped the tails behind his waist, but they were still two feet too long. He wrapped them around his back and front again where he tied them in a bow above his naval. He was ready. Two steps behind Alfonso, he tried to keep up with the Spanish gibberish the young guy spat.

"Wait. Get back here," the brother said.

"Is something wrong?" Morris asked.

"Great. Already in trouble. I told you this was stupid," Oscar said.

"The emergency contact. I need an emergency contact number, or you can't work here." Mr. Saki held out the clipboard.

Beads of sweat formed along Morris' neck. The people, the noise, the idea of working for paltry cash. These things unnerved him as did the idea of Larimore seeing him in the grungy apron slopping coffee. But he persevered in the name of love. *This has to work.*

"Look, man. It's not like I'm going to call the number. I need it in case someone comes asking. So put something down. Anything."

"Sure. I got distracted. That's all." Morris laughed like they were best pals. In the blank spot, he wrote the first three digits of his number and made up the rest.

"Amigo, we're out of hairnets. Buy more. Vamanos," Alfonso told the brother as he yanked a sweaty smelling ball cap over Morris' head. "Who cut your hair, man? It's all crooked in the back."

Before Morris could respond, Alfonso ushered him into the dining room and spent the next three hours instructing Morris on the craft of coffee making. Alfonso was a certified barista, having attended a three-day training in San Diego, courtesy of the Saki brothers. He had a certificate with his name on it. Alfonso promised to show it to Morris someday when they had more time.

Steamed milk, lattes and cappuccinos, iced versus hot, mochas, white, regular, and dark, all with additional flavors upon request. Alfonso showed Morris the difference between cup sizes and where to wash the ceramic mugs they provided to customers who dined in. Morris learned how to use the bus bin to collect dirty dishes and how to wipe down the tables and chairs. The menu consisted of prepackaged sandwiches heated in one of three microwaves that graced the "kitchen," and fruit that required washing and chopping before being scooped into plastic containers. The baked goods arrived frozen and were thawed each night before the early morning shift started.

"The most important thing to know is this. Show me the dinero," Alfonso said with a grin as he pried the plastic lid off a large coffee can. Taped to the can was a ratty piece of paper with the word "tips" scrawled across it. "Tips" was also spelled out three times on the lid where a ragged slit was cut. "This is where the customers put the tips when we give good service."

"Who gets them?" Morris asked, feigning interest.

"Up until now, we split fifty-fifty between me and old Jimbo over there. Now that you work here, we split them three ways. Even Steven."

Alfonso's trainee frowned. "Three ways? What does Steven get?"

Alfonso looked quizzically at Morris as he waited for the punchline. When Morris didn't explain, Alfonso laughed. English was his second language, and some things didn't translate well. "You loco, amigo?" He slapped his leg. "Jimbo, you gotta hear what this crazy guy said."

Oscar bristled at the word 'crazy,' but Morris ignored him. If nothing else, Morris hoped the constant noise of Saki Brothers would quiet the sound of Oscar's voice and the memory of his morning lesson. Morris wouldn't let Oscar end this relationship as he had done in the past. And he'd be damned if he was going to let Oscar's evil side convince him to kill his girlfriend.

CHAPTER SEVEN

The first time Starr cut herself, it was an accident. She had been angry and upset and had gone to the kitchen of her apartment for a snack. In an attempt to be healthy and not eat her feelings, as she'd done so many times in the past, Starr chose a Granny Smith apple. She favored the crunchy, tart fruit and thought the sharp flavor might help her mood. Her need to slam a door or throw something made her reach for a paring knife. She would chop the apple, cut it to the core, and enjoy the satisfying sound of the knife slicing through the fruit.

She didn't remember the feel of the knife entering her skin. The cut wasn't that deep. Instead, she remembered an awareness of the penetration and the slight sucking of her breath when she'd realized what had happened. Robotically, she set the knife down and pushed aside the apple on the cutting board. The wound was on her left forefinger. She held it close to her face, and a dark drop of blood oozed to the surface. She watched it bubble and felt the emotional release clients had often told her about. The same emotional release she'd suggested they find healthier ways to achieve.

It'd been ten days since Geoff left for Alaska, and Starr fought a daily battle against the desire to self-harm. Today was day eleven. Her white flag of surrender would make the perfect tourniquet. The first four days Geoff called or texted with every detail.

ON THEJ PLAN[E]. LUV U. / MADE IT TO SETAC. MISS
YOU / GOT U A GIFT! / WEATHER DELAY /
BOARDING / WINDO SEAT [PIC INCLUDED] /
LANDED / VILLG WEATHR / COUTING THE DAYS
[RING EMOJI]

She scrolled through the texts. She saved the voicemail
message he'd left when she was busy with patients. She called
him back. They talked for thirty minutes. She texted pictures of
herself. Some racy, others playful, and some with Bridgette lying
across her feet. The whole experience reminded Starr of when
they'd made the decision to take their relationship to the next
level while determined to make a long-distance romance work.
Then his last message came.

ONWARD FOR THE LORD / WILL CALL WHEN CAN

Cell coverage was spotty where he was headed out among the
Native people in far flung villages she couldn't picture. Every so
often she picked up her phone, checked for battery life, tapped
the phone icon, and searched for a missed call. The message icon
for a missed text. Nothing was there. Geoff was gone. He had
replaced her with a zealous servant's love for this God she didn't
know.

It was ten o'clock, and she was already tired. After a fitful
night's sleep, she'd risen early and worked on the plan for her
new private practice before coming to work at Cloverleaf. She
was a mere six weeks from starting her own business, and her list
of clients at the center was winding down nicely. She had a few
appointments on her calendar that day, and one client had
canceled, leaving her with a coveted block of precious free time.

Starr twisted her bracelet and reminded herself. "Tonight, it's
Oliveros and wine. Tonight, I won't hide behind my jewelry."
She shuddered at the thought of her two guilty pleasures,
knowing they'd lead to a little emotional relief. She was almost
glad Geoff wouldn't be home. There would be no need to hide

her cigar or feign exhaustion to be alone.

Behind her, Sdax squealed and clapped her hands. The wisp was a blue blur. She'd barely had to coax Starr at all since Geoff had left. "Thank you, Starr. I've been so good."

"But first, coffee," Starr said. She pulled her tote bag out of the bottom of a file cabinet and fished inside for her keys. She hadn't been to Saki Brothers in months.

****

Morris wiped the faux granite tabletop with a dingy rag. The cloth smelled like one-part Clorox and ten-parts water—the standard cleaning ratio. The people who had just vacated the dining room were pigs. Morris hated society more than people. At least he thought he did. It was the proverbial chicken and egg conundrum. Did society create materialistic, nonsensical, shallow people? Or did those people create a society that continued to spiral downward until it reached a point somehow worse than Dante's seven levels of Hell? He rubbed furiously at a stubborn blob of coffee mixture—raspberry syrup, half-café, and whipped cream—the life of a barista/bus boy was hell.

Most days Morris was plagued with the daydream of Larimore arriving at Saki Brothers. She would see him and realize their lives were better when they danced their romantic waltz where he served her and she let him. He knew she would acquiesce once she saw the dirty apron and sweat-ringed ball cap. Then she would regret refusing him with her two-step strut that resulted in their angry blowout. Most of all, she would regret any mention of Harold and come back to Morris. She would drop tender kisses along his strong jaw line and apologize profusely in her gentle whisper. Morris would slip the diamond ring on her finger and forgive her. This rotten job was his means to that end. Larimore wouldn't settle for being in a relationship with a man who wore a stained uniform and slopped coffee, albeit fancy coffee, for others. He was hers, not theirs, and once she realized her deep love for Morris, she'd recommit to him.

Oscar trailed behind Morris, scuffing his feet along the floor.

"If she loves you at all."

"She does," Morris said quietly, his eyes trained on the table. "She most certainly does."

The door to Saki Brothers opened with a jingle. Morris held his breath as he waited a millisecond for Larimore's voice to call him. When again she didn't materialize in front of him, Morris grimaced. In a few short weeks, he'd begun to experience a Pavlovian response every time the door opened, and the ridiculous bell rang, letting in the smell of the outdoors and the sounds of people and the city. His demeanor shifted in response to the physical sensation that came. First, the headache and with it a sense of loathing for his masters that came in droves for the coffee he had to serve them. Second, a congenial smile he'd trained himself to form, followed by an odd and unusual sense of humility. Finally, a slight bowing of the head paired with crouching shoulders. The shame he felt morphed him into a lowly no one. This version of himself went unnoticed. He asked the master how he was doing and listened for a response. Yet the master did not reciprocate. Morris handed coffee over the bar, yet he rarely received a word of gratitude. He bid the master, "Good day," and the master dismissed him without a word.

At Saki Brothers, Morris was a non-person. An unnoticed, unworthy lackey sentenced to a life of servanthood.

"Just like at home," Oscar said.

"Shut up," Morris muttered.

"Pardon me. Is this seat taken?" He raised his eyes without raising his head. The epitome of the subservient role. "No, ma'am," he said. The congenial smile spread itself across his face.

Look at me. I'm a good boy.

"Let me finish cleaning this up," Morris said. He touched his hand to his forehead as the headache blossomed behind his eyes. The Clorox smell from the rag he held wafted upward through his nostrils. He looked at her closely as if he would be quizzed later about her features. It took a second, but the headache stepped back. Her features sharpened in front of him like an old Polaroid picture.

The woman was lovely. Her clothes were soft and flowing

from the peasant blouse to the long, gauzy skirt. He imagined her with a crown of lavender flowers on her head. Her hair cascaded past her shoulders. She wore colors like the Earth—a chestnut colored skirt that matched her hair and eyes. A chunky bracelet was a shade lighter. She'd cinched herself at the waist with a matching fabric belt. Someone had stitched row after row of daisies up and down the skirt, which stopped at her calves revealing shapely legs and a thin, silver bracelet on one ankle. He worked his way back up the length of her body. She was thicker than Larimore. Not heavy but curvy.

"You're so sweet. I'll throw my stuff down and get a coffee. Thank you," she said and went to order.

"My pleasure," Morris replied. He was surprised at the stirring inside his chest, at the sincerity with which he spoke. He turned back to his cleaning, careful to wipe the table until it was spotless. It wasn't attraction he felt. Yes, the woman was nice looking, but he only had eyes for Larimore.

Oscar wiped his shaggy hair from his face to reveal an adolescent smirk. "Ring a ding. Fuck her. Then maybe Larimore will see that she needs to treat you better," he quipped.

Morris ignored Oscar and examined the strange woman's belongings. Her satchel was beautiful. He couldn't help himself. He caressed it lightly. It was soft like melted butter. What was it about her that was so captivating?

"Break time, amigo," Alfonso said, interrupting Morris' internal curiosity.

Morris turned. His skin felt hot. He hoped Alfonso didn't see him touch the bag. "What?"

"Break time. I got." Alfonso reached for the damp rag and handed Morris a cup of coffee.

At Saki Brothers, the owners believed they'd build a loyal customer base if their own employees drank the coffee and sat among the patrons. Breaks were given twice during an eight-hour shift and staggered among the staff. Breaks were also required to be taken in the coffee shop—no outside smoke breaks, no leaving the premises, and absolutely no working while on break. The Saki brothers had been sued previously when they allowed workers to eschew their breaks, resulting in a lawsuit payout that nearly broke them their first year in business. The brothers even encouraged the staff to role play if they didn't have an engaging coffee shop persona—laptops, earbuds, notebooks, FaceTime, adult coloring books, sketch pads, friends. Whatever it took to create a Zen-like quality that made people sit down and drink up, the Saki brothers supported their staff. This was the hardest part for Morris. Well, one hard part. He liked music, acrylic paints, and even coffee. But he did not like people surrounding him, breathing near him, or talking to him or at him. He preferred the quiet solitude of the library or walking through the city on chilly, dreary days when the number of people on the sidewalks was few. Those locations gave Morris room to settle in to whatever part he chose to play.

Today Saki Brothers was packed. Tables were full except for one that stood in the center of the room. Morris had no interest in being on display there. He considered sitting at the bar, but he disliked the idea of facing the wall. The Saki brothers' rule was on repeat in his brain, and Morris, a rule follower by nature, considered breaking it when a harmonious voice broke into his thoughts.

"Shall we turn this into a table for two?" The stranger was back. She smiled at him.

Larimore was in Morris' heart, and this woman, this goddess, was in his sight. He could hardly breathe.

"Let me shove this stuff over," she said and pushed her bag aside before he could protest.

Morris blushed. "I don't want to intrude."

"Don't be silly. You cleaned the table. The least I can do is share it with you." She scanned the room. "Besides, this place is packed."

"Yes, ma'am."

She sat and smiled up at him as she cradled her large mug between both hands. The steam rose, and her nose was dotted with perspiration. She had long eyelashes and a pleasant laugh. It was their private joke. "Ma'am? I don't look that old, do I?" she asked.

Morris shook his head and breathed in her scent, hazelnut and some kind of coconut lotion. "Not at all." He pulled his gaze away from her lips and her nose and looked into her eyes. "I meant no disrespect."

That's when he saw it. The pull she had on him. It was her eyes. Coffee with a generous splash of cream. They drank him in, and he felt as though he might drown. With one hand, he lifted his coffee to his mouth. With the other, he gripped the edge of the table to steady himself.

"Good," she said and leaned in close to read his name tag. "That's the last thing I need, Morris." She smiled.

Morris found himself at ease. No underlying sense of frustration was projected on him. There was no need for him to feel anxious or worry about upsetting her. She was guileless and wanted him to feel the same. She hugged the satchel to her side and pulled her sunglasses case, keys, dogeared notebook, and cell phone closer to her chest until she'd created an opening. For him. For their conversation. For the unexpected. She waved her hand at him and the chair he stood behind.

Sdax had nagged her all the way to Saki Brothers, leaving Starr feeling more alone than she'd felt all week. The coffee shop was overflowing, and there wasn't a free table anywhere. If someone real or someone tangible would talk to her, she might be able to lose her wisp in the crowd.

"You're welcome to sit down," Starr said to Morris. She'd seen the intense look he'd given her and felt a little thrill up her spine at the attention he gave her. He was her saving grace. "If you want."

As the sights and sounds of the cafe dulled in the presence of this woman, Morris did as he was told. Morris didn't have old friends. No one from high school. No childhood playmate that he got together with for boys' weekends. No college roommate to meet at sporting events. He had nothing to compare this encounter with, but he thought if he did have any or all of those other things, they would be like this. Easy, spellbinding, and quirky. Full of depth and somehow lighthearted at the same time. He didn't have much to say, but she seemed to want to know everything. He found himself eager to provide.

"Morris. What a great name. Unique," she said with a tilt of her head. She put out her hand. "I'm Starr. With two r's." She held up two fingers.

The night came to Morris in a sudden burst of a vision. A cluster of trees stood nearby, and their empyrean music played softly in the background. An ebony canvas stretched above them as he and Starr sat together on a blanket. They gazed upward toward the heavens he didn't believe in though if she asked him to, he might reconsider. He pointed, and she looked up at him and tilted her head back. In the sky, an array of constellations splashed a brilliant white contrast. She scooted closer to him, a sign of her undivided attention, and in the vision, his mood buoyed.

"Thank you," he murmured.

"Don't you just love this place? It's not anywhere near my house or my office, but making time to come here is worth it." Starr sipped her coffee. "Hazelnut. It's an actual tree nut. Not like the peanut, which is a legume even though it has the word nut in its name."

She smiled. "I suppose you know all the dirty secrets about coffee from working here. Blame it on the trade, huh?"

Morris shook his head. "You wear it like a perfume, Starr."

Her cheeks turned a soft shade of pink. She could tell him that was Geoff's line, but then she'd have to explain who Geoff was and why she was having coffee alone. "It's my vice." Starr fiddled with her phone, embarrassed that she'd been called out so bluntly.

"There's a seed in it," he explained. "Like this." Morris made a fist. "Pretend this is the hazelnut seed, see? Around it is a layer of dry fruit." He put his left hand over his fist.

Starr couldn't help but stare at Morris' hands. "You're married?" Never in her life had she been so forward with a man, and now she'd sidled right up to another woman's husband. The coffee soured in her stomach. "I'm sorry. I didn't realize that. How embarrassing." She shrunk into her blouse.

With her, he was more than a servant. More than a gopher.

He was unique and fascinating, a real individual, and she was a shooting star. Morris flicked away Oscar's lewd suggestion and set the conversation straight.

"No. Don't be. I'm not—"

"You're wearing a ring," Starr admonished and pointed.

"Right, but this isn't wrong. It's coffee." He wrestled his tongue to come under his command. "You invited me to sit down," he insisted in defense.

"Vamanos, amigo. My turn to sit," Alfonso said, interrupting their dispute.

Morris frowned. He wanted to set the record straight. To find resolution with Starr in a way he had yet to do with Larimore. How could he explain this convoluted situation with his coworker? "I just sat down."

"Yeah, fourteen minutes ago. Time to punch the clock. See the line?" Alfonso pointed to the waiting customers. "Move. I'll keep your new friend company."

Another Saki Brother rule: Don't leave the customers waiting.

Morris had no choice but to leave her. Leave the moment and this chance at opportunity. The night sky faded to gray. The stars turned into plain, ceramic mugs. Starr remained on the blanket, looking up. Only now her attention was on Alfonso and his goofy smile. She'd tuned in to the sound of his voice and brushed Morris aside. A philanderer. A wandering eye.

"See that?" Oscar asked. He pointed wildly at the table. "Her business card. Ask her for it. She acts all innocent, but she's into you. I can tell."

The day was too much between the crowded dining room and the woman's accusations. Now Oscar had to chime in, rile him up, and cause the pulsing headache to increase in strength.

"Starr, would you like me to take your card?" Morris asked. She shielded it with her hand.

"Look, I said—"

He whipped up his customer service smile. "For the coffee drawing. It's a Saki Brothers tradition." "Oh, I'd almost forgotten," Starr said. "I can take it up later. I'd hate to bother you."

"It's no bother. Morris likes taking care of his customers." Alfonso beamed like a proud parent.

Morris bowed his head and shifted his gaze to the floor. "It's my pleasure," he said. He stretched out his hand and waited for her to drop the card into his palm. Tentatively. Without making contact. Like a timid butterfly afraid of being crushed. He turned and walked away with the treasure in his hand. He hated society and people equally. His reverence for Dante increased tenfold.

CHAPTER EIGHT

After three weeks of Larimore working late and eating dinner out with colleagues, Morris took matters into his own hands by firing off a text of his own.

MORRIS: Working late, my love.

He made sure to add the endearment. No sense in fanning the argumentative flame to the point of an uncontrollable forest fire. After several tense moments (Morris had a tendency to lean toward anxious when waiting for a reply from her when he knew he was being antagonistic.), she replied.

LARIMORE: Meeting tonight. Harold. I'll try not to wake you when I return.

Morris spent the remainder of his work day seething, and when a Saki brother fished for a volunteer to do the week's deep clean, Morris agreed to help. He didn't need the extra pay, but he was determined to stay out past Larimore. By dinner time, he'd gone home, changed clothes, and checked the security devices. When he returned to the coffee shop, he locked the front door, put on an urn of coffee, and retreated to the brothers' office.

Every so often, Morris tapped the Wink app on his phone. It told him when the front door of the condo was unlocked. He'd been using this covert way to keep an eye on Larimore's comings and goings since long before Harold came into being. The app was one of Oscar's ideas, left over from Morris' previous relationship that ended in an explosion of name calling and accusations made by Morris and a restraining order put into place by a tearful Faye. She denied her adultress ways right up until the end, and Morris, not having known about Wink, had no proof other than Oscar's constant reports of her slutty behavior.

Countless times Oscar ruined Morris' relationships, forcing him to shift erratically from being accusatory and hateful to clinging and weak. Morris was helpless against his wisp and struggled to keep his emotional state on an even keel. It was always something with Oscar—a look, a feeling, an insistence that Morris had blindly overlooked something obvious. Morris followed his lead, anything to shut him up. Almost anything. To date, Morris had not succumbed to the directive to harm a woman. He'd thrown things and threatened a girl once but never followed through. The thought made Morris nauseous. He didn't care for violence.

Then Morris met Larimore. When he moved in with her, he added the locking device as a precautionary move. Larimore had been hesitant at first, but he gushed about the benefits. "It's to improve security," he'd told her as he punched in the code and indoctrinated her on the importance of keeping the information private. Larimore submitted to his instruction and lavished praise on him for taking such good care of her. Their lovemaking that night had been fierce and brought on by Larimore's desire to show him her appreciation. Afterward, when she'd bid him ado, Morris had retreated to his own room on the other side of the condo, somewhat convinced that perhaps he was overreacting and letting Oscar get the best of him.

Enter Harold. An egotistical tightwad, Harold was Larimore's executive assistant. She'd hired him shortly after Morris moved in with her and even had the nerve to bring him home for dinner. Insisted Morris trail along behind them as she gave Harold the grand tour. When she opened the door to her bedroom and invited Harold to take a look, Morris was hurt. When she touched Harold's arm as she told him about the nuances of her stately king-size bed, Morris was angry.

It took Morris several weeks to complete his research, but a new pattern had definitely developed. There were late nights at the office. Several times Larimore had returned home intoxicated, and Harold had brought her to the door, rang the bell, and smugly handed her over to Morris. The security camera was installed, completely hidden from view. He took note of the discrepancies between the Wink lock and the new cameras on a regular basis, especially after the marmalade incident. Tonight, he would stay out until after he saw her return home. No matter how long the wait.

The Saki brothers' office was as messy as the day he'd interviewed. Alone in there, Morris breathed better. It was peaceful in the closet-sized room. He closed the door behind him. He preferred miscellany over conversation, and people insisted on conversation. How are you? Who are you? What do you do? He answered only when necessary. At other times when his benefactors weren't present, Morris pretended he didn't hear the incessant inquiries. His bosses cared only how he carried himself when he was on the clock and customers were watching. Tonight, in their space among the detritus of this so-called American dream, he was alone with his thoughts and his camera lens as he laid in wait for his love. Morris pushed aside a clump of dogeared documents. He needed room to spread out.

He'd finished the deep clean in record time, and his reward was to continue his analysis of an array of coffee mugs he kept hidden in a large canvas tote. Customers purchased the totes and filled them with bags of coffee beans, ground coffee, snacks, and an assortment of coffee mugs the brothers displayed in baskets and on shelves for purchase. Morris and the other workers were encouraged to sell these items, all of which Morris found unnecessary. Some days he sold more than others. Most days, he didn't have to try. The customers clamored for the overpriced mugs and discount marked bags of coffee without any input from him.

Morris tapped the refresh button on his Wink app and

prepared himself. No change. He was relieved. He set the phone on top of the highest pile of business paperwork and dug into the bag for his treasures. There were five containers inside, and he lined them up by size on the laminate desktop.

The office door opened, and Morris cringed. "This again?" Oscar asked.

"We're up to five now," Morris answered. He tried hard to fight the agitation Oscar evoked in him.

"We? I don't want to do this." The wisp climbed up on the tall file cabinet. He banged his feet against the drawers and kicked up a blue cloud. He knew the noise would bother Morris.

"You're a part of me, no? My inner self? My wounded demon? My fucking mini me I can't rid myself of?"

"Demon? If you say so."

"I say so," Morris said as he moved each item into the exact spot he wanted them. One cup was too close to another. He lifted it up, pushed his glasses up on his nose and carefully set the cup down again.

"Maybe," Oscar acquiesced. "But at least I'm not crazy."

"Have you forgotten? There is no diagnosis of crazy."

"Crazy." The wisp kicked the cabinet for another minute and then leaned his head back against the wall. He watched Morris intently.

When each cup was in its assigned spot, Morris opened a notebook and continued writing his philosophy of people as identified by their coffee mugs. Occasionally, when the right words failed him, he picked up the mug for inspiration. He turned it in his hands, sniffed it, rested the chalice against his cheek, and closed his eyes as he conjured the type of person who drank from it.

The first in line was a twenty-ounce travel mug. The outside was royal blue, the inside stainless steel. The cup was both heavy and thin in nature. Morris filled it to the brim with fresh coffee from a carafe and twisted the lid into place. The coffee was the darkest silk they carried. He swished a mouthful as if tasting a fine wine. When he swallowed, it scalded the back of his throat and, he grimaced with the burn. Morris considered the heat of the liquid against the structure of the mug.

"Thin," he decided and wrote the description in his notebook.

Morris pictured the front door of the coffee shop and watched as a tall man entered. The man's head was smooth like butter, his cheekbones high. The man approached the counter, paused, and retraced his steps. He bent low at one of the cup displays and lifted a travel mug. After a quick inspection of the price tag, he returned to the counter and produced a wallet. "Drip coffee. Medium," he ordered in a high-pitched voice. The man plucked a credit card from its slot and handed it to Morris. The man's skin was pale to the point of translucent.

As Morris filled his cup, the man's phone rang. He answered and tucked the device against his shoulder, listening intently. "Room?" Morris asked, knowing full well the man would nod and say yes without really knowing what he's saying yes to.

The man bobbed his head vigorously. "Right. Right. I know." He cupped his free hand and made a "Come on" motion to Morris.

"Here. Let me," Morris said and took the cup as he turned away from the counter. His back to his imaginary customer, Morris filled the mug as high as he could with steaming coffee, leaving no room for cream at all. Attempts to add anything, cream or otherwise, would cause an overflow. He replaced the lid but refrained from screwing it on tight. There was enough space that one tilt, one finger gripped in just the right place and well...Morris smiled at the thought.

"I'm coming. I'm coming," the man said into the phone. His voice raised an octave with each word. "I'm late, kid," he snarled at Morris.

Morris felt the shame that came with his servant's role trickle down his head like rainwater. "Yes sir," he said and gingerly carried the cup to his master. "Careful, it's hot." Morris set the travel mug on the counter and eked out a weak smile.

"I'm not an idiot," the man said and took the cup. "But thanks to you, I'm late."

"Yes, sir."

As he stalked off, Morris embraced the scenario and sipped

his own coffee. He'd watched this scene unfold in real life and found just as much enjoyment in the imaginary version of it. He conjured up his next customer. She was necessary.

A harried and heavy woman jostled the tall man with her collection of shopping bags that bumped her legs as she entered Saki Brothers. His travel mug made contact with the door handle. It exploded. The man screeched and hurled angry words at the large woman and her coffee splattered bags. His face was crimson.

"What the hell is the matter with you? Don't you see what you've done? I'm already late and now look at me." His voice alternated between red-faced shouts and snake skin hisses. "You're nothing but a cow. Too fat to even see where you're going, and innocent people like me have to suffer. Heifer," he hurled over his shoulder as he rushed out the door, leaving the spilled coffee and travel mug on the floor. They were offerings at the woman's feet, but no redemption came.

Morris pitied the woman. As he waited for her to approach the counter, he picked up his pen and crossed out the word 'thin.' In its place, he wrote: Reedy. Transparent snake skin. Fragile.

He put down his pen and the travel mug. The Wink app called him, but he resisted. Morris picked up the next cup. It was made of recycled paper and sported a plastic snap-on lid with a brown recycled sleeve. For this next customer, the woman, he must leave the brothers' office. Morris headed to the pseudo-kitchen behind the bar. His supplies awaited him, and he deftly gathered them. He paused and glanced out the door the angry man had exited. Morris caught a glimpse of thick clouds and a smattering of rain. The woman was cold, and she ached from the harsh chastisement, her trophies unable to warm her. Morris knew the words would come to him.

Oscar rubbed his hands together, and a blue spark crackled in the dim light. Morris' coffee philosophy had begun to change even him. "This might be good," Oscar whispered.

Behind the counter, Morris selected a sturdy paper cup from the middle of the stack. Each cup faced downward, a tower of white with the Saki Brother logo on each one. When he served customers, Morris chose the cup on the top. He did so hurriedly as if frazzled and chaotic, mimicking the frazzled and hurried customers. They were eager to prove they were in a rush, moving about hither and to. Morris was the invisible lackey. The customers didn't care if he was tired. They would continue to bustle about, and he would continue to deal with it for this was the law, the crux of master/servant coexistence.

Morris looked up. The woman lumbered toward him. Her bags slapped against her thick legs. She was worn and frustrated. He tossed the cup in the trash, turned, and went back for a larger size. In front of him were two square plastic tubs. A metal scoop laid on top of one. Morris could see they'd been lazy, using the same scoop for both the chocolate and the white chocolate granules. He wrinkled his nose in disgust. "

Flavored coffee is for the weak," he whispered as she approached.

"For the weak. That's a good one," Oscar agreed.

"A mocha please," the woman practically shouted. "Bastard," she quipped, looking back at the now empty doorway.

"Large?" Morris asked, putting on a furrowed brow of concern.

The woman looked like she might cry. She untangled herself from the shopping bag handles and let them sink to the floor. The bags spouted names of high-end stores, places Morris avoided. Larimore shopped for the both of them. Or sent one of her minions to shop for them, he wasn't sure. From the looks of the tired woman's face and the number of sacks at her feet, she'd spent all day gathering. He wanted to ask her why. He wanted to know what the packages represented and what void they filled. But he resisted. He was a servant, not an interrogator.

"That would be great. Thank you." She sniffled and dug into an oversized bag. She pulled out a cellophane wrapped package, which she demolished in order to retrieve two delicate pieces of tissue. She wiped her face and spoke again.

"People are so rude these days. Only thinking about themselves. Can't they see anyone else? Do they think the world revolves around them? I wasn't being rude. I'm never rude. I'm a rather pleasant person to be around. I care about people." She nearly shouted that last barb and looked over her shoulder while she said it as if the reedy male was still in the listening vicinity.

The woman fell silent and watched with great interest as Morris held the frothing cup under the spigot. The whirring sound was loud, and the steam rose off the milk. Morris was a fan of the frothing cup. He preferred the sound of it over the sound of people's mindless chatter. It soothed him. He made a show of pouring steamed milk into her large cardboard cup. He wouldn't admit it, but he enjoyed pouring from a great height. He never splashed or spilled, and younger children tended to stare in awe. Not that they ever spoke to him. No. Their parents instilled stranger danger fear in them, and Morris became an odd combination of scary and servant. Unworthy of being treated like a person, yet no one feared he'd poison their drinks.

The woman snorted. "You can't be serious," she said, pointing a stubby finger at the gallon of whole milk sweating on the counter.

"I beg your pardon?" Morris, ever the servant, asked.

"You used whole milk."

"Are you asking me if I did or telling me you wanted me to?" He hated being confused.

"What's the difference?"

Morris knew the difference, and despite the woman answering his question with a question, he was sure she knew the difference, too. He had no time for riddles. He had to decipher enough of them at home. He took a deep breath and counted to ten. Slowly, so as to make her wait as punishment for her inconsiderate behavior. The customer service protocol, as told to him by the Saki brothers, was to become apologetic. The customer was always right. Or so the brothers told him. He tried again. "Ma'am, have I used the wrong milk?"

She smacked her chubby hand on the counter top, and Morris saw the way her costume jewelry dug deeply into the skin on her middle finger. Around the fake gold ring, her skin took on a greenish hue. It was tarnish, but he hoped it was gangrene.

"Why are you such an imbecile? I thought you'd be a better

barista. Can't you see I'm already in a bad mood?" She waved a hand in front of her face, and Morris was reminded of the ASL sign for beautiful. He smirked. "Oh, fine," she said. "I see how you are. Just because I'm not a fucking size two, you assume I'm some kind of fatty who doesn't know how to choose skim milk? You think if I don't come in here showing skin that I'm not decent looking?"

Morris wanted to respond, but she wouldn't stop talking.

She jerked at the hem of her blouse and hiked it up three inches, exposing a slab of colorless skin. "How about that skin, huh? Let me tell you something, jerk. It's people like you that make life hard for the rest of us. It didn't occur to you to ask me how I want my coffee. No. You think you can tell me what to put in it because you assume things about me. Like that I'm fat because I make poor choices, not because maybe I have a thyroid problem or because I'm big boned. No. You put up these stupid assumptions, these unrealistic, shitty expectations on people all because you think every woman is supposed to look like fucking Barbie or something and—"

Ding.

Like an oven timer, Morris' cell phone chirped a notification. The woman evaporated into nothing. Her shopping bags melted into the floor. Morris was alone with Oscar who sat at one of the tables tracing his finger along the granite design in the way someone might be aware of a small cut that's begun to scab over. The pain from the injury had subsided, the injury still visible on the skin. The scab was nothing but a mark—left alone, and it would continue to heal. Dig at it, peel it back, scratch at it with a fingernail or something sharper, and the skin would open up. The pain would return.

Ding.

Morris set the mocha on the counter. His hand trembled. He didn't believe in social media. He found it a stage for fake news and fake people. An atrocity against rational thinking. An emotional quicksand—get too close and you could never get out. He inched toward the phone. He was being summoned.

"It's fine," he said to the empty room. "She's home and

probably wondering where I am. She's asking me to come home. She misses me. Yearns for me." The words poured out of him, unbidden. Unrelenting. Morris despised when people rambled and despised when his behavior mimicked theirs.

He pressed the home button and watched as the screen changed from black to the home screen. His wallpaper bore an image of Larimore. She was scantily clad in a string bikini, her hands on her waist. Her back to him, the ocean in front of her, unaware that he'd been snapping her picture from behind as the sun kissed her face.

Covering the wallpaper were his most used icons and sprinkled among them, the unused. The camera function with its partner, the photo library. The calendar where he kept track of his shifts at Saki Brothers. The clock, the phone, the Internet browser—these remained unused most of the time. Morris preferred an old-fashioned watch. The sound of it tick-tocking the time away soothed him. Larimore did not make phone calls, preferring to text him, and Morris had no one else to call. He found the Internet to be a time waster, much like social media. The iTunes app sat innocently enough, and he wished he could tap it right now—forget what he'd been waiting for all night and lose himself in music. But he couldn't. He had to know the truth. He tapped the little blue pentagon on the Wink app.

Larimore was home. The front door had been unlocked, and she had used her code to gain access to their home. He checked his watch against the time she unlocked the door. It'd been less than two minutes. Morris swiped the Wink app away and opened the one that let him see inside the house. His breathing picked up speed. He had to see her. Now.

The front door was closed, and she leaned against it. Her hair was loose around her face. For a minute, he thought she knew he peered in at her. That somehow, they had locked eyes, and the gentle look was her way of letting him know she missed him. Or that she knew he missed her, ached for her.

"What is she smiling about?" he muttered. He cursed the limitation of the camera angle. If he repositioned it now while she was in the room, she might hear the faint noise the camera emitted when it shifted. He watched for several agonizing seconds until he caught a glimpse of movement.

There, just inside of the camera lens, a hand reached out. A finger touched Larimore between her breasts and trailed the length of her sternum. She trembled at the touch. Her hands were behind her back, and her smile turned into a serious look. Not a frown exactly but a sober look as if trying to see inside of something. Or someone.

Morris knew it was not possible to feel his heart moving, but he could swear the scene before him yanked it two inches to the right. Someone was in their house. Someone had his hand on his love's body. He tried to steady himself. He had to call her. He had to call someone to alert them to the problem. His job was to protect her and, he'd failed.

"I have to get to her."

He stood straighter and looked around as if a pair of car keys or a space ship would materialize out of thin air and transport him home. The counter held only the fat lady's mocha. His keys were in the office. Morris hurried back to the solace of the cluttered room, bumping against a table along the way. His anger at the intruder increased as sharp pain radiated along his hip bone. He would save Larimore. He would find the bastard and make him pay for touching her. He would make him experience pain ten thousand times over.

The keys had disappeared of their own volition, and Morris knew it was because he wasn't focused. "Slow. Focus," he instructed.

Ding.

He was paralyzed by the sound of another notification. Had the intruder locked her in? Had she managed to get him out of the house? Was she safely locked inside and trying to reach Morris who had promised to protect her? Had someone else punched in a code in an attempt to gain entry?

He picked up the phone. It wasn't the Wink app. The camera app was trying to tell him something. He tapped the living room icon and took in the scene.

Morris watched the jerky movements. He saw Larimore and a

man with his back to the camera lens. Slender and tall. His hair was cut short and parted on the side. Morris could not see his face as the man leaned down and touched his lips to Larimore's.

"No. No. This is a mistake. This is wrong. Get away, my love. Try to get away."

Larimore did not hear him. She did not try to escape. She returned the man's kiss, and when Morris was sure his pulse could not go faster without bursting out of his chest, they embraced one another. She let him lift her off the ground. She wrapped her legs around the stranger's waist, and he carried her out of the view of the lens.

Morris tapped relentlessly at the refresh button, but his efforts went unnoticed. The couple did not return to his view. In his gut, he knew they'd retired to Larimore's boudoir, the one place in the house Morris had refrained from putting a camera. If someone other than himself ever gained access to Morris' phone, he did not want them to see into the room when he was there, so he'd respected Larimore's private quarters out of concern for his own. He regretted that decision now.

Oscar took up residence in Morris' body and held firm to his human's mindset. The wisp refused to let Morris exhaust himself in a fit of childish rage. There would be no throwing things and no glass breaking. Morris would not be given an opportunity to temper tantrum. Oscar was done with this servant-like charade of obedience to Larimore. She was a tramp. A whore. She did not deserve Morris, and Morris did not deserve this kind of treatment. Oscar would make her pay and, he would use Morris to get the job done.

Unable to process his next move, Morris sat in the desk chair. His car keys were in plain sight where he'd left them, but he was in no hurry to go home. The scene there was not something he wanted to confront. He almost wished he could go back in time and recreate the reedy man and the beefy woman. Almost. To distract himself, he turned his attention to the tray of coffee mugs. There, to the far right of the tray was the smallest one. Minuscule really.

"That is what I need. That will help," Morris said to Oscar.

"It's good we saved it for last," Oscar replied. "Go ahead."

The small cup had no handles. It was ceramic with painted stripes all around. Earth tones—brown, green, red, brown, green, red. Morris cupped it in his palm and rubbed the cool ceramic against his mouth and nose. He craved the burning liquid. But instead of pouring hot coffee, he reached into the back corner desk drawer where the Saki brothers kept a bottle of liquor hidden. It was mostly full. Morris had waited weeks before one of the men had cracked the seal and poured himself a finger's worth of bourbon. Since then, whenever no one was looking, Morris helped himself to the private stash. Never much. Just a lick and a taste from time to time.

"May I?" Oscar asked and filled the cup to the brim. He approved of this shot of liquid confidence. He held the cup to Morris' lips. Decision making was a battle, and Oscar had to ensure his carapace was up for the job. Morris had to be well informed, well educated, and knowledgeable before he acted. It was the wisp's duty to pave the way.

Morris licked his lips and stared into the cup. "One. Two. Three," he counted and coated his throat.

The burn was instantaneous followed by a solution to his problem. The resolution was so clear, so concrete in his mind, there was no questioning what had to be done. It was the same vision he'd seen each time something like this happened to him. This time, he was determined to see it through.

"Alright then," he said. "So be it."

"That's better," Oscar said.

"If things were left up to me, I'd never get out of these messes."

"What about her? She deserves this, no?" Oscar fed Morris his lines.

"There is no better way. I know that." He put away the cups he hadn't used. He stuffed the tote back where he'd found it and made a mental note to throw out the large mocha in the dining room. He picked up the smallest cup and examined it.

Painted on one side was an outline. The state of Alaska. He hadn't noticed it before nor had he noticed the cup wasn't for espresso like he'd originally thought. It was a shot glass. Despite the morose situation, he laughed. He laughed until there were tears in his eyes.

"It's like it was meant to be. This is made for alcohol. This is right, but it doesn't belong here. Not in a coffee shop."

"Don't worry. I'll help you."

"You will?" Morris asked. "No matter what I ask you to do?" He stuffed the Alaska cup into the front pocket of his jeans.

"Yes, sir," Oscar said and hung his head, servant style. It was imperative he conveyed a sense of helping Morris, or Morris would never go through with the plan.

As Morris pulled his hand out of his pocket, a crumpled card came with it and fell to the floor. He retrieved it and flattened it against his palm. On the back, centered boldly in the middle, was a phone number. Above the number, the words "Crisis Line" were written in dark black letters. He flipped the card over. On the front, Cloverleaf Counseling was advertised in all caps. Beneath it, in feminine script, the name Starr Randel. Her phone number and email address were listed along the bottom.

He smiled at the memory of the daisies on her skirt, and he worked his way up the memory of her figure. He saw her pretty smile and her lovely eyes. The woman who'd shared a table with him. The woman who'd noticed him. Her name was Starr, and she had a number.

"Thank you," Morris whispered and pressed his lips to the card. Maybe she could help.

He left Saki Brothers through the back door. Halfway home, he remembered the cardboard cup, the mocha souring inside it and tried to forget about Larimore and the strange man who carried her out of his sight. He held Starr's card in a tight grip against the steering wheel. The card was wrinkled beyond repair, but he wasn't worried. Her office address was burned into his brain. It rested nicely beside her phone number. He'd made sure to commit them to memory before he'd gone to his car. He had quickly scoured the brothers' messy desk to locate his paper application and hurriedly scrawled Starr's office number as his new emergency contact. He would call her tomorrow.

The wisp hovered in the passenger seat, the faintest streak of blue. He'd play along for a while and then get the job done.

****

The next day Morris entered the library and scanned the area for an unused computer. He was anxious and unhappy with Larimore. Her behavior caused him to be here, out in the open with his back to windows and doors. Because of her, he had to sit next to someone in the library to use the Internet. He'd become so angry he'd thrown his laptop and broken it.

The computer room buzzed with activity. The clicking and clacking of fingers against keys. The almost silent rumble as people scrolled the mouse up and down, down and up, sounded like delivery trucks rolling their cavernous back doors up and down on the tracks. He listened for delivery men shouting directions but heard none. He cleared his throat, but no one turned. Could they tell he was a barista? Did he have to produce a library card to use one of the machines? The library was his stage, not a facility he knew how to use.

To his right, a woman with a nest of curls on her head pressed buttons on an industrial-sized printer. She wore a contraption on her back and in it was a child. It looked sluggish as if drugged. Its eyes were cloudy blue. A dribble of milk rested on its chin. The woman pressed more buttons, consulted the printer's screen, bit her bottom lip, and leaned forward to check the tray. It was empty. When she noticed Morris staring, she gave him a nervous laugh.

"These things," she said, indicating the printer. "You need a degree to operate them, I swear."

Morris hated when people did this—said they swore when really they hadn't. "They have manuals."

"Right?" she said and poked the buttons again. A coin purse covered in intricate beading rested on a large textbook that sat on the printer. She consulted the purse for change. "I don't suppose you have a nickel," she said.

"Are you asking or stating?" He wished people said what they meant. Be clear, he wanted to shout at her. People aren't mind readers.

"What?" she asked.

Before Morris could explain, the baby erupted in a scream. Every head in the room turned toward the commotion as it arched its back. Morris was sure it would fall right out of the backpack and drop to the floor on its head. He didn't move to catch it. *Where do such small people get such grandiose lungs?*

"Braxton, honey. Mommy's here," the woman said in a voice that betrayed her chaotic attempt to gather up her belongings.

She opened the tote bag on her arm and shoved the textbook into it. Wrinkled papers accepted the book into their bent and wayward arms. A receipt flew out and fluttered to the floor, unnoticed by the woman. She jabbed at the printer buttons a few more times in desperation as the child continued to bellow as if it was in great pain. Fat teardrops rolled down its cheeks and met the drop of milk on its chin.

"Come on already," the woman instructed the printer. "Don't cry, Braxton," she cooed to the baby.

She stuck the fingers from one hand into the coin purse and feverishly shoved coins into the slot. She prayed for the jackpot with the random selection. With her free hand, she stroked the baby's leg that dangled against her back. The baby kicked her hand away, determined to cause a scene.

Morris wanted to walk away, but his legs wouldn't cooperate. Did people think he knew the woman? Would they frown at him if he didn't offer to help? As he was about to step forward and do something, though he wasn't sure what, the baby's pudgy hands raised up as if in praise and grabbed hold of the woman's hair. It wrapped all ten fingers around the locks and yanked with superhuman strength. The woman arched her back. Morris saw tears come to her eyes. Her lips parted.

"Shit," she whimpered.

Now she swore, and Oscar grinned at the show. Hurriedly, she grabbed the coin purse. Coins clattered to the ground.

"Braxton," she said, beseeching the child to release her as she ran from the room.

Down the hall they went, the cries of the monstrous baby getting fainter and fainter with every step the woman took until at last the cries were silenced by the deep thud of the women's restroom door.

Library patrons clucked their tongues and shook their heads like disappointed hens. As they returned to their activities, their annoyance faded into forgetfulness.

Morris startled as the printer beeped and whirred. A bundle of papers spurted out and landed in the tray. He nodded his approval and headed to a nearby computer. When he'd called the number on Starr's card, a receptionist had answered and taken his number. She said Starr would call him back, but his phone had yet to ring. Not to be deterred, he resorted to sending an email.

CHAPTER NINE

Cloverleaf Counseling was small with only three mental health therapists, an office assistant, and Julle, the intern. Cloverleaf was also old school—no electronic health record. Starr balanced the eight-page, double-sided packet on her knee and twirled her hair absentmindedly as she read her new patient's admission packet. The client, M. Oscar Wilde, had reached out to her via email. If he'd called the center, he would have been directed to the other therapist. With less than two months to go, Starr wasn't taking new patients.

Her legs were crossed, and her skirt covered them nicely. She always dressed modestly. She used a toe from her right foot to scratch the calf of her left leg. The nail was painted the color of wet clay. If only she could shake the distractions that threatened to close in on her. With no one to hide from at home, she'd nicked her ankle with a razor that morning. The wound called out to her, exacerbated by Sdax's behavior.

"Why are you staring at me?" Starr whispered as she checked to make sure her office door was closed.

"I'm   not,"   Sdax   retorted.

"Yes, you are." She despised the fact that she was so easily roped into arguing with a child.

"Because I can. That's all," Sdax said. She'd been sulking all morning. Ever since Starr had taken a hammer to the razor blade and thrown the pieces into the trash.

Starr turned around and faced her desk. At home, she was constantly plagued with Sdax. Her tantrums and constant demands for a death party were exhausting. She found most of her peace by going to the office or zeroing in on her client work. Geoff often accused Starr of having no work-life balance. She'd never bothered to tell him that it was her only way to keep the little brat under control. These days, even work didn't help. Sdax was everywhere, pushing and pleading. She was so convincing Starr had begun to think that just maybe the kid was on to something.

"See? You are staring. It's creepy. And rude."

"You're rude," Sdax said. She stood by the sandbox, her hands on her hips.

"I'm reading. That's not being rude. Besides, this place is for grown-ups. You shouldn't even be here."

"You brought me here."

"Shut up, Sdax. I'm trying to work, okay? This is my work, and I don't have time for you."

The wisp's lip quivered. She started to cry. "You hate me?"

"Damn it. Fuck. I never said that. Just—" Her desk phone rang, and she jumped. She shushed the wisp as she hit the speakerphone button. "This is Starr." Without thinking, she reached down and scratched at the cut on her ankle. Anything to shut Sdax up. "My 1:30 is here now?" She sighed. "Agitated? Did you offer him coffee or anything? I'm not done reading his intake packet."

A light on her phone blinked, indicating a second call. Starr checked for a number. Unknown caller. She considered putting the receptionist on hold and answering, but the caller hung up before she could.

"All right. I'll be right out. Thanks."

Getting calls from the receptionist used to be her favorite back when Geoff was the one telling her about her clients' arrivals. Brandy, the fourth receptionist in the last year, was better than the previous three. She'd lasted the longest in a demanding position, and Starr tried to be friendly.

Sdax pleaded, "Can I come, Starr? I'll be nice."

"Don't bother. And try to be quiet for once," Starr whispered.

Early clients were an interruption. Starr was more upset about this client showing up early than she was about Sdax. Was it wrong to want a cup of coffee between appointments or to be able to go to the ladies' room before the need became an emergency? Her daily goal was to have a positive attitude regardless, but it wasn't always easy. Her new client hadn't even bothered to give his first name on the admission packet, and now she'd be forced to call him Mr. Wilde. She had half a mind to make him call her Ms. Randel.

With the desk phone headset plugged into her ears, Brandy tidied the waiting room, which was in total disarray. The Fica plant in the corner was missing a leaf and a small amount of potting soil sat on the striped carpet. Children's books that Brandy kept sanitized and regularly rotated were scattered across the vinyl sofa. Thankfully, only Starr's 1:30 was present to witness the mess.

"Mr. Wilde," Brandy said when Starr stuck her head out the main door.

Half in and half out of the private hallway that led to the inner offices, Starr tried to maintain her composure. Separated from the clients by a solid door with an opaque window, the door was locked from the inside for security reasons. Whenever a client arrived, Brandy pushed a small button under her desk that unlatched the door. The therapists all had keys to the main building, the suite, and the door Starr held open.

"Are you ready?" Starr asked. The man looked familiar, but she couldn't place him.

"It's not one-thirty," he said. He stared at her but pointed to his wristwatch.

"True. It's a little early. You're welcome to come in, though."

"Will that count?"

"Will what count?" Starr felt like she was being asked to solve another of Sdax's riddles.

"It. Now. If we start now, will it count against my time?"

"I explained that he has a ninety-minute appointment with you that starts at one-thirty," Brandy said.

"Exactly," Mr. Wilde reiterated. "Will starting early count against my time, or will I still get ninety minutes?"

"Is he sad?" Sdax whispered.

Starr ignored her wisp. "Not at all," she said and offered Mr. Wilde a smile.

"So I won't get my ninety minutes?" His face turned red, a shade just lighter than his hair.

It was Starr's turn to blush. "Mr. Wilde, I have you scheduled for a ninety-minute appointment. If you'd like to start early, we'll likely end early, but I assure you, I won't cut your time short."

He scratched his neck with a vengeance and tugged on his slate gray tie. "Thank you," he said and opened the main door to the suite.

"Mr. Wilde, it's this way." Brandy pointed to Starr.

"I'm going." He paused and traced the letter C etched into the door. "To the bathroom," he finished and stepped into the main hall.

Brandy caught the door and pulled it shut with a click. The door closer was broken. A work order had been placed the day before to keep it from banging shut. Another nuisance that came with working in community mental health where funds were not altogether generous.

"What was that about?" Starr whispered.

"You've got a winner, Starr. Seriously," Brandy said, shaking her head.

"I wonder what triggered him."

Brandy gave an annoyed shake of her head. "No idea," she said as the door handle turned under her hand. "Oh, shit."

Starr's heart thumped wildly in her chest. She hoped he hadn't heard them.

Mr. Wilde walked in. "I'm ready now," he announced.

"Certainly," Starr replied. She ushered him back to her office. "Brandy, if I get any calls, will you take messages, please?" It was standard practice for Brandy to hold therapists' calls when they were in session, but Starr wanted Mr. Wilde to know she took his appointment seriously.

"Sure," Brandy said and followed Mr. Wilde through the door to her desk. "Mr. Wilde, I almost forgot. You dropped your phone. Earlier. Would you like me to hold it?"

"Right. I." Mr. Wilde reached for his device. "My call was ignored," he muttered and shoved the phone into the breast pocket of his shirt.

Upon entering Starr's office, Mr. Wilde stood as if puzzled by the furniture arrangement. The door opened inward to the right. The walls were the same tan color as the rest of the suite. She'd gotten rid of the traditional love seat her first week there and traded it in for two chairs with a small table between them. Aside from the twelve-hundred square foot home Starr shared with Geoff, this room was her favorite place on earth. Soon to be replaced by a much smaller space, but she would think about that later.

Starr smoothed her hands down the front of her skirt. "Feel free to make yourself at home," she said.

"You let your patients sit at your desk?"

"Clients. I'm not a doctor," Starr corrected. "And no. Why?"

"Then I can't really make myself at home, can I? If I could, I'd get to choose where I want to sit. What you really meant to say is that I should take a seat. There or there," he said, and in a single fluid movement he turned to face her. Then, he sat stiffly in a chair, his spine straight and inches from the seat back.

"Mr. Wilde."

"You don't remember me. Do you?" he asked.

Starr racked her brain. Not from the grocery store. She'd been ordering groceries in since Geoff left. Post office? No. After Geoff's first two postcards, none of which mentioned the care package she'd sent him, she hadn't sent anything else. Where else did she go anymore besides work and home?

"I thought you'd recognized me, and that's why you wore the

same outfit. From when we met. Before."

"Same outfit?"

"Yes, remember? I mentioned it in my email requesting services. About how daisies are my favorite flower."

She remembered that from an email. Had thought it strange the author felt it pertinent to write "Favorite flower: daisies" at the bottom of the inquiry for services. So strange, she'd thought some kind of bot had filled it out. She hadn't even replied. "That was you?" she asked.

"You didn't reply, so that's why I had to call Brandy. That's her name, isn't it? The woman at the front desk?"

"Yes. Brandy schedules all my appointments." She waited for Mr. Wilde to say something else, but he didn't. "You said we've met before. I'm sorry. I'm having trouble remembering." She put her hand to her head. She needed a cigar. "Can I get you a coffee? We always have plenty."

Mr. Wilde looked at her and nodded. "That's it. That's how we first met."

Coffee? Plenty of it? His deep green eyes. The red hair. His tie hidden behind a messy brown apron as he scrubbed the table. She'd sat down and thanked him for his customer service.

"Morris. What an unusual name," she said warmly and put out her hand to shake.

He took her hand, and the vision of their starlit night exploded behind his eyes. She remembered him. It had taken a minute, but she knew. Her subconscious knew enough that she'd worn the same brown skirt with the daisies. He wished he'd brought them both coffee. Hazelnut for her, black for himself. "Coffee would be great, ma'am."

She tilted her head and shook her finger at him. "Nonsense. Call me Starr. Two seconds, I'll be right back," she said, wagging two fingers at him for emphasis. "You can read through these while I'm gone. Patient confidentiality, non-discrimination, all that fun stuff."

Morris took the sheaf of papers from her and relaxed in the chair. He'd done it. He'd one-upped his wisp.

The coffee was in the break room along with a variety of

mismatched cups. Starr placed two on saucers and filled them to the brim. In her head she carried her initial plan for Morris. He was sweet enough and seemed lonely. She'd double check his admission packet for any signs of crisis and talk about coping skills and discharge planning. They'd spend a few weeks having coffee and increasing his support network, and then she'd transition him to Julle. Three weeks tops and she was done. She had to be. It was evident she'd overreacted at the coffee shop, making assumptions and accusations. Community mental health was tough work. She needed something less intense.

"Knock-knock," she said quietly and pushed open her office door.

Tucked inside Cloverleaf's intake packet were line after line of monotonous drivel. An incoherent pile of mumbo jumbo lumped together to tell clients about their patient rights, how to file a grievance, information about the no-show policy, and of course, the sliding scale fee policy. In all Starr's years as a therapist, including those as a graduate student intern, she'd never before seen someone read the pages as if they were going to be quizzed on them later. Except for Morris Wilde. So taken aback by his concentration, Starr set the coffee on the table and snatched up his paperwork to search for a clue about this interesting man.

NAME: M. (Oscar) Wilde.

She wondered what the parentheses were about.

DATE OF BIRTH: 3/1/82

Thirty-six. His birthstone was aquamarine. Zodiac sign: Pisces. Starr made a mental note to learn more about the fish. She had a vague memory of Pisces being moody or whimsical. Whimsically moody, perhaps? Or that could be Aquarius. She couldn't remember.

OCCUPATION: Customer Service

He'd called her ma'am that day at Saki Brothers, too. He'd smiled and had a humble quality about him. She'd be sure to frequent the café more often. Leave big tips. That would help him feel more confident and reduce his need for therapy.

MARITAL STATUS: Single

Not single-cohabiting. Just single. Starr made an asterisk next to the word. She'd be sure to talk about his support network. Create a network map on paper. She had construction paper and markers for things like that. The bigger his support network, the less he'd need services. She was curious why he wore a ring if he wasn't married.

"Have you gotten to the part about why I'm in therapy?" Morris asked.

"What's that?" She felt strangely suffocated as if he'd been reading over her shoulder.

He'd scooted his chair next to the end table where she'd laid the coffee tray. His knees touched the table, like an overgrown schoolboy in a desk too small for his frame. The intake forms were on the floor under his chair, neatly folded in half.

"My reason for treatment," Morris prodded. "Have you gotten to that part? The reason I self-referred."

"No, I haven't," she said. He must have been to therapy before. He knew the jargon well enough. Starr made a note to ask about his previous therapist and why he didn't return to him or her. She tried to put a pin in the nagging worry that tried to skate to the front of her mind. If Morris had been in therapy before...if he knew his way around proper diagnosing coupled with the perfect cocktail of antipsychotics or opioids to reduce the sting of an ailment—physical or mental—why was he here? Schizoaffective disorder, the bipolar kind, and the standard bipolar disorder diagnoses rolled around in her head like pool balls.

In the corner, Sdax was mesmerized by Oscar. The boy wisp checked the end of his pool stick and rubbed a healthy amount of blue chalk over the tip. He blew on the end and got into position. Sdax crouched lower in the corner. Something about him bothered her and, she was reluctant to ask if she could play. She'd have to remember to mention him to Starr tonight. Until then, she'd hide under Starr's desk and fade into the color of the wall. Sometimes it was better to remain unnoticed.

Morris crossed one leg over the other and reached for the coffee. "It's kind of embarrassing actually. The reason I'm here."

"There's no need to be embarrassed, Morris," Starr reassured him. "People come to therapy for many reasons. Society is the problem with all the stigma that's attached to taking care of our mental health." She brushed off her soapbox and tapped the attached microphone. "Mental health is just as important as physical health. You wouldn't ignore low blood sugar because someone said diabetes is caused by weight gain, would you? Getting an emotional checkup is no different than getting a physical, having your teeth cleaned, or getting an eye exam. We aren't ashamed of taking any of those preventative measures, are we?"

"No," he said and hung his head properly chastised.

"Okay, then." Starr moved to the seat across from Morris. "Now, let's have some coffee, and you can tell me why you're here."

"Do you have any cream?" he asked.

Oscar struck the eight ball, and it sailed into the corner pocket. This was part of the plan. Morris was here to get help. Here to keep himself from going through with it. As long as Starr Randel did her part, Larimore wouldn't have to die, and Oscar wouldn't have to kill her as an atonement for her sins. Everything would be okay.

"Oh, before I forget. Three things: I can't tell anyone about you or your sessions without your written permission unless you tell me you're going to hurt yourself or hurt someone else, or you're being abused or neglected. Then all bets are off, and I'm obligated to keep you safe. Understood?"

"Of course," Morris replied.

"If a court were to subpoena your records, I'd have to testify in court even if you didn't want me to."

"Not if I can help it," Oscar muttered.

"Understood," Morris repeated.

"Cream?" Starr grinned, glad the basics were present and accounted for. "Promise to keep a secret?" she asked conspiratorially.

"What a charade," Oscar said into Morris' ear.

"In the break room, all we have is the plain kind. So, I keep my own stash in here. See?" Starr lifted the cabinet where she kept her cleaning supplies. In a small wicker basket beside them sat two plastic containers of hazelnut powdered creamer. She grabbed one and flipped open the cap. "Want some?"

Morris chuckled. "You won't run out, will you?"

"This is the first thing on my grocery order every week." He held out his cup, and Starr poured.

"So, there you have it. My big secret. Now, what's your big secret for needing therapy? You didn't specify an actual problem on your paperwork," Starr said, glancing at him as she stirred her coffee.

"Not exactly my kind of tit for tat," Oscar muttered.

Starr was right. Morris had only checked the boxes for "work problems" and "relationship problems—not marital." Nothing that sounded serious enough for weekly therapy.

He kept his coffee cup in front of his face, his eyes averted, as if ashamed of what he was about to divulge. "The woman I want to marry turned me down."

"Oh, Morris. I'm so sorry. That must have been really hurtful." Starr sat in the chair opposite him, a peer chatting over coffee. "Rejection isn't easy."

"I'm a mess about it," Morris said. He set his cup down and looked her in the eyes. "Will you help me, Starr?" he as his eyes pooled with tears.

"Morris, goodness. Of course, I'll help you." She patted his arm. A mother hen consoling a wayward chick.

In therapy, people work hard to find a path. A lane. Be it direct, circular, or a veritable zigzag through a desert and over a mental mountain range. That was Starr's goal. To help her clients find their path to get to the answers hidden inside. Morris referred to her as an expert, but he didn't realize he was the expert on himself. He knew what he needed, where he'd been, and what his protective factors were. Starr's job was to help him resurface the things that were hidden beneath the anxiety, trauma, depression, or, in his case, the rejection. No matter the cost.

"It's a lot of little things just adding up. Like a mountain of things." Morris looked ready to launch into a diatribe of issues but stopped. "You're not going to write this down?"

"I don't usually. I'll summarize in the progress note."

"Oh." He appeared insulted.

"Would you rather I did?"

"It seems taking actual notes demonstrates concentration. A focused sense of urgency on my problems, if you will. At the cafe, we write down the customers' names on their orders. So we don't forget," he said. "How do you think I remembered your name?"

"I assure you I have a very good memory, Mr.—Morris."

He looked wounded. A child told no when he really wanted to hear yes. Starr felt the taut rope of the therapeutic relationship constrict against her rib cage. Her hope of building rapport and making a quick difference before moving on to suit herself tumbled to the pit of her stomach, an avalanche that would weigh her down with guilt for weeks to come. She averted her eyes and reached for the notepad on her desk. Extracting a ballpoint pen from the cup on her desk, she flipped the notebook to a clean page. The picture from her business card, the words Randel Counseling, flashed through her mind. She shoved it aside, silently ashamed of herself for thinking she was good at this. Her watch said they had sixty minutes until her schedule shifted to administrative duties, a time that was considered a mental reprieve from the days' clients. Silently, she rolled the time back and restarted the clock for Morris' ninety-minute session. It was a small sacrifice that she hoped would show him the fullest extent of her regret. His needs were greater than hers. She'd stay late into the evening to do her paperwork if she had to. He was the client, she only the counselor.

"Shall we begin?" she asked and let the session start in earnest.

CHAPTER TEN

Starr took a deep breath and tried to find her center. Grace Wu was the last teenage client on her caseload at Cloverleaf, and she was a pill. Starr had hoped the sixteen-year-old would be farther along in her progress by now, but today's session had not proved fruitful thus far. In fact, she and Grace were deadlocked and had been for more than ten minutes.

"I think if you'd let yourself feel something different, you'd feel better. You might even be able to see this from a different perspective," Starr suggested. She remembered how long it took her to convince Rachel James to feel something and tried to focus on the potential for progress.

The girl barely moved her mouth, but her words came through clearly. "No. I don't need to cry. No more homework. And no family therapy."

"Grace, you aren't an adult yet. Inviting your father in for your sessions could make a huge difference. Why not give it a chance?" Starr asked. She hated it when clients made her beg.

"Then I'll get emancipated."

"Because you don't want to talk to him? Doesn't that seem rather extreme?"

"Other kids have done it," Grace said.

Starr folded her arms across her chest and leaned back in

her chair. This was the longest session she'd had all day, and she was only fifteen minutes into it. "Kids you know?"

"Who cares if I know them. Other kids have done it. Like that one from the movies. I'm not any different from him. Besides I'm almost eighteen, so it makes sense." Grace punctuated every sentence with a finger stab. She stabbed the air in front of Starr, the computer monitor, and the calendar. Always stabbing with her finger.

"Macaulay Culkin? From *Home Alone*? That's who you're comparing yourself with? Grace..." Starr couldn't think of a way to finish her sentence. She wanted to tell the girl she was being ridiculous, but who was she to judge? How many times had she herself wished a different kind of life when her parents were alive and fighting? Well, her father fought. Her mother dug herself deeper into a cocoon of silence.

Grace stabbed herself with her finger. "I thought you were supposed to help me. That's what you always say. You're here to validate my feelings, to help me grow as a person. Yet it feels like you're trying to sacrifice me and what I want to please my father."

Starr's heart sank a little. Had Grace's sessions always been this difficult? She'd played cards with Grace and colored with her. They'd even tried knitting a couple of times before Grace deemed it old-ladyish and said she wasn't interested. For every sixty-minute session, Starr prided herself on getting a solid five therapeutic minutes with Grace. Starr felt the chances of a breakthrough were ticking away with the hour on the clock.

"I'm sorry. You're right. I wasn't validating your feelings. I'm trying too hard to get you to see things from my perspective," Starr said.

Grace tightened her ponytail. "I want to know what it takes to get emancipated." She opened the notes app on her phone, ready to make a list of tasks.

"A few things."

"Like?"

"Paperwork. A court hearing. You'd have to prove you have a job and money." "I can get a job. What would happen in the hearing?" Grace asked without looking up.

"You'd have to prove to a judge that you don't need financial or emotional support from your parent."

Grace stopped typing and glared at Starr. "Parents. I have two you know. Just because my dad wrote my mom off doesn't mean you get to do the same."

Starr bit her lip. "Of course. Parents."

"Will you help me?"

"Talk to your dad?" Starr asked, hanging her hope on a thread.

"Get emancipated," Grace said. "Will you help me do it?"

In that moment, Starr decided she would not take adolescent clients in her new practice. It would be adults or little kids accompanied by adults. No one in between. She gave the shopping list for her new practice a mental perusal and crossed several items off of it. No need for a dictionary of slang words or card games. She wouldn't need any of those things, which meant she could put her money to better use by purchasing nice journals for the adults and dolls for the little kids.

"Can we get blocks, too?" Sdax asked. She sat beside Grace with a piece of paper and a crayon taking her own notes.

"Grace, you know I can't do that."

"It's a coping skill, isn't it? I don't like how my dad treats me like a prisoner, so I want to cope by becoming an adult."

"Coping is experiencing the prisoner life. Embracing it. Exploring it with your dad in family therapy. You know, figuring it out and working together. Emancipating yourself is running away."

A stubborn tear rolled down Grace's cheek. "You're like all the others. All the other therapists he's dragged me to over the years. You tell me one thing and then do the opposite. You don't know what it's like. Living by his rules. Not having a mother."

"Remember to use 'I' statements, Grace." Starr spoke as gently as she could and bit the inside of her cheek to stop herself from saying anything more. To stop herself from feeling.

Grace jumped out of her chair and went to the window. The blinds were down in an effort to keep out the stream of sun that caused a glare on Starr's computer screen. Grace wore a t-shirt, jeans, and flip-flops. Though she didn't wear makeup or dye her hair in bright colors like some kids, on the outside, she looked like an average teenage girl. Her long, straight hair was pulled into a high ponytail, and she carried a nice backpack and cute cross-body purse. In Starr's opinion, everything about the girl was as ordinary as any other. She had a strict father and an absent mother. In less than a year Grace would be eighteen, and she could go find her mother if she wanted to.

"I hate coming to therapy. I think you're in it for the money, not to help people. I want to find my mother, and you don't understand. No one does." Grace twisted the rod making the blinds open and close. "I have a right to know my mother."

"Grace, please. You're blinding me when you do that." Starr shielded her eyes with her hands.

"Use 'I' statements," Grace said in a mocking tone. She yanked the cord. The blinds slapped each other on their way to the top of the window box, and then she threw herself back down in her chair. "*I* like the blinds *that* way," she muttered.

Starr savored the pinch of her cheek between her teeth and counted backwards from five in her head. Coping skills were in abundance, and it made no sense why Grace couldn't put them to good use. "Grace, I understand you're upset. I appreciate you sharing your feelings with me." She rose and went to the window.

"But?" Grace said.

"But in my office I'd like you to respect my space by leaving the blinds alone and using a respectful tone. Your father isn't in here, and I realize he's the one you're angry at. We could work on resolving that anger if you invited him to a session. Finally, in my office—"

"In your office it's your way or the highway. I get it," Grace said. She watched Starr release the blinds back to their original position. The rest of the signal, just like she and her uncle Don had talked about.

Don was her mother's half-brother, someone Grace had met accidentally through a friend of a friend when she'd snuck away and ended up at a college party. He worked in the green building next door. A month of communication, him feeding her information from her mother, and they'd devised the signal. When she was ready for him to take her to Montana, all she had to do was let him know. Lowering the blinds again had been the last indication, and while Grace was uncertain if she wanted to make the plunge, she'd decided to let Starr make the choice for her.

"There. That's better now, isn't it?" Starr asked.

"Do you know your mother, Starr?" Grace asked, fueled by a strange new curiosity mixed with fear that she had just committed to running away from home.

"I did."

"Is she? Gone?" Grace hated the word dead.

Starr listened for the sound of gunshots. The quiet pop-pop that always came with the memory of her parents' last moments on Earth. She'd been at a sleepover the night before, and her friend's mother had dropped her off at home. Excited to tell her mother all about the slumber party, Starr waved away the woman's offer to walk her to the door.

"It's okay. I'll run up," Starr said. With her backpack slung over her shoulder, she impatiently waited for the vehicle to come to a stop before yanking the door open. She hit the ground and ran up the path as fast as her legs would go. From behind, her friend Kelli yelled goodbye, and Starr threw her hand up in a backward wave.

Three more steps and Starr reached the doorknob. Her parents were expecting her. The party invitation had said Kelli's mom would drop her off at eleven, and they were right on time. Kelli's mom had honked the car horn when she drove up, which made the next sound all the more strange coming from inside the house.

"Mom?" Starr called as she pushed the door open.

Starr never understood how Kelli's mom had gotten to the front door so quickly, one hand on Starr's shoulder, the other pulling the door shut despite Starr's frantic attempts to push it open and rush to her mother's side. Starr never understood why her father had chosen that moment to end their pain and suffering. Did he hate her as much as he hated her mother? Was the timing her punishment for being a bad daughter? The questions lived beneath the surface of the memory. Ocean creatures waiting to pull her beneath the undertow of the trauma if she allowed herself to get too close.

"She's passed, yes. A long time ago," Starr said calmly. Now was not the time to resurrect the memories or solve the mysteries of her youth.

"Oh."

"Does that put things in perspective some? Your mother is alive. Waiting a few more months until you're an adult is an inconvenience. Frustrating maybe. But she's out there."

"Was your mom sick when she died?"

Starr's heart sped up. The conversation bordered on an inappropriate amount of self-disclosure. "My mother isn't the focus here, Grace."

"So she wasn't sick. Did you get to say goodbye?"

"Bye Mom. See you tomorrow," Starr yelled on her way out the door.

"What? No hug?" her mother asked.

"Okay, but hurry." Starr turned and let her mother hug her. As she ran out the door with Kelli, Starr realized that was the first time in a long time her mother had initiated physical affection. As she climbed into the car, she looked back at their house and blew a kiss to her mother. Clothed in pajamas and a tattered robe, her mother pressed her fingers to her mouth. She smiled and waved.

"If we can't talk about your mother and we can't talk about mine, is there anything left to say?" Grace asked.

She had a point. She didn't think emancipation would help, but she'd been wrong before. "We still have two more sessions together."

The silence bounced off the walls. Starr waited, determined to stay the course with Grace. Unwilling to hand her off until she completed her part of the deal. *If Grace wants out, she'll have to make the first move.*

"You're going to transfer me anyway. Why not get it over with?"

Starr kept her composure intact. "Oh. If that's what you want. Would you like to meet Julle today while we have a few minutes left?"

Grace's demeanor went from stubborn and determined to nonchalant and dismissive. "Yeah, cool. I'll get my dad. He'll want to meet her," Grace said.

Rejection hurt no matter who it came from. Starr screwed the lid tight on her mother's memory and silently patched the hole in the wall of her feelings. If Grace wanted to be emancipated, Julle could   do   the   dirty   work.   Starr   was   tired.

CHAPTER ELEVEN

Every time Morris made coffee at Saki Brothers, he thought of Starr. The sound of her voice. The tip of her head—she tipped it to the right when she was deep in thought. The brush of her Bohemian skirts as they rustled against her legs. Never in a sexual way. He didn't feel that way about her though he did sense their connection. When she shook his hand or leaned in as he spoke, he felt the connection. She was a dew drop resting on the edge of a green leaf. He, the dry and dusty road beneath. When she could cling no longer, she dropped. On contact, Morris exploded with sensation. She made him feel alive.

His previous session, hardly his last, had become particularly intense. It thrilled Morris to think about it and how things had progressed. The start of the session and the disgust he felt toward himself and Starr when she'd mentioned the word discharge still made him angry. Angry to the point of rabid if he allowed himself to dwell on it. So he didn't grant that allowance. Instead, he steered far from it, focusing on what had happened after she'd introduced the idea of Gestalt therapy and the empty chair technique. Morris knew if he dwelt too long on his anger, it became an open invitation to Oscar and his ideas to grow.

Starr situated their chairs differently, asking demurely for Morris' help to shove the end table out of the way. That was tough. Her office was big but not massive. They tried putting it under the window, but that backed Starr into a corner. Next to her desk was no good because she said she'd be sitting at her desk and needed the two client chairs to face one another.

"Not too close but close enough," she instructed. It was then she explained the empty chair concept. How she wanted Morris to sit and talk to Larimore, tell her what was on his heart, so that he could eventually graduate from therapy and feel confident that his time with Starr had been beneficial.

"That's when another lie of omission presented itself, right?" Oscar asked as Morris wiped clean a corner table.

The patrons who'd sat there had no regard for the service industry. They'd torn open sugar packets and shredded their napkins into long strips. The napkins reminded Morris of the jeans women wore—the kind with torn hems, jagged as if a bear had mauled them from the toes to the ankle bone before deeming the wearer unpleasant for eating and lumbered away. All around the garbage were spots of dried coffee. The patrons had used straws to hold bits of the steamed milk and coffee concoction only to release them drip by drip all over the table. Like the old decoder messages kids played with that used invisible ink. He'd watched them do it from his place behind the counter.

"The omission?" Oscar asked, eager for the story to be told again.

After the typical pleasantries and his presentation of Saki Brothers' coffee for the two of them, Morris explained, "I want to propose to Larimore again. The right way, where I focus on her needs and not my own. Not like last time."

"Morris, that's wonderful. That will work perfectly for this exercise." Starr grimaced. "All we have to do is get this furniture arranged."

Morris took it upon himself to sort through that dilemma. He gently tucked Starr's sandbox, situated on a rolling cart, near her desk. He noticed she liked to rake through the sand when they talked. The movement soothed her. In fact, he'd noticed at times she was so enthralled by the sensation that if he raised his voice at all, it caused her to jolt back into reality as if she'd forgotten exactly what their roles were and had to be reminded she was the therapist and he the client.

"If we put this right here," Morris said, "we can put the end table here." He positioned it close to the office door.

"That blocks the exit, though," Starr said thoughtfully.

"You are staying in the room, yes? To coach me through this empty chair process?" he asked, pretending to be nervous at the thought of her abandoning him to an empty room.

"Of course, I'm staying. Don't be silly," she said and rested her hand on his shoulder.

Morris was somewhat irritated that anyone, especially Starr, would consider him behaving in a manner that suggested silliness, but he forgave her at the feel of her hand. "Right. What was I thinking?" he replied, looking into her eyes. "I know you won't leave me."

Starr surveyed the room one last time. It jangled her nerves to have her exit blocked. It went against everything she'd been taught in therapy school. She had even stressed the importance of this to Julle a few days before. Yet here she was, a competent and experienced clinician, going against what her gut told her was wrong.

"Well, it *is* a bit of a hazard. You've done all the heavy lifting, though," she said, considering the other side of the situation. She twisted her bracelets a full two circles around her wrist. *He's so eager to try this new technique. Now isn't the time to tell him that in a few short weeks he'll be working with Julle.*

Morris sensed her hesitation. "It's only for this little bit. Right? And if it helps me get better." He shrugged.

Starr smiled. "Fair enough. We'll leave it for a few minutes. Here's how the empty chair technique works." She led him to the chair on the right where she instructed him to sit and envision Larimore sitting across from him. She, Starr, would sit out of the way at her desk while Morris spoke to Larimore.

"This will be your opportunity to practice asking her to marry you. To talk through any residual conflict you all might be experiencing and break through any final and lingering barriers. In a way, it'll be like having Larimore right here with us."

It took three attempts and pleading from Morris to actually try the technique. He had to reposition the chairs twice until they were the perfect distance from one another. He asked Starr how he should start the conversation and if his tone was accurate. He reached up to tweak the position of the blinds, reducing the amount of sunlight streaming in. Then Morris went for the jugular.

"Starr?"

"Hmmm?" she asked, keeping her eyes focused on the sand.

"This is hard. I can't." He scratched his head. "I can't picture her."

"Think of what she'd be wearing. Imagine her smile. You can even close your eyes if you'd like. It might help you visualize her better."

"That would help. But can I hold your hand? Please?"

Morris' request stunned her. She stopped raking, and Morris saw her hand twitch. His scheming mind almost felt bad knowing his request meant Starr worried about the blocked exit. There she was, trapped inside her office with a man and no route of escape. Morris had scared her. He felt a tingle of thrill skate up his insides, through his belly, and up his esophagus until he had to bite the corner of his tongue. Then he let out a sharp laugh because he had no intention of frightening her. None at all. He wanted Larimore back. He wanted a pure, unadulterated commitment from her. Starr was the only one who could help him, and Oscar was on the verge of screwing up everything.

"Not like that, silly," Morris said. "I don't mean...like...that."

"Morris."

He tried hard to show her the predicament he was in without divulging the presence of his fickle and unstable wisp. "Will you sit here? I can't picture Larimore with this empty chair. If I hold your hand, I can close my eyes and speak to her. I know I'll be able to. Please. Will you?" He begged. "How will I ever get discharged if I can't conquer this, Starr?"

Starr hesitated. The point of the chair was that it was empty. The space was there to free up the client's mind and shore up his confidence enough to speak plainly. It wasn't about holding your therapist's hand and pretending she was your partner. "Morris, I don't know."

He closed his eyes and held out his hands. "Larimore, I want you to know." Pause. "A lot of things." Pause. "You're important to me. I mean, you're important to other people, too. Like at work. And at the gym. But with me." Pause. Morris stopped talking and put his hand against his forehead.

Starr waited. Morris wasn't her first client to have trouble articulating his feelings. She had waited out others, and she would do the same with him. In a few weeks, he'd transfer seamlessly to Julle. He'd get better, even without Starr's help. She made a mental note to talk to him about the frequent gifts of coffee and the way he looked at her recently. It seemed like things were shifting for Morris and not in the way she'd intended. She hadn't realized it had come to this.

Quietly Morris began to weep, and Starr's resolve crumbled. A man's gut-wrenching cry over the loss of a woman. Rare and beautiful. The kind of ache she wanted Geoff to feel for her. A mystery that most women didn't believe existed. She rose as if triggered by something greater than her and inched the sandbox away. She took a seat in the empty chair across the man who was once M. (Oscar) Wilde to her but had become a faithful client. Her heart thudded in her chest. She felt the shock and awe of therapists everywhere, their judgment raining down on her for breaking the code of being an objective bystander. She had taken an oath to do no harm. To Starr, letting this poor soul sit and cry in anguish was doing harm.

"It's okay, Morris," she said. "I'm here now." Starr steadied herself. If he was bluffing, she would know as soon as he took his hand away from his face. If he was faking it, so help her God, she would send him away immediately. Banish him to a canceled session and transfer him to a male therapist. The latter thought made her gag just a little. Made her feel less than, as it always did if a male client caused her discomfort and had to be reined in by someone of his own kind. Sexism was rampant even in the manipulations of mental health patients.

Morris lowered his hand. Slowly, afraid that she might

disappear. The whites of his eyes were red. His lids had started to swell, and angry tears collected below his bottom row of lashes, matting them against his cheeks. Morris' mouth twisted into a grimace, a sorry attempt at a smile. "You're here? Are you sure? I don't want to make you uncomfortable."

Starr reached out her hand. "Close your eyes, Morris. I'm not going anywhere."

Morris held his hand face up under hers, gently cupping her fingers that curled softly into his. He leaned forward, closed his eyes, and spoke. "I've been trying to say this to you in so many ways. Making meals, cleaning the apartment, and doing laundry. I've always thought I could put my feelings into action and let those things speak for me. But I know now, actions aren't enough. I can't cook my way into your heart or scrub the floor to make you know what I feel. I have to connect with you. Physically. Emotionally. I can't go off and do my own thing without considering how it affects you. I'm sorry. I'm really sorry."

"Sorry for what," Starr prompted him.

"For so many things, really. I'm sorry for not listening. For not validating your feelings when you shared your heart with me. For being distant and cold. Emotionally cut off. You remind me constantly to do better. To be better. Even when you nag and yell at me about it."

"Use 'I' statements. Don't attack me. Her," Starr murmured.

Morris flicked open his eyes. "Right. Starr?"

"It's okay. Keep talking."

He continued but kept his eyes open and watched her eyes dart from side to side beneath closed lids. "I know you've explained to me that you need...more. That I need to be more spontaneous. Confident. And I didn't listen. The few times I did, I didn't focus on...us. I thought only of myself. I should have tried harder. I should have been more thoughtful in how I interacted with you."

Starr's emotions battled for control. Tears tracked her cheeks. She held her breath to keep from sobbing. Either her mind was far away in deep pain or the words he spoke touched her deeply.

He thought of how frequently she touched his hand or his shoulder. The way she looked at him when he spoke as if no one else on Earth existed. He remembered the way she started their first conversation that day at Saki Brothers. The way she'd exploded like a million bright stars across the canvas of the night sky. Since then she popped into the cafe at least once a week, always making sure to seek him out and exchange hellos.

"I'm changed now. I'm a different, better man, my love."

It was the term of endearment that broke the dam. The fact that Morris wasn't embarrassed or ashamed to use a sweet nickname with the woman he loved. He knew his shortcomings and faults. He openly admitted and accepted them and was willing to change. Starr felt the pressure build behind her eyes and in her throat. What she wouldn't give for a real conversation like this with Geoff. For him to own up to his flaws and be willing to talk to her—really talk to her for once. If he did, she might reciprocate. She squeezed Morris' hand to show him she was proud of his progress.

"Starr?"

She blinked rapidly and tipped her face to the ceiling, trying to stop her running nose. "It's okay, Morris. I'm okay." She laughed. "Gosh, that was crazy. I'm sorry for getting all emotional on you. I—" She tried pulling her hand back and felt resistance. "Morris, no," she said in as stern a voice she could muster.

He knelt before her on one knee, her hand still in his and a ring box in the other.

Starr rose and yanked her hand back. This isn't right. She was frantic at what her colleagues would think when she staffed Morris' case for transfer next week. They'd think it was her fault. That she couldn't keep her own boyfriend happy enough to stick around and marry her, so she had to go after an innocent and troubled man.

"You shouldn't have let him hold your hand, Starr. Look what you did," Sdax reprimanded from beneath the desk.

Starr's cheeks flamed red. "I should have insisted you use the technique the proper way. This is wrong. You don't feel anything for me, Morris. This is transference. That's all. You're transferring your feelings for Larimore onto me. It's completely normal and not your fault. It happens sometimes. And it happened now, but it won't happen again. Do you understand?" She pushed her desk chair into its rightful place and dumped her half full coffee cup into the trash. "I never should have agreed to this. It was wrong, and you need to understand that."

"They're going to talk about you now, Starr. Rumors and bullying. HIPAA and malpractice. People will laugh at you," Sdax babbled.

"God, this is the kind of thing lawsuits are made of, Morris. Do you realize that? I could lose my license over this," she hissed branding him the one at fault.

Morris stood up when Starr pushed the end table back into place. He had trouble keeping up with the conversation. "It's not like that. Please, Starr. I wouldn't sue you for having feelings for me as long as you understand that I love Larimore. I could never break her heart by having an affair."

"I could never break her heart by having an affair," Oscar mimicked in a whiny voice as he stepped out from behind Morris. He laughed behind Morris' back. "You're too weak even for this boho type. Do better, Morris. Find your spine."

"Fuck you," Morris whispered at Oscar. To Starr, "No. It's not like that. I wasn't trying to do anything."

"That's all well and good, Mr. Wilde, but you should know, I'm an engaged woman. I'm in a happy relationship with someone not in this room. You—"

"She isn't even wearing a ring," Oscar said, pointing.

"Geoff loves her, stupid," Sdax yelled.

"See?" Starr held up her finger, glad that Sdax had her back.

And for the first time, she did see. The ring Starr wore was one of her own. Shiny cubic Zirconia in the shape of a heart. It was the kind of jewelry a child wore or perhaps a teenager full of youth and infatuation for a boy smitten with her. A cheap promise ring at best, a child's play thing at worst.

Morris touched her finger. "You're a kind and considerate woman, Starr. The last thing I want is for you to feel unloved. This is not an engagement ring," he said gently. His words caressed Starr's bruised heart. "Not like this. This is a real ring. The kind a man gives to a woman he's committed to. The kind of ring a man gives to the woman he's going to make his bride."

She couldn't take her eyes off the diamond. It was thick and along each side of it, three small stones. The band was made of white gold. "I said I'm engaged," Starr squeaked.

Morris continued. "This ring you're wearing is the kind a woman wears when she's been deceived. Or the kind a scorned or lonely woman might wear. The question is which one are you?"

Starr said nothing as she tried to decipher whether his question was rhetorical. It wasn't often the tables turned, and she became the client.

"See?" He turned her hand over, palm up. Faint green marks were visible against her pink flesh. "Fake like a fairy tale. Unfortunately, there's no cure for fake, Starr. No coping skills or therapy techniques. Fake is fake as fuck." He slid the costume jewelry from her finger. "There. Now doesn't that feel better?"

Starr nodded dumbly. The diamond ring he placed in the center of her palm was a dead weight in her hand. She trembled when he closed her fingers tight around it.

"It's okay," Morris said. "It's all going to be okay. Consider the ring my payment. I think I should go now. Take care." He pocketed the Cubic Zirconia he'd slipped from her finger and let himself out, at peace with his decision.

"Don't worry. He's gone now," Sdax said as she crawled up into Starr's lap and faded into her form. "So pretty." She touched the shiny new ring. She slipped the ring onto Starr's finger, and the two sat there until it was time to go home. Later she would tell her about that awful Oscar.

SHOOTING SDAX

CHAPTER TWELVE

Starr arrived home as the sun began to set. She both loved and hated this time of day. With Geoff gone, the evenings were lonely. The nights that followed, even lonelier. She tried to focus on the positives—the countdown to starting her new practice, the days slipping by on the calendar, the sunsets. Though her practice and Geoff's eventual return provided her with a mixture of happy and anxious thoughts, the sunset did not disappoint. It was a medicine ball of fire situated between the city's tall buildings. A perfect circle the color of blood that sunk lower and lower until it hung inches above the population. When she saw it, she stopped what she was doing. Be it talking on the phone, reading a journal article, or singing along to the radio, everything stopped when the sun set. When it was gone, so was her reverence for it. She hated the sun as much as the lonely nights and the bureaucratic red tape that came with working in community mental health. Once the sun was gone, she was left to fight the loneliness and the darkness that swallowed her whole. She was Jonah, and the night was her whale.

Starr pulled two paper bags of groceries out of the cab. "That didn't last long," she lamented when the sun hunkered down behind the horizon after a mere three minutes.

She reached through the window and paid the cab driver. Her rocky relationship with Geoff rubbed off on all her actions, including choosing public transportation over driving his car.

The vehicle sat along the street as if mocking her and the ache in her back. She didn't know why she'd purchased a large bag of frozen chicken breasts or a whole watermelon, both of which rode together in one sack and weighed her down. In the other was a gallon of ice cream. She didn't need to examine the rationale behind that purchase. She'd long since stopped believing in the happily ever after Geoff promised her the day he left. It was time to sever the relationship she shouldn't have agreed to in the first place. "I should have just ordered in," Starr grumbled. She hoisted the bags higher on her arm and dug in her purse for her keys.

Next door, Ms. Caulton sat with her head and arms out the windowsill. "In my day, women cooked, and men went to work," Ms. Caulton said. A cigar hung from her wrinkled lips, and she worked to strike a match.

Her wisp, Jomi, sat on the sidewalk with her back against the house. "Don't get her started."

"I guess it's not your day anymore, Ms. Caulton."

The two women had some commonalities that Starr had come to grudgingly accept. They were both women who lived on the same block. Both were fending for themselves, and both had a pet that greeted them each morning and laid beside them each night. Twice since Geoff's Alaskan departure, Ms. Caulton had invited herself over for coffee, and twice Starr had let her in. It helped that they shared the same affinity for Oliveros cigars.

"Looks like you're having a party," Ms. Caulton said.

"Nope. Just little ole me."

"In my day, women knew how to throw a party. Gin and tonic. Hor d'oeuvres. Music." Ms. Caulton swayed to an imaginary band.

"If I had a party, there would be cupcakes," Sdax said. Her hair was neatly braided down her back. She wore pink leggings and a gray striped sweatshirt. "And I'd wear a party dress," she added.

"Make sure you know what you're wishing for," Jomi said into the night air. "Parties aren't all they're cracked up to be."

"It's just me, Ms. Caulton," Starr said. *I prefer the independent lifestyle. I am a feminist. Hear me fucking roar.*

Inside Bridgette barked, and outside Starr juggled her bags. She'd been out later than usual, and it was past time for Bridgette's dinner and walk. The watermelon bumped against Starr's leg. She felt her key ring but couldn't wrap her fingers around it.

"These days women think they have to be independent. Feminists and lesbians and such."

Starr wondered if the old lady had, in fact, already had a gin and tonic. Or two. "Nothing wrong with being independent, Ms. Caulton. Or with being a lesbian."

Bridgette scratched the door. Starr's purse slipped down her arm, and she shoved it back into place. Turning her head, she put the purse strap between her teeth and crammed her left hand into the gaping mouth of her bag. The pointed end of her nail file rose up and stabbed the soft bed under her nail. Tears sprang to her eyes.

"Maybe. Maybe not. Course maybe that's why your honey up and left you. Did you ever think of that?" Ms. Caulton asked. She poked her nose into the window screen.

Starr looked skyward. She bit her tongue to keep from swearing. The last thing she needed from Ms. Caulton was a lecture on manners. *This is not how my evening was supposed to go. This is not how my life was supposed to go.* She gripped the keys inside her purse and decided she'd had enough. "No, I have never thought of that because he didn't leave me. He's on a mission trip. Besides, even if he had left me, it's none of your damn business. Nothing about my life is ever your business, Ms. Caulton. Not what I'm eating or what time I get home from work or whether I'm in a relationship or not. So stop talking to me. Just stop."

Sdax winced, to avoid any further confrontation, rushed past Starr and passed through the door. Immediately Bridgette's bark quieted to a soft whine.

"You don't have to get all worked up," Ms. Caulton said, annoyed. She reached for the top of the window to close it. "I just said it was a possibility."

Thoughts—none of them kind—raced through Starr's mind as she jammed the house key into the lock. The faster she could remove herself from Ms. Caulton's presence, the better it would be for all of them. She'd take Bridgette to the backyard to relieve herself. Thankfully it was a Friday night. There would be no need to go anywhere for the next two days. The less she had to interact with Ms. Caulton, the less frustrated she would be.

The bag with the ice cream ripped open, and its contents hit the sidewalk.

"Cheez-its!" She yelled. "I don't need this." She threw the accompanying bag of watermelon and chicken to the ground, too.

There's a funny thing about being a mental health therapist. People who know you think one of two things about you. Either you have a slew of emotional issues that you're trying to cure by treating others or you have reached a kind of inner Zen status that prevents you from having a meltdown of any kind. You can be an educated therapist, knowledgeable about a vast array of healthy coping skills. The one thing people don't think about is that therapists are human. All humans reach their limit.

"Then why did you buy it if you don't need it?" Ms. Caulton asked.

Starr jumped. The woman stood right behind her, leaning heavily on her cane and peering down at the ice cream. Ms. Caulton grabbed the container and lifted it to eye level. She twisted and turned it to make sure there weren't any cracks.

"How did you do that?" Starr asked.

"I'm old, not dead. I can pick up ice cream," Ms. Caulton said. She looked at Starr over the top of her bifocals. "Besides," she said, tapping the ground with her cane. "You don't want to leave it on the ground. Ants'll get it if you do."

"I meant, I didn't hear you."

"Huh. And people think I'm old."

"Well, thanks. You didn't have to do that." It was hard getting rid of someone after they were nice.

"Your watermelon doesn't look too good," Ms. Caulton replied.

The melon was broken in half. Part of it teetered on the sidewalk's edge. One poke into its busted side, and it would be in the gutter, its sticky sweet pulp covered in dirt.

"Ants'll be on it in no time," Starr agreed.

"Might even be there already. Hard to tell in the dusk," Ms. Caulton said.

The bag of chicken laid at Starr's feet. The plastic was still intact but at risk of an ant infestation due to location. Starr felt a migraine coming on. "Would you like to come in?" she asked Ms. Caulton.

"Suits me, I suppose."

Inside it didn't take Starr long to complete the essential tasks. She put the ice cream away, walked Bridgette, fed her, and walked her again. Afterward in her room, Starr changed into yoga pants and an oversized sweatshirt and sank onto the bed. She pulled on house slippers and hugged her knees to her chest. The ache was particularly deep tonight. She wanted nothing more than to be alone, eat ice cream, and plot an end.

Sdax sidled up beside her and curled herself around Starr's yarn doll. She shimmered when Starr pulled the doll close and, in doing so, snuggled the wisp tight against her frame. This was what Sdax wanted if she couldn't have a party. To be loved and held. To be protected against all the bad and scary things in life.

"Geoff didn't call again today," Starr said. "No postcard or letter all week either. Now we've got cranky Ms. Caulton in the living room expecting to be entertained." She wiped her nose on the neck of her hoodie.

Sdax turned until she faced her person. She placed gentle kisses on Starr's forehead and cheeks.

Starr rubbed the kisses away, annoyed. "Dog hair." She wiped her hand across her face and paused at the cool feel of her bracelet against her skin.

The bracelet was made of tiny brown beads, the size of Sixlets candy pieces. In the center was a large square piece with soft, rounded edges. In the center of the square was a marble design that was smooth to the touch. Oddly enough, it rested on the underside of her wrist, not on top where it should have been.

Come to think of it, her wrist had bothered her all day.

"That's weird. I must have put it on wrong this morning," Starr murmured and peeled the jewelry off.

"Ooooh, pretty." Sdax pressed her bow tie lips against the underside of Starr's wrist. Her eyes twinkled with delight. "So pretty," she gushed.

The line was razor thin and red. Starr touched it with her index finger and traced the wound from end to end. She licked her lips nervously. "I must have gotten cut. Or Bridgette scratched me." On the bedside table her empty wine glass from the night before sat intact. "I don't remember getting a sliver."

Sdax tilted her head and asked, "Doesn't it feel better?"

"It feels okay. Just sore," Starr admitted.

In the other room Ms. Caulton talked to Bridgette. Her esophagus, scratchy and hoarse from years of smoking, hindered her sing-song voice. The sound, not entirely unpleasant, interrupted the place Sdax wanted to take Starr.

The little wisp flickered her hazy blue aura and begged, "Talk to me. I'm here. I'm hurting, too. Let's make it better."

Starr brushed her voice away. She was tired of being sad. For the first time all day, she was hungry. Her mouth watered at the thought of fried chicken and ice cream. She'd ask Ms. Caulton to stay for a girls' night. Determined to cover her feelings of despair and sadness with seasoned flour and fry them up, Starr stretched and stood. "That's what I need. A girls' night. I'm not going to let a guy bring me down. I just won't. I can beat this. I teach my clients to overcome things like this all the time. So I will, too."

Decision made, she felt lighter than she had all day. She checked her reflection in the bureau mirror and smiled. She pinched her cheeks the way she remembered her grandmother doing. On impulse, Starr picked up a blush brush from her usually ignored makeup kit. She swiped it across her cheeks and begged her mouth to smile more.

"We can do this," Sdax needled and willed herself to take charge.

Starr wiped at a stubborn splotch of blush, and her fingers returned to the cut. As if listening, her hand slowly and softly traveled north along her arm where it pushed at the worn edges of her hoodie. Her fingers took hold of the material and pulled it upward revealing her naked skin. A freckle here. A sparse field of arm hair released from the confines stood at attention.

Sdax held her breath as she guided Starr's arm and turned it. The flesh was fairer skinned along the soft underbelly. Hairless, blemish free. It was soft as butter. Sdax pulled back the sleeve until Starr saw the faint, silvery lines above the inner elbow. Hidden secrets from the world forever covered with long-sleeved peasant blouses, jackets, and light sweaters. Starr's San Francisco attire was perfect for covering up years' old self-inflicted imperfections.

Starr stopped pulling when she met resistance. The sound of tinkling wind chimes floated along the peripheral. She licked her lips and counted feverishly. "One, two...thirteen...seventeen. Twenty." The lines intersected, crisscrossing a pattern on her skin like a mash of waffle fries. In between them, unharmed tender bits of flesh called out to her. Starr's resolve to push away the negativity that plagued her faltered, and she dug deep to resist.

"I've got issues," Sdax sang, her eyes fastened on the marks. "So do you…"

"Fake it 'til you make it." Starr whispered and yanked the sleeve down over her past. She faced her reflection and squared her shoulders. "Ms. Caulton," she yelled. "Want to stay for dinner?"

"You've got them, too," Sdax said from her place in front of the mirror.

Starr ignored her. "No kids allowed," she said angrily as she shut Sdax in the bedroom by herself.

The smell of fried chicken lingered. Together, Starr and Ms. Caulton fried the entire bag of chicken breasts. Half was gone, shared between them and Bridgette. Four pieces were burned beyond recognition and laid like lumps of charcoal in a skillet on the stove. A bottle of wine was on the coffee table. They'd drank most of it, and Ms. Caulton had twice reported it was time for her to head next door and check on Clarence. But Starr didn't want to be alone. In between the cooking and feasting, she'd kept her dark thoughts at bay. With only four hours left before the sun made its appearance, she needed the woman to see her through to the end.

"I could be a bartender with these skills," Starr said with a giggle as she eyed the bottle of red and expertly poured half into her glass and the other half into Ms. Caulton's.

"Shit Sdax. You're right about that. But I think I've drunk my fill." Ms. Caulton moved her head from side to side as she tried to gauge the whereabouts of her cup. She zeroed in on it and lifted it to her lips.

"Cheers." Starr clinked the empty bottle against the woman's glass.

"I haven't had this much to drink since my honeymoon."

"I didn't know you were married." Starr said. She sat up and cradled her drink, intrigued.

"Forty-two years and a month when he dropped dead of a heart attack." Ms. Caulton crossed herself. "God rest his soul."

Forty-two years was a lifetime to Starr who wished Geoff would properly propose so that she could revel in forty-two days of being his fianceé. Forty-two years was how long it seemed since she'd spoken to him. Alaska was far away.

"That's nice," Starr slurred, thinking of a young and pretty Ms. Caulton saying her vows to a dashing new husband.

"It was, and it wasn't."

Several minutes passed with no conversation. Starr watched her guest nod off a few times, only to jerk herself awake again. She held her glass in one hand, a smoldering cigar in the other. Though Starr's thoughts and mannerisms were wobbly at best, she knew she was losing her audience. With luck Ms. Caulton would pass out on the sofa, and Starr wouldn't technically be alone.

"She might catch the house on fire," Sdax said from where she sat in her favorite corner.

As frustrating as the wisp was, she had a point and increased Starr's level of anxiety by three degrees. Starr also considered the fact that if Ms. Caulton fell asleep, Starr would be alone with Sdax. Left to their own devices. It was hard enough to keep the witchy little Sdax under control when she was sober. Imbibed Starr wouldn't be able to keep her in check or those nagging worries that came out of hiding and took up residence in her heartbeat, her dormant goosebumps, and her range of hearing. Catastrophes found Sdax no matter where she hid, and when they did, Starr had no choice but to react as instructed.

Under the roll top desk, Bridgette snored, oblivious to her mistress' quandary. Starr took another sip of wine. It was warm, and she rolled it around on her tongue, swishing it softly against the inside of her cheek before arching her neck and swallowing. She imagined all of her worries as miniature people on an equally miniature raft falling over the back of her tongue. Down, down, down, the waterfall. Until they splashed into her stomach.

"This is nice," Starr said to her wine glass. She let her eyelids close and allowed herself a cleansing breath. But she did not rest. The tiny worry dolls took up their wooden oars and used them like pick axes. They were determined, those worries. She felt them chop their blades into the sides of her throat. Up, up, up, they climbed. No matter how hard Starr swallowed, they persisted. Alive inside her, she felt the truth of her shame coming closer to her mouth where it would force its way out. Wasted and half asleep, she knew Ms. Caulton would hear the words as they tumbled out. She had to stop them.

"Geoff asked me to marry him," Starr blurted. The words ricocheted through the room causing Bridgette to stir.

Ms. Caulton jerked herself awake. "What's that?" She slugged her wine and flicked ash from her cigar.

Starr winced when it landed on the sofa between them but didn't move. She counted to three waiting to see if a spark grew. Nothing. It faded into the upholstery.

"What if the next one doesn't?" Sdax moaned. She blew furiously at the black mark.

"Are you done with that?" Starr asked. She leaned forward and took the cigar. "You're not too tired, are you?"

"No. No. I'm wide awake," Ms. Caulton replied as she

struggled to keep her eyes open. She relinquished the cigar.

Starr ignored the moist end covered in Ms. Caulton's teeth marks and clamped down on the borrowed cigar. "Good. I can tell you all about the wedding. We're both excited. Maybe you'd like to come to the ceremony?"

"'Course I would. Not that I can dance anymore."

"Sure you can," Starr said, knowing full well the woman probably couldn't.

Ms. Caulton made a noise. Her eyes flashed. She was awake now, defensive. "Back in my day, there was real dancing at weddings. Jitterbug, the two-step. Waltz, too. Not like they do now-a-days—grinding up against each other and half naked to boot. Disgrace."

Starr leaned back against the sofa's arm. She imagined Geoff holding her. Really holding her, not supporting her like he always claimed to be. She puffed on the cigar and tasted the memories of a grandmother long gone. A conversation tickled her nose, and Starr slumped into it.

"Who's that?" Starr asked her mother, pointing to a wrinkled, faded picture. She ran her fingers along the torn edge of it.

"My mother. Your maurluq. Your grandmother."

"Maurluq," Starr repeated.

"They called her Betty Bob," Starr's mother said angrily.

The mother/grandmother stood in the picture and stared into the camera lens. She wore a dress uniform and held a baby. But instead of smiling like Starr did when someone said "Say cheese," the woman looked sad.

"She had dirt on her," Starr said, and rubbed Grandma Betty Bob's face in the picture.

"Not so hard," her mother admonished and smacked Starr's hand.

Starr jerked her hand back. "Is she holding me?" She touched the baby in the picture, gently this time.

"No."

"Is she holding you? Are you a baby in the picture?" It was

hard for Starr to imagine her mother as a tiny baby. She wished her mom would have a baby, and then Starr would be a big sister like her friend Carrie. Two girls would make Starr's mom laugh and smile and go to the family playdates at the park.

"That's my brother."

Starr was confused. Her dad had a sister that Starr called Aunt Cecilia. But Starr's mom had no one since Grandma Betty died. Starr missed her grandma even if she did have the big scar on her face. Starr thought Grandma Betty Bob was pretty. She liked to trace the scar on her grandma's face because it made Grandma Betty Bob's lips curl into a sort-of smile. And Grandma Betty Bob never smiled. Just like in that picture.

"Is your brother in heaven? Like Grandma Betty Bob?"

"If he is, I'm sure she's happy now."

"Where's her scar?" Starr turned the picture over as if her grandmother's picture was a mystery game of hide-n-seek.

"She didn't have it then."

How could a dirt splotch be there one day and a scar the next? Was it like her mother's hair spots? One day there was hair, and the next day she had bald spots. Starr's father had caught her yanking her hair one day and scolded her. He'd said that just because Starr's mother had to pick hers didn't mean his daughter was going to end up crazy, too.

"Did she pick it?" Starr asked.

Starr's father came home, and her mother quickly shoved the picture into a cigar box with other private stuff and never said another word about it. Her silence frustrated Starr who had so many questions. Could she meet her mother's brother? Didn't he like to come visit them? If Starr had a brother, would she be able to see him? Why was Grandma Betty Bob sad? Why did Starr's mom say Grandma Betty Bob went to heaven, but Starr's father said Grandma Betty Bob had gone to purgatory? Would Starr's mom have to go there, too, since she picked her hair like Grandma Betty Bob picked her scar? Would the car that killed Grandma Betty Bob kill Starr and her parents some day if they sat in the garage too long?

But Starr never got to ask her questions before her parents died, and she was sent to live with her aunt. Any questions she tried to ask went unanswered because Aunt Cecilia was angry at Starr's mother for going to Heaven. Well, purgatory first, and then heaven after Aunt Cecilia got to know Jesus. By then she was able to forgive Starr's mother, but the cancer had gotten hold of Cecilia's mind. Starr was too busy trying to figure out life to worry about something that had happened years before. Nor did Starr have time to explore that past now. She was too busy trying to keep Ms. Caulton's attention.

Starr wiggled her finger to let the diamonds in her ring sparkle and grabbed hold of her Midwestern roots. "It'll be glorious. We can have the ceremony in a barn with the door flung open to the outside. We'll choose a crisp, fall night, so we can have fire pits set up all across the pasture for the reception. The band will play in the loft, and the music will float down and serenade the guests."

"How many?" Ms. Caulton mumbled.

"Hundreds. Ours will be the ceremony of the century. All of Geoff's coworkers. The church congregation. People from Cloverleaf."

"And me."

"You. Bridgette. Clarence." Starr giggled. "We can have dog and cat ring bearers." She clapped.

"That sounds lovely," Ms. Caulton said. Starr drifted off to the sound of a cello lulling her. She exhaled and blew into creation a hundred fire pits, surrounded by people sharing thoughtful remarks about the beauty of her wedding, the evening, and herself, the bride. She radiated peace and beauty in a flowing gown as she crossed the barn's threshold. A smile spread across her face as she gazed up at her new husband.

"Isn't it everything you dreamed it would be?" Starr asked.

Geoff nodded and caressed her face. She sunk into the crook of his arm as they entered the pasture, ready to greet their guests. Night had fallen. Stars lit up the sky as if switched on one-by-one, courtesy of the Creator. The wind picked up, and Starr sniffed. Her nose twitched at the smell of burning cedar. The fire pits. Out of control, they blazed in fury, and thick tendrils of smoke reached heavenward. Starr gripped the lapels of Geoff's tuxedo.

"We have to evacuate," he shouted.

Her dream was literally being consumed by the stench and clouds of smoke. Guests screamed in alarm and drowned out the sound of Geoff's words.

"What?" she yelled.

His mouth turned into a scowl, and he shook her furiously by the front of her dress. He shouted again, and she flinched at the words he spoke. "Look at what you're doing, Starr. You're ruining everything. Get out. Get out!" Geoff pointed to the open window and shoved her to its edge. She looked out at the burning pasture. The flames gobbled up the hay bales and chased wedding guests. Scared, she spun around desperate to cling to Geoff's strong arms and chest. He put his hand out to stop her, and then he grabbed her by the arms. With venom in his voice, he shook her like a rag doll. "You're not marriage material, Starr. You're not marriage material."

Starr's eyes watered, and she shook her head against his hateful words. If she wasn't careful she'd lose her footing and fall out the window. She blinked hard and fast. The smoke burned her eyes and choked her lungs. The bright light of the moon turned a brilliant blue and danced a psychedelic jig that threatened to blind her. Then, poof. Geoff, the wedding scene, the blazing furnace—they all disappeared.

Ms. Caulton's voice sliced through Starr's nightmare. "You're burning the couch material, Starr! Look what you're doing! Get up!" The older woman pulled at the front of Starr's clothes and yanked her off the sofa with strength Starr hadn't thought the woman capable of possessing.

"What? God. What?"

"Get up."

With a final yank, Ms. Caulton pulled Starr to half standing. A thin stream of smoke rose from the cushion, and a handful of sparks flickered. Pinpricks of pain danced up and down one leg as Starr stumbled toward the kitchen and fell. Ms. Caulton clucked her tongue at the scene and snapped the throw blanket from around her shoulders to stomp out the fire. Bridgette looked on from under the desk, unnerved by the chaos.

"There. I think I got it."

"Thank you," Starr murmured.

"I have to get to Clarence," Ms. Caulton said.

Starr didn't move. She didn't care about the ruined couch or the lonely cat next door. She didn't say goodbye. When the door shut behind Ms. Caulton, Starr didn't hurry to twist the deadbolt. She stayed where she'd fallen, shivering uncontrollably.

"Geoff's not coming back. He doesn't want to marry me," Starr said to the empty room.

Sdax shimmered into view and knelt beside Starr. She stroked her human's hair and let the tears fall.

CHAPTER THIRTEEN

On her second to last day at Cloverleaf, Starr lingered at the office as long as she could without picking up loitering charges. She had boxed up the majority of her therapy books and carted them, one slow trip after another, out to the rental car she'd secured to avoid having to move out in a hurry with an Uber waiting. The vehicle would come in handy for apartment searching, too, which she planned to start as soon as possible. For now, she pretended the rental was hers and quite enjoyed the frivolity of the whole experience. By the time she finished dusting her office, reviewing her last two charts for the following day, and writing long and detailed transfer summaries, she locked the office door. She'd saved the hardest task for last.

She had to return Morris' ring. Since their last session, she'd worn it like a woman in love, admiring the way the diamonds twinkled and shined in the sunlight. The ring fit her finger perfectly but not her life. Each day brought her closer to the truth. Geoff didn't call or text her anymore. Morris had ousted Starr from her fantasy and taken her cheap, fake gold ring with him. When Julle had noticed the sparkling half carat resting on Starr's ring finger, she'd let Julle believe it was "the ring" from Geoff. Starr would be lying if she said she didn't enjoy the attention and admiration from the young woman.

"Do we have to give it back?" Sdax asked.

"Yes, you know it goes against the rules to keep something of this value. Besides, Geoff didn't give it to me, remember? Tonight this goes in the mail to Morris, and tomorrow we go on our merry way of starting over."

"Aren't you going to miss it?" Sdax talked around the thumb in her mouth. She'd spent the day dragging herself behind Starr, who went back and forth from the office to the parking lot. "I am."

"Suck it up, little one. That's life," Starr said as she sat down in Brandy's desk chair and unlocked the file cabinet in search of Morris' street address. She shoved the ring inside a ring box and then into a larger box. She scribbled his address in black marker and returned the paperwork with his address on it to its rightful place. "Tomorrow Brandy can take it to the post office, and this will be just another bad memory."

Starr thought back to her first day at Cloverleaf, and the warm welcome the other staff members had given her. She thought about the day when Geoff had sent flowers to her office for some silly, made up anniversary they shared. He'd made her feel loved and noticed that day. As she sat and reflected on her time there, other older memories surfaced. There was a time when a man had shown up at her old agency.

She hadn't recognized him at the time. At their first meeting the man had been timid, afraid of his own shadow. He'd lived in a rundown motel and eked out a living in some remote work-from-home job he hated. After months of therapy, he was a new person. He was well dressed and had a wide smile and a firm handshake. He brought her a small gift and when Starr explained she couldn't ethically accept it, he assured her it was worth less than the twenty-dollar limit imposed on therapist-client gift exchanges. Starr had finally relented, and the man pressed a business card into her hand. His business card for the business he had started after completing therapy with her. A simple startup that held promise. He told her he was getting out more and had finally found his courage. He'd only come back to thank her for believing in him. The entire interaction had lasted less than thirty minutes but left a strong impact on Starr. The man's belief spurred her into believing she might be able to make a living at her own private practice. He planted a seed, and for a long time Geoff watered it.

"Maybe I'll miss it a little," Starr said.

"Should we stay then?" Sdax asked.

Starr found herself reconsidering. She could say she chickened out or it wasn't the right time. She could wait for Geoff to come home, so they could work on their relationship before she hung her shingle. Or she could call him and tell him about the turmoil she struggled with. She could seek the help he was always offering her.

Then she remembered—there was no guarantee Geoff would come home to her.

There were so many simple things she loved about her role in Geoff's life. Like when they grocery shopped together and he amused her with his manly explanations about the best cut of beef. The way he danced with her in the kitchen before hugging her tightly and slipping a twenty in her hand on her way out the door. He knew she liked to stop for a hazelnut coffee and tip the barista. Likewise, Starr loved that he knew that about her and his non-verbal show of gallant affection warmed her heart. And the way he trailed behind her at night, locking the front door and checking that the windows latches were in place as he followed her up to their bedroom.

"But he stopped doing that and decided to sleep alone," she whispered and focused on her new version of reality: that no one really cared about her. Not Geoff. Or Morris. Not Grace who transferred to Julle's care without looking back. She'd even declined a final goodbye session with Starr. There were no guarantees in life except that Starr could and would find her own way for once.

She knelt before Sdax. "No, staying would be like saying we're giving these people another chance, Sdax. They've used up all their chances. They don't have any left. Understand?" Starr rose and took the wisp by the hand. She let them out the back door and locked it. She would go home and take Bridgette to the little coffee shop across the street. She'd force herself to like something other than Saki Brothers. She'd sip a latte or a cappuccino and search for a new apartment—one that allowed cats. Then she would start to feel better.

"Then why are we sitting here?" Sdax asked from where she sat buckled into the backseat.

"Because I said so, okay? I'm allowing myself one last look at the agency that was supposed to be my place," Starr snapped.

As she put the car in reverse, she noticed the green building next door. Number 1046. She hit the brakes and stared. "That's probably my biggest regret. Not knowing what's in that building."

When Starr thought about her life in the community mental health business, the one thing she wished she'd done different was put herself on her schedule. Like so many others, she rarely put a lunch date on her calendar or took the time to leave early for a day of exploring and adventure. If she took a long bathroom break, she was plagued with guilt and made herself work an extra thirty minutes to make up for it. People in the helping profession were the ones who needed help figuring out how to live life out from under the weight of their clients' problems. Not in a way that disregarded those problems or cast them aside as irrelevant, but in a way that allowed therapists to balance them, to be able to bear them with the client while separating oneself enough to not be crushed in the process.

She had yet to find that balance and hoped in her new practice, where paperwork would be less burdensome and her hours more flexible, she'd be able to carve out a life. The feeling of unfinished business and the loss of a quirky opportunity washed over her and settled on her shoulders. This was a weight she didn't want to forget. She wanted to carry it with her as a faithful and somber reminder that each day should be treasured. That even she deserved to experience daily drops of joy in whatever shape or form they presented themselves.

"Like this building. This unknown," she said to the empty parking lot.

"Oooh. Like a mystery?" Sdax unbuckled herself and popped her head up over the front seat. "Can we go inside?"

"Sort of like a mystery. Why shouldn't we be the ones to solve it?" Starr asked as she resolved to snatch up this tidbit of joy on her last day at Cloverleaf.

"Yes! We can solve a mystery!"

"Sit tight. I'll see what I can sleuth up." Starr removed her seat belt and climbed out of the vehicle. She strode to the dumpster area that separated the two buildings and their respective lots. "Looks like an ordinary dumpster," she said.

"Yep," Sdax agreed.

"I thought I told you to stay in the car."

"Guess there's no mystery."

"I guess not."

"Nothing 'cept a bunch of trash and a teddy bear. Please can I have it? Please?" Sdax pleaded as she jumped up and down in her patent leather shoes.

"Aw, look. Someone left a teddy bear out here."

The bear had muddy brown fur and glass eyes sewn into its head. His round matted ears gave him a dopey, friendly look. Starr smiled at the forgotten animal. "No sense in leaving him out here all by himself is there?"

"Yes, I have a bear." Sdax pumped her fists into the air and snatched the stuffed animal. She crushed the bear to her chest, and it emitted a crunchy sound that got Starr's attention. Sdax squeezed again.

"That's odd," Starr mused. She poked the bear and looked around as if a random parent might present him or herself on a hunt for a bear they'd mistakenly left behind in their hurry to get somewhere. "Oh, shoot," Starr said when her thumb went through the bear's chest.

"Here. Just tape it," Sdax said pointing at a piece of duct tape that hung from the side of the dumpster.

"What?"

"That's where I found it." Sdax wiggled herself into a bright blue haze as she tried to take the bear back from Starr. "I found it. Let me."

Starr peeled off the tape. The bear had been left on purpose. Taped to the side of the dumpster. She looked more closely and saw the writing on the tape. "DAD" was written in blue marker.

"It was the girl. The one with the snacks," Sdax said knowingly.

"It couldn't have been. That's nonsense." Starr reached into the bear's chest and pulled a Lay's potato chip bag out of the cavity. Inside was a note.

Dear Dad—I love you, but I can't do this anymore. It's not fair to me or my mom. Uncle Don told me about her. I know she's not as bad as you think. She loves me. Please don't come after me. Give me a chance to get to know my mother. It's the least you can do. I'll come back someday. Don't worry. Uncle Don will take care of everything. —Love, Grace.

The note was dated that day.

"Please can I have my bear now?" Sdax whined.

"No, you can't have it." Starr's mind raced as she refolded the note and stuffed it back into the bag, then stuffed the bag back where she found it. She pulled the seams together around the opening. Finally, she retaped the bear until it looked just as Sdax had found it – lonely, alone, and stuck to the side of a dumpster. "I have to get out of here," Starr said and hurried back to the car so fast that Sdax had to run to keep up with her.

At home, Starr flipped on the news channel and waited for the announcement of the runaway girl while she did a Google search for 1046 Cloverleaf Drive. She waited for the police to knock on the door with accusations and demands. She waited for the authorities to subpoena her records. Would she be arrested or have her license suspended or revoked, leaving her penniless and working in a fast food joint to pay rent? She wanted to call Geoff, but couldn't risk the thought of leaving him a voicemail with that kind of message.

Starr waited for the phone to ring with the sound of reporters' voices on the other end full of invasive questions. *Did you know Grace Wu was going to run away? Did you give her money? Was this part of her treatment plan? How many times has Grace's uncle been involved in her therapy sessions? Why didn't you include her father? Will you continue to practice therapy? Are you worried about Grace's safety? Does this have anything to do with Rachel James' case?*

"I can't believe this is happening," she moaned and popped open the website for green building labeled 1046. She muted the television and read: fraud, insurance cases, child custody, infidelity, or surveillance needs, we've got you covered. The private investigators we hire are thorough, professional, and capable of finding the missing piece to your puzzle.

Starr fretted inconsolably. "If the licensing board doesn't get to my therapy notes, the private eyes at 1046 will."

All evening and long after she should have been asleep, Starr waited for something to happen. When the fear and panic threatened to drown her, Starr gave in to Sdax's demands until she fell into a troubled sleep. The guilt and stress left tears on Geoff's pillow that she clutched to her chest.

Hours later Starr woke from a deep sleep to Bridgette licking her arm. The dog's saliva made the swollen cuts sting, and she tapped the dog's nose to make her stop.

"Leave me alone, Bridgette," Starr mumbled. She rubbed her tear-stained face. Even with her eyes closed, Starr knew the cuts were there. One crisscrossing the other with dried blood that had trickled from her inner shoulder in tiny rivulets to the eyes of her elbows. The cuts were not deep, but they were haphazard and full of anger and frustration. After she had sliced one arm, Starr had flipped the razor to her other hand and punished herself some more.

"I guess it's long sleeves today," she said.

In the corner, Sdax sat hunkered down and quiet. She stroked Bridgette's silky fur and sucked her thumb until it was raw and bulging. She'd taken to sucking her thumb when Starr's cutting had become increasingly violent. Though Sdax still wanted her party more than anything else, she wanted it to be a peaceful event. She hated the way Starr dug at her skin while cursing and calling herself names.

It took Starr three tries to find a blouse that covered the

marks. The second one had been long enough, but the elastic bands on the sleeves pinched at her skin and puckered until the wounds throbbed. With the longer blouse, Starr put on an ankle length skirt. It was one of her favorites, and she was pleased with how the soft material matched the pale pink blouse. Her face, on the other hand, was not as easy to put in order.

She looked into the mirror above the double vanity and scowled at her reflection. "Tired eyes. Puffy face. Great. I've even got a zit to match my adolescent behavior." Starr ran her fingers through her hair, which looked decent. "No need to shower, huh, kid?" she asked Sdax who stared up at her with wide, dark eyes.

She'd come across a "no shampoo" website during one of her middle of the night Internet binges that promised lustrous curls and had given it a try. The first few days her hair had been oily. She caved under the beads of hot water and a palmful of her favorite shampoo, feeling relieved that no one had mentioned the state of her hair. The following day, she read through the site again and started the challenge anew. Though she could shower without washing her hair, the temptation to lather up was there. It was an odd realization how much concentration it took to not wash her hair. Determined to not have to start over with the no shampoo routine, Starr had taken to sponge bathing.

"It's easier this way," she told Sdax, who frowned in confusion when she watched Starr pull powder scented baby wipes out of a plastic tub and rub them across her chest, up and down her legs and arms, and into the crevices of her womanly shape. "You wouldn't understand. You're just an annoying, tag along, whiny, no good kid. And I'm the unlucky woman who got stuck with you," Starr told her.

Sdax was furious. "I know what you're doing." She took her thumb out of her mouth long enough to spit out the accusation and pop her thumb back between her teeth.

"You think you know? Because you don't. You're a child. And what I'm doing is what a grown-up needs to do. It's called coping, Sdax. I'm using coping skills to get through this...this shit Sdax kind of life I have to live. You got it? I don't care if you sit there like a freaking little princess and judge me for it." She breathed harder with every sentence and winced in pain when she jabbed at her arm, piercing the tender flesh with her nail.

"You're not coping. You're settling because you're too afraid and it's not fair. You can fix it, if you tried," Sdax insisted.

Straightening up, Starr looked into the mirror and examined her features. The bloodshot whites of her puffy eyes. Her hair hung limply down her back framing her tired face. "You're right. I can fix this," Starr said to her reflection.

She pulled up her limp hair and knotted it into a messy bun, piled high on her head. She fumbled along the countertop like a blind person, shoved aside the hand soap, the bar of soap, and the hand sanitizer, wondering why she had so many soaps on display. Starr removed one of her bras that had found its way to the sink top and pushed aside a bottle of lotion, two bottles of hair spray, a hair brush, some eyebrow tweezers she never used, six bottles of nail polish (black, pink, mauve, lime green, dusty rose, and chocolate brown), and a bottle of clear topcoat. Finally, she located the small makeup bag tucked behind a sack of unused cotton balls and another bag of dental floss sticks.

"There it is," she said with a bright smile. "This stuff always helps. It's like Aunt Cecilia used to say: If you don't feel it, fake it." Starr swiped blush across her cheeks and applied a healthy amount of apricot colored eye shadow across her lids. With a careful hand she drew a thin, black, almost straight line along the bottom lid of both eyes. The right side was thicker than the left, so she grabbed a cotton ball and moistened it with water. Leaning closer, she wiped the eyeliner until the strip of black matched the thickness of the line beneath her left eye. Satisfied, Starr went for the mascara and lengthened her lashes until they stretched out from the depths of her eyes like spiders' legs reaching out to catch someone walking through its dew-covered web.

"I'm not dismissing you, Sdax. I want you to stop insisting that death is the only way out. As a therapist, I spend my livelihood encouraging others to cope with the abundant struggles in life. I stake my belief system on people's ability to change and grow and develop. Why can't I feel the same way about myself? Don't I at least deserve the chance to try?"

Sdax planted her feet in resistance and refused to talk. This stubbornness was easier to deal with than her full-on tantrums where she carried on about killing herself, which often caused Starr to waver in her resolve. In Starr's mind cutting was enough—an easy middle-of-the-road compromise to stop her wisp's pouting and pleading. Starr wanted it to be enough so that eventually she could choose healthier coping skills because deep down she believed she was capable of being happy.

"While we're at it," Starr said gaily, "I'll clean this bathroom sink since I've managed to wake up early for once." She straightened the bottles of polish and lotion into little lines like soldiers ready for battle. She tossed out the used cotton ball and stuffed each of the makeup items back into their designated bag. When everything was in its rightful place, she reached into the back corner of the bathroom cabinet until her fingers latched on to the elusive container that held cleaning wipes. She bought them periodically when she was tired of cleaning the bathroom the old-fashioned way—with a scrub brush and proper cleaning supplies. "Got you," she said to the tub.

Her thoughts turned to Geoff and their looming separation as she cleaned.

"Don't. Think about what you're doing. How you're getting a fresh start. You're a strong and independent woman capable of cleaning up the mess you've gotten yourself into. Embrace it. You can do this." It was her best pep talk to date.

For the next two minutes she did do it. She cleaned and wiped and pulled out another lemon-scented wipe when the first one became covered in dust and soap scum. With the second towelette Starr reached into the far corners of the bathroom. It was no use reprimanding herself for neglecting the space. She scrubbed a particularly stubborn spot of mint-flavored toothpaste and nudged an object hidden beneath a dried up washrag.

"Gross," Starr muttered and with her free hand plucked the rag off the counter and tossed it on the floor behind her. "Next is laundry." But her train of thought stopped there when she saw what her fingers had butted up against.

The hard plastic case meant to hold five razor blades was almost empty. They were Gillette brand, yet another change Geoff made since moving to San Francisco. Before that, he'd been a fan of the Dollar Shave Club. Back in Indiana, he'd triumphantly hold up his brown cardboard package that he received around the fifth of each month as if it was a great and wonderful gift sent to him by a long lost relative. She paused her cleaning and savored the memory.

"Do you know what this means?" Geoff asked Starr.

"What?"

"It means I'm in. I'm a card carrying, dues paying, legit member of the a shaving club. That's what it means. I'm part of an elite group," he said, laughing as he tore open the package, excited as a kid at Christmas.

"What exactly comes with being part of this elite group?" she asked.

"What, my fair lady, doesn't it come with?" He ticked off each aspect of the membership for her listening pleasure. "A monthly supply of razors, which every man needs. All of them packaged neatly and safely in this one of a kind carrying case. It comes with oils, salves, and good smelling lotions."

"That every man needs?" Starr asked mischievously.

"Absolutely."

"Wow. All for a dollar?"

"Well, the potions and things require a bit more of an investment, but they're well worth it," Geoff assured her. He held up a handful of razor handles without blades attached. "For just a small, small price, you can purchase razor handles to go with said razor blades," he said.

"That's amazing?" she said, confused. "So, the razor handles don't automatically come with the blades?"

"Trust me. It's what makes a man's business a profitable man's business. No need to worry your pretty little head about it," he said, patting her in a faux patronizing mode on the head.

"Well, then you've sold me on the wonders of this amazing

little club. How do I get in on it?" Starr asked, plucking a razor handle from his hand.

"My dear, sweet Starr," Geoff said frowning. "It's a man's club. You are not a man. I am forever grateful for that. Because if you were, I wouldn't be able to do this."

The kiss took Starr's breath away, but it started and ended before she could think. As they stood in Geoff's small bathroom, it became awkward between them, the way a shift in a relationship has a way of doing. She, missing the feathery feel of his lips on hers, held the razor handle, uncertain what she was supposed to do next. He rocked on his heels like a college professor trying to figure out a complicated math problem. Then, they both spoke at once.

"And the—" Geoff said.

"Well, I—" Starr began.

They laughed, somewhat embarrassed at themselves, yet both eager to stay in the moment. To keep it alive and explore the idea of them as a couple without having the courage to say it.

"You go," Starr said, hopeful a romantic conversation would blossom out of this odd and silly talk of men's clubs and shaving supplies. Truth be told, she didn't really know what she'd intended to say. Well, I'm supremely interested in shaving clubs. Well, I can't imagine such a thing as a shaving club. Well, I never thought something as interesting as shaving clubs would end with a lovely kiss like that. Well, I liked kissing you, I hope you liked kissing me, and maybe we can kiss again. Someday. Soon. Nothing she came up with sounded intelligent or romantic, so she insisted he speak first. Even when Geoff protested, Starr held her ground.

"Seriously, Geoff," she said, looking at him shyly. "I want to hear what you have to say."

He was flustered. "The best part of the, uh, club, is the booklet."

"The booklet?"

"Oh, yeah. They send this booklet every month with the blades. It's pretty cool. It has cartoons and articles that men find interesting anyway. Quizzes and, you know, stuff," Geoff said.

His words tumbled out faster and faster as he spoke until the last few words sounded more like "yaknowstuff," and Starr had to silently work at separating the syllables until she knew what he'd said.

She stumbled for a recovery response. "Sure. The booklet. I imagine that's the most important part of any club. Maybe even the most important part of all clubs the world over. Right?"

They laughed again—her a little more forcefully as she struggled not to ask questions about the kiss. Questions like: What did it mean? Are we dating now? Have we crossed from friends to more than friends? Are we dating now? Will you kiss me again? Should I kiss you?

But neither of them mentioned the kiss again, and the sound of the coffee maker brought Starr back to the present.

"Obviously, the kiss meant nothing. I mean, look at us now. Him thousands of miles away and me sitting here, waiting for my career to explode in my face." She shoved the razor box with its lonely, shiny razor blade into her skirt pocket. She had to turn on the news to find out what had happened to Grace. "First things first. Call in sick, have coffee, and then watch the news," she said, turning her back on the vanity.

Starr scrolled through her contacts. Cloverleaf, Crisis Line, Caulton, Ms... All of them nosy. All of them necessary. She held her finger above them all, trying to decide who would do the least damage to her already fragile state. In the corner, Sdax pouted and used one of Starr's lipsticks to draw a picture of a coffin on the bathroom mirror.

CHAPTER FOURTEEN

Morris sat in the waiting room of the Cloverleaf Counseling Center, but he didn't sit still. He fidgeted and twitched almost uncontrollably until the kid he recognized from a previous visit got up from where he sat on the floor using a plastic end table for his coloring activity.

The boy took three steps, and without looking Morris in the eye or speaking very loudly, he said, "Want to color with me?" He thrust half a crayon in Morris' personal space. The crayon was hunter green. The boy's intrusive conversation penetrated the anxiety that crawled through Morris' veins, and his fidgeting came to a screeching halt.

"What are you coloring?" Morris asked, surprised to find himself a little bit interested in the boy's response.

"*Hello Kitty*. But it's something to do."

Gingerly, Morris accepted the broken crayon and edged himself off the vinyl seat where he'd been waiting for Starr to come to the inner door and invite him in. Though he'd abruptly ended his sessions, today he needed to see her smiling face. He needed to hear her reassuring voice. Oscar's taunting was strong, and Morris was afraid something bad would happen if he couldn't subdue his wisp.

Uncomfortable kneeling on the floor, he dragged his chair close to the end table. His knees touched it, and he had to lean over, hunched back, in order to share the coloring book. The boy was right—it was something to do.

The boy picked up a brown crayon, pointed to the page opposite the one he was about to color, and said, "It'll be okay. There's still some uncolored parts on your page."

The large cat (presumably *Hello Kitty*) smiled at him and hugged a smaller cat. Both had bows in their fur next to their pointy ears. Some of the page had been colored in by a small or reckless kid with no regard for the black outline of the figures. The scribble marks frustrated Morris almost as much as Starr's absence, and he hesitated to make his first mark.

"I know. It's a girl book. I asked my dad to let me play video games, but he said no. So..." The boy didn't finish the sentence as if he'd clearly explained himself, and his new friend would not have trouble putting the pieces of his unfinished verbal puzzle together.

"Why not?" Morris asked as he began to color in the smaller cat's bow.

"I dunno. Screen time or something." The boy scratched his eyebrow with one hand and continued coloring with the other. "You got ADHD?"

Morris looked around. Couldn't the boy see that he had nothing? Well, his wallet and two coffees, but otherwise nothing. "Did you see me come in with something else?" he asked, mildly uncertain that perhaps he had, in all of his distress, brought something with him into the counseling center and now couldn't remember what it was.

"You can't carry ADHD. It's something you just...have. Like a sickness. That's what my mom says."

Morris stopped coloring and examined the boy. He saw no distress in the kid's face. He didn't appear gaunt or disheveled or otherwise ill-looking. No tubes protruded from his body. Nor did he see casts or splints on the kid. "You don't look sick," he said to the boy.

"Isn't that what my mom says?" the kid asked the man sitting across the room.

The man uncrossed and crossed his leg again. He flipped through the pages of a People magazine and didn't look up. "Mmmm hmmmm."

"See?" the boy said to Morris.

Morris was knowledgeable about many things, but he was unfamiliar with ADHD or how one contracted it. For a minute he worried that perhaps the kid was contagious. Until he remembered where he was—at a counseling center. A community mental health agency. Quickly he set the crayon down and dug in his back pocket for his wallet. Star's business card rested in the first slot right where it had been since the day they'd met.

Yes. Confirmed. Since Morris thought of counseling as a way to get Larimore back, he hadn't given thought to his, or anyone else's, mental health. He hadn't given any thought to how Starr might have diagnosed *him*.

"Excuse me," Morris said to the boy. He shoved his chair back and headed to the check-in desk.

Starr was out sick for the day, and Morris was her second client to show up unannounced and unscheduled.

"Is Starr coming? I need an appointment today." Morris spoke in hushed tones.

"Your therapist will be with you in a little bit, sir. She's—we're running behind today. That's all." She glanced at the clock on her desk and willed the numbers to move faster.

"My mental health therapist?" Morris asked.

Brandy pretended not to hear. She checked the calendar on the computer and rifled through papers, hoping someone else would come through the door and need her assistance. When Morris didn't go away, she blurted out the next best thing. A decoy she'd used many times with frustrated and upset clients. Coffee. Coffee was her saving grace.

"Would you like some coffee, sir? While you wait?" Brandy smiled. "I made a fresh pot." She turned away from Morris, ready to rise from her chair and bolt down the hall in search of the perfect cup. She would gladly fill it to the brim in order to staunch some of his frustration over the long and annoying wait for someone who wasn't coming.

"No. I don't want any coffee. I work in a coffee shop. Don't you know that?"

"She's just like the rest of the women in your life, Morris. Ignorant. Determined to use you until there's nothing left."

Morris jumped at the sound of Oscar's voice. For two days Morris had evaded his wisp. Miserable at parties, Morris accepted Alfonso's invitation to celebrate his son's birthday. It was an extravagant family gathering with food and booze. Morris mingled among his coworker's family and eventually passed out on Alfonso's sofa. The next day he camped out in the ER with Alfonso and his sick child. Afraid to be left alone with Oscar, Morris refused to leave even when the lobby was filled to overflowing with people vomiting and crying from their pain and ailments. He bought new clothes in the hospital gift shop hoping Oscar wouldn't recognize him. On the way to Starr's office, he took different routes on the bus system knowing Oscar preferred it when the two were alone. But Oscar found him in the one place Morris had hoped he could find solace.

"Sir, you'll have to be patient. We're doing the best we can," Brandy said.

"I'm scared," Brandy's wisp whimpered from behind the desk.

"You should be," Oscar said.

At the far end of the inner hall, Julle hurried out of her office. The couple she'd met with thanked her for their session and left through the back door. As she closed it behind them, Julle straightened her blazer and brushed her hands together, freeing herself of the responsibility of the clients she'd just ushered out.

"Good morning, Mr. Wilde. I take it Brandy has explained that Starr isn't in today? Not to worry. I'm aware of your case. You're welcome to come back, and we can get started." Julle plucked Morris' file from the rack on Brandy's desk and welcomed him in.

On each door was a sign that read either "available" or "in

session", and it appeared there was an equal number of therapists in both statuses. Morris wondered who had moved into Starr's office. He didn't want to talk to this strange woman, but his growing concern about his mental health and the need to escape Oscar gave him the courage to follow her. Then he stopped, turned, and surprised himself.

"Don't forget this," he said to the young boy who had shared his coloring book. "Your crayon." He held it out for the boy to retrieve.

The boy ran over, holding his coloring book the whole way as if he was afraid someone would come along and steal it if left unattended. "Cool," the kid said. "We can color next week, too. Right, Dad?" he asked his father.

"What? Yeah, that's fine." His father never looked up.

Once the door was closed behind him, the fight or flight hormones took hold, and Oscar used them to his advantage. "See that? All you have to do is grab her from behind. Squeeze her neck and shake her like one of those bobble head dolls." Oscar matched Morris' stride and raised his hands to show Morris how easy it would be to snap Julle's neck.

Morris could see it. He clenched his hands and realized he'd left the coffee in the other room with the boy and his father. He forced his hands open and stretched his fingers until they hurt. He couldn't give in to Oscar's schemes.

"When we leave, you can take the computer monitor from that receptionist and beat it against the desk until it splinters. Brandy the bitch. Look at her, I dare you. She's afraid."

Brandy hadn't looked afraid to Morris. Bored maybe. Irritated. Morris didn't look back, and he didn't argue with Oscar. He was afraid he wouldn't win.

Julle's office was nothing like Starr's. The two floor lamps and an overhead fluorescent light bulb were too bright. There was a small window in the office door, and he kept looking at it, wondering if someone peered in at them. Julle's chair was a swivel seat on wheels with no back. She seemed to enjoy whirling from her computer to him as she threw rapid fire questions at him. Morris felt like he was juggling live grenades.

"So your last session with Starr went well? She spoke highly of you. How are you feeling today? Any agitation? Mood swings? You're feeling safe, right? No worries about self-harm or suicide? Aren't you the coffee guy? How's that going? Must be nice to get a day off. Sometimes people serve the same thing day after day, like burgers or something, but they hate burgers. You know, because they're so tired of cooking them or smelling them or whatever. Is coffee like that for you?"

Morris sat stiffly on a straight-backed wooden chair tucked into a corner with one of the floor lamps behind him. He felt like a scolded school boy on display under a heating lamp. He tried not to squirm. He responded, desperate to complete his time with her, yet equally afraid to leave.

"Yes. That's nice. Okay. Some? Not really. Sure. Yes, coffee. I do. No, it's not."

"Well," Julle said. She put her elbows on her knees and her face in her hands as she assessed the situation. "Starr's out today. Obviously. It's her last day so no one's really forcing her to come in, you know. She didn't have any clients anyway. I mean, until you called."

"Her last day?"

"That reminds me. Starr said she'd discharged you. Did that not work out? Like you want services still? Again?"

Oscar sighed. "Last day. Wow. She didn't even tell you."

"She didn't tell me it was her last day."

Julle flipped through Morris' file. "Yeah, well, don't take it personal. It's not unusual for therapists to want out of the grind of community mental health. Too much paperwork, not enough...of anything else. You're welcome to re-enroll, though." Julle skimmed a few pages in his folder. "Looks like Starr completed the discharge paperwork yesterday. Administrative discharge, which means you stopped coming in. I can amend it, and you wouldn't have to do a whole new intake packet. Assuming, of course, you plan to keep your appointments."

Morris didn't know how to respond. He couldn't believe Starr had gone through with it. Discharged him completely with no intention of coming back.

"How about we keep it short today? I can schedule you for next week. Tuesday? I can fit you in at three."

"Dang. How does that feel? She can 'fit you in.' Like you're nothing but an afterthought."

Morris silently cursed Julle for upsetting Oscar. Now he'd have to really keep his hands to himself. He splayed his fingers against his knees. I will not choke her. I will not. Starr never treated him like leftovers. She always let Morris choose when he wanted to be seen, no matter what her schedule said. Nine in the morning? Certainly. Three-fifteen? Not three, not three-thirty. Of course. Eleven forty-five? "You got it," she'd say. Starr would make a show of using ink to add him to her calendar—yet another indication that she had no idea of erasing his name or canceling on him. Starr never shortened his sessions or hurried through their conversations.

"Until today. She didn't bother to show up. She wasn't even thinking about you," Oscar reminded him.

Morris hadn't thought of that. Nor had he thought Starr would end up in Oscar's cross hairs. He wished he could rewind Julle and her series of questions. He would answer them differently this time.

"So your last session with Starr went well?"

"Not really. She was upset. I think I upset her."

"She speaks highly of you."

"Did she tell you what I did? I made a fool of myself. And her."

"How are you feeling today? Any agitation? Mood swings?"

"Not well. Really agitated. I'm afraid of what I might do."

"You're feeling safe?"

"No. Maybe for myself, I mean. But I'm afraid of what I might do to someone else."

"No worries about self-harm or suicide?"

"No, nothing like that."

"You're the coffee guy, right? How's that going?"

"Yes. It's bad. I have to work the late shift tonight, and I'm afraid."

But Morris didn't ask Julle to review her list of questions. He didn't let her know that his anxiety had reached a boiling point he couldn't control. He didn't tell her about his wisp or how Oscar had changed from a wimpy, scared kid to that of a frightening voice that insisted on doing things his way. He didn't tell Julle about the visions he had following her into her office where Oscar literally pulsed with life and anger.

"Is there anything else?" Morris asked quietly.

Julle thought for a minute. Then she asked, "Would you mind updating this emergency contact form? Just a formality."

Morris took the paper from her and balanced it on his knee. Every word was spelled correctly. He wrote the number he remembered from her business card. Oscar told him to. Had whispered it in his ear. Morris hoped Julle would see it, that she'd call Starr and warn her.

But his new therapist slid the paper into a folder with his name on it without reading what he wrote. "All done for today then," she announced, and the session was over. She opened the door and directed Morris to the back exit when Brandy hurried down the hall.

"Wait, Julle?"

"Yes, Brandy? What is it?" "There's a package here. It has his name on it." She waved the bulging envelope in the air. "I almost forgot about it."

"What is it?" Julle asked.

"I don't know. But it was on the desk when I got here this morning," Brandy said.

"I guess if it's yours," Julle said and handed it to Morris.

After Julle ushered Morris out of her office, she reviewed her conversation with Morris. Partly she was annoyed with Starr. For someone who had spent time lecturing Julle on the intricacies of being a good therapist—listening with the third ear, making clients feel like the only one, giving appropriate homework—Starr had missed the boat on this one. Discharging a client who clearly wasn't ready. Yet there was something else. Something Julle felt she'd forgotten. An uncrossed T or an I not dotted. She couldn't put her finger on it though.

CHAPTER FIFTEEN

The goodbyes were hard. He started with Larimore. His anger released its grip on him as he packed up his clothes and toiletries, leaving nothing behind to remind her of him. Their morning rituals and his scent would fade from her memory over time if they hadn't already, replaced by Harold and whatever activities made up their relationship. Harold. He was a joke. But so had been his relationship with Larimore. It was unhealthy. He knew that now. He would miss her. At the last minute, Morris put an unopened jar of marmalade on the counter with her spoon resting beside it.

At the library Morris sat behind a computer monitor with earbuds plugged in and cranked up to drown out the intrusive sound of Oscar's voice. His wisp was relentless, and Morris' agitation ratcheted up like notches on his belt as he tried to keep the montage of vile instructions at bay. Kind and compassionate Starr. He had to tell her something. He had to tell her the truth. Morris felt she deserved that before the end came. It was the least he could do.

The ring he'd placed on her finger had been their undoing. He shouldn't have upset her. He began his email to her with an apology and ended it with another. In the body were his truths about the proposal, Oscar, and the worry of his pending actions and how the potential for disaster consumed him. The voice of his wisp was at fault, triggered by whatever childhood past he couldn't recall and fueled by Oscar's hatred toward women. *We're an unlikely pair*, he wrote. *Our only true connection is the name. This is the only way I know to remove his control over me. I think this is what sacrifice means.* He didn't mention the diamond ring that he'd shipped back to Cloverleaf with a handmade receipt that read: payment for services. He would have to trust Julle and Brandy to make sure she received it.

Morris killed time in Buena Vista Park listening to a local band punctuate the evening with woodwinds and strings until it was time to put the last part of his solution into place. Getting hold of Alfonso was easy.

MORRIS: I can come in tonight and do the late cleaning.

ALFONSO: You sure, amigo?

MORRIS: Si. ALFONSO: Can come by finish last part together.

MORRIS: No need.

ALFONSO: It no problem.

MORRIS: Stay home. Con su familia.

The night was unusually dark, and as the hour grew later, the dew point slowly fell with the temperature until both were within a few degrees of one another. The stars blinked out behind a thick layer of clouds. The moon, brighter than the twinkling stars was much more difficult to camouflage. It hung above the city until it too was covered bit by bit until the moon was a circle the size of a coin.

Morris finished the cleaning duties at the cafe, priding himself on being a man of his word. He told Alfonso that he would clean and he'd meant it. He cleaned every inch until the dining area was gleaming top to bottom. Oscar tried to distract him, but for once,

Morris didn't engage with him. As resolutely as Morris had been about completing the cleaning tasks, he was resolute in his decision that this—the anger, the confusion, the constant pressure to do what Oscar wanted—had to end. Tonight.

He tossed out the dirty mop water at the back entrance and let himself into the manager's office. The room was still cluttered, the desk piled high with outdated papers and receipts. Old invoices, charge slips, and inventory lists—some crumpled, others flat as if they'd been starched and ironed—were situated among the piles that weighed down the old wooden desk, the centerpiece in the small and crowded room.

"What are you doing?" Oscar asked. He could hardly see where Morris was bent over, huffing and puffing, as he tried to dig something out of the crevice between two towering file cabinets. "We need to go. She'll be home soon, and you have to make her pay. Have you even checked the camera tonight?"

"What do you think?" Morris asked. He gave a final tug, and the file cabinets released a long flat wall mirror with a wicked crack across the top corner from their grip. He propped the dusty item against the back wall.

"Looks like junk to me. Come on. Check on her already." Oscar pointed at Morris' phone.

"It doesn't have to be shiny and new."

The last time Morris cleaned the coffee shop, he'd ransacked the place after learning of Larimore's infidelity. Busted out a couple of windows, broke some dishes, and trashed the Saki brothers messy office. When he was confronted, Morris weaved a tale about a couple of thugs who'd come along and broken out the security camera before they made a mess of the place. "I was lucky they didn't do any worse," Morris had said, portraying himself as a scared employee who felt threatened and uncertain about whether or not he should go to the police. Worried about the ramifications they might experience if Morris was hurt in their facility and worse yet if Morris reported that they'd done nothing to protect him, the brothers took it upon themselves to ensure the safety of all their employees.

They said they'd get more cameras. New ones capable of

taking sharper images than the last one and placed them in more discreet locations to prevent potential thieves from damaging the lenses. They made promises to hire a security guard to patrol the perimeter when staff were required to be there after dark. In the end, the brothers only had enough money for one thing. A small, inexpensive gun. They scrounged up enough cash for a box of ammunition that they kept locked in one of the desk drawers.

"You don't even have to load it," the brothers explained. "Just scare them. That's all."

Morris hadn't cared one way or the other, knowing there hadn't been any vandals to begin with. Now in front of the broken mirror, with the coffee shop sparkling, he faced his reflection. He pointed to the mirror, and Oscar entered until the two were the same image staring at one another.

"What now?" The wisp's eyelid twitched. Morris was behaving funny. "Why are you acting like you're in charge?"

"Nothing to worry about, Oscar. This is business. It's the solution to a problem."

"This wasn't the solution. We were supposed to make them pay. Larimore for rejecting you. Starr for discharging you," Oscar sneered.

"That was how you wanted to solve the problem. And I can't do that."

"Can't? Or won't?"

"Does it matter? I've decided this is what I have to do. Me. And you have to listen this time."

For a millisecond Oscar's demeanor went from cavalier to cowering. Then Morris pointed the barrel of the gun at his temple, and Oscar fought back. He kicked and shoved Morris, bent his arm into a twisted pretzel shape. The gun clattered to the floor, and Oscar prayed it wouldn't fire.

"It's the only way," Morris said through clenched teeth. "Leave me alone."

"No, I won't," Oscar spat. He kicked the firearm out of Morris' reach.

"We have to do this!" Morris shouted as the gun slid between the file cabinets where it wedged in, handle first. He crouched on the floor, his cheek cold against the concrete. "It's the only way." It wouldn't be clean, but it would end his despair. It would keep Larimore and Starr safe and unharmed.

"Unless you end up grossly disfigured. Kept alive by machines. Don't you see why my plan was better?" Oscar stood in front of the door, blocking Morris' access to any other means. "When you're ready to do things my way, we can go."

Morris moved quickly and quietly. With his employee file updated and resting on top of the debris, he stood on the folding chair. He scaled the tower of old paperwork where he grabbed the power cord from the electrical job still in progress. Morris twisted one end of it around an industrial hook in the ceiling, then reached up, and looped his necktie into the fray.

At the door, Oscar continued to grumble about the situation.

Morris put his head through the noose. He kicked aside the pile of papers and watched as they floated down, down, down around the desk.

He reached out as far as his legs would let him, straining to reach the wooden lip.

Oscar sprang to his feet. His cheeks turned as red as his hair. "No! No! Fuck you. Fuck you. I'll kill them anyway. I'll wring Larimore's scrawny neck while she sleeps. Watch me. I swear I'll do it. I'll find Starr and I'll—"

Morris grabbed a toe hold on the corner and toppled the desk. The landslide of paperwork made a whooshing sound. His legs jerked. His torso began to sway. The Alaska shot glass slipped from his grip and shattered into pieces.

Oscar and his plans for revenge were silenced.

CHAPTER SIXTEEN

Geoff woke with a start triggered by the sound of breaking glass. His heart raced and he was covered in a film of sweat. The crunch of metal that twisted and snarled in on itself and its victims followed. Over the years the true order of that night's events had begun to play tricks on his brain. He laid there trying to still his heart and mind. Somewhere in the tundra, a stray dog barked and didn't stop. Geoff plugged his ear with his finger to drown out the buzz of a persistent mosquito. Lately the bad dreams visited him every few days.

"Something wake you?" Alexie Daniels asked from across the room.

"Just the good Lord getting my attention, I suppose," Geoff said. His stump throbbed. He thought about Starr and how she asked him to rate the pain. Today it was an eight.

"You been ignoring Him something fierce?" Alexie Daniels, Geoff's roommate, was an older man in his late sixties or early seventies. No one seemed to know his exact age. He'd been taken into custody by the village public safety officer (VPSO) for threatening his daughter after the two of them had gotten into an argument. The kerfuffle had amounted to nothing more than angry voices, a few swear words, and the elderly man telling his daughter he ought to "show her who was boss." But the young woman didn't stand for it. He lived in her house, and she had two young sons to raise. She refused to let her boys think it was okay to drink and cause trouble. Besides, this wasn't the first time Alexie had gotten carried away. Nor was it the first time his daughter, Minnie, had taken action. The VPSO showed up and told Alexie he had to find a place to stay or he'd have to take him in.

Geoff felt sorry for the old man and convinced the officer to release him to Geoff's custody. He offered Alexie the spare bed in the small house one of the school teachers had vacated for the summer. The VPSO had raised his eyebrows at that but didn't object to the arrangement. It meant he could go home instead of staying at the village jailhouse keeping an eye on Alexie—something he'd done before.

In Geoff's charge, Alexie sobered up. The next day Alexie asked for some of Geoff's food, and Geoff obliged. The man was no trouble. Quiet and calm when he wasn't drinking. Yet he wasn't inclined to return to his daughter's and work things out as Geoff had suggested. It wasn't really a bother to share the space with Alexie, but it did put a crimp in Geoff's evenings with his missionary partner, Penny.

The two missionaries ate together, went over their daily activities, and prepared for the following day. Geoff's favorite thing about his evenings with Penny was their prayer time. She was fervent when she spoke to God. Passionate about her faith and the mission field. About everything really. It sparked an energy in Geoff he hadn't experienced in a long time. He hoped today Alexie would go back to his daughter's.

Geoff rubbed his aching leg. He wished often that the lower half was there even if it was useless. There was something strange about the painful sensation of something that didn't exist. "Never said that."

"You didn't not say it either," Alexie pointed out.

Geoff was in no mood for Yup'ik riddles. "Sometimes the Lord gets our attention because He wants us to pray. Or praise Him. Share our testimony with someone who needs to hear it. That's all. It doesn't have to mean we've been ignoring Him."

"Why'd He wake you up this time?" Alexie asked. He had a twig in his mouth. One that he'd whittled into a sharp point from the pocket knife Geoff had loaned him earlier. Alexie behaved like Geoff was the law. He never went more than a few feet from Geoff.

"You imply He's woken me up before. What about you? Seems like you've been awake all night."

"Sometimes God wakes us up. To pray or praise. To share our testimony. Remember?" Alexie giggled like a schoolgirl.

Geoff felt a stern retort crawl up his throat and stand on the edge of his tongue like a diver ready to jump off the diving board and into the pool. Then he remembered his role in the community and bit back the response. He tried in vain to ignore the burning sensation in his missing leg. "So which is it?" Geoff asked. There was no sense in trying to sleep. He prepared himself for one of Alexie's stories. Most of the Yup'ik people Geoff had met were storytellers. It was part of the culture.

"To pray." He felt guilty for assuming differently. Then annoyed. "And you can't do that silently?"

"I was. But you cried out. Acting like someone was after you. Ircinrraq? A little person? Calling out to you from the grave?"

Cold chills ran through Geoff's body, and he hugged himself for warmth. He tried to remind himself that per the village folks and the local, but spotty, news station, it was an unseasonably cool summer. "I don't believe in ghosts. Unless you're talking about the Holy Ghost and He—"

"Never said nothing about a ghost."

Geoff sat up in his sleeping bag and pushed himself against the wall. He and Penny had been in the subregional village of Hooper Bay for three weeks. Longer than they'd been in Nunapitchuk, Kwig, and Quinhagak. Pastor Rudy felt it important for them to get more time there since it was one of the larger, more populated communities that made up the Yukon-Kuskokwim Delta and acted as small hub to the surrounding hamlets situated in southwest Alaska. The remote locations reached far and wide, the Yukon and Kuskokwim rivers snaking along and among them.

Hooper Bay was made up mostly of young people, and the missionaries of LifeSpring Church felt strongly about providing Biblical education to the youth. The Vacation Bible School events were a chance for the team to share the Gospel and gave the Native children fun activities to participate in. Rain and fog had prevented the team's planned departure. If the weather cleared, they'd fly back to Bethel the following day and then travel to two more villages on the itinerary before they returned to California.

With two weeks left before going home, Geoff wasn't sure how he felt. Would Starr be there? Did he even want her there? He'd grown close to Penny as they shared the Gospel together. Several times community members had mistaken them for a couple. While Penny blushed, Geoff politely corrected people at first. But after the first few times, he simply said, "How sweet" or "God bless you." It was easier than explaining how he'd ended up in Alaska with a woman who wasn't his fianceé. Eventually, the thought of Penny and him as a couple sounded nice. When he told the Bible story of Ruth and Boaz to a group of youngsters one of them asked if he and Penny were like them. When Penny brought it up later, he danced around the conversation—waiting to see if she'd come to the same conclusion he was. That maybe they were meant for each other and God had brought them to the far-flung corners of Alaska to bring them together.

Geoff tried the servant role with Alexie. "Is there something I can do for you? A glass of water? Something?"

The old man ignored him the patronizing ways of this strange kass'aq. Alexie should be at home. Growing old with the woman he loved, playing with his grandchildren, and teaching them Native ways. But a war, a world war at that, did more than destroy a nation. It separated loved ones and families. It changed everything in a way no one could fathom.

"I'm not supposed to be here," Alexie said. He was tired of the pain, tired of the past. Only booze dulled the ache and blurred the memories. His body had shrunk and withered over the years. His clothes hung on his frame. The old flannel shirt was worn, and a hole had begun to wear in the right elbow exposing his dry and mottled skin beneath. Alexie's daughter would have clean clothes waiting for him when he returned. She always did. She was a good girl who took care of him despite his shortcomings, which were many.

Geoff voiced one of his many mantras of the faith. "The good Lord has a purpose for all of His children if they come to Him and repent."

"Repenting is easy. I have apologized many, many times. Promised to be different. Make new choices." Alexie shook his head, still covered in dark hair with only a few strands of gray peeking out. "So many times I promised. Like raindrops coming out of the sky."

Geoff didn't say so, but he understood. How many times had he made promises to be different? Only to return to his same old ways. He remembered when he was a teenager and how difficult he had made his high school years for his parents. Demanding, yelling, throwing his weight around when he didn't get his way. Sneaking girls into the house, going to parties without permission. When he got caught, he'd beg and bargain with his mother. Promised her he'd never do it again if she'd forgive him. Believe him this time. She'd cave and convince his father that this time Geoff would get it right. Sometimes he'd last a week. Maybe two. Then he'd be right back at it all over again.

"You know anyone like that?" Alexie asked. "Good intentions. Hard time showing love in action."

"We are all sinners, my friend." Geoff felt a strange kinship with this man who irritated him. "Is that woman your wife?" Alexie asked, and the subject was changed on a dime.

The book of John rattled around in Geoff's mind until the words and his wisp took charge.

"You know the scripture," Ian said glumly. He sat next to Alexie and recited,

"Jesus said to her, "Everyone who drinks of this water will be thirsty again, but whoever drinks of the water that I will give him will never be thirsty again. The water that I will give him will become in him a spring of water welling up to eternal life. The woman said to him, "Sir, give me this water, so that I will not be thirsty or have to come here to draw water." Jesus

said to her, "Go, call your husband and come here." The woman answered him, "I have no husband." Jesus said to her, "You are right in saying 'I have no husband'; for you have had five husbands, and the one you now have is not your husband. What you have said is true. (John 4:13-18)"'

Following on the heels of the Samaritan woman's shame was an image of his last morning with Starr. Geoff bit back the sweetness of her name. His cheeks burned as if she knew. He was grateful for the darkness in the room.

"Penny is my sister in Christ. We're here to evangelize and share the Gospel. Remember?" He said to Alexie and Ian.

That was a statement Geoff had made many times since being in Alaska. But persecution happens to those who love the Lord. Trials, tribulations, accusations. Challenges everywhere they turn. Serving the Lord was not easy. Geoff could attest to that. He blessed those who persecuted him. Turned the other cheek. Took the high road. When all else failed, he prayed for his enemies. He served because he had to.

Tonight Geoff excused his attitude with the sleepless night, his nightmare, and the fiery ache in his leg. He sent up a silent prayer for forgiveness. He hoped God would understand.

"Eee. Servant of the Lord," Alexie murmured.

"Exactly," Geoff muttered. An urge to explain himself further surged through him, but at the last second decided the Lord probably wanted him to rest for what would likely be a long day ahead.

They were scheduled to pick berries. A back breaking job in the tundra. At eleven Geoff was scheduled to call in to court with Alexie. He'd been given a reprieve from flying in for the hearing due to the cost of airfare. Alexie would be back in his daughter's house by evening but still had to make amends with the legal system. Then there was the evening Vacation Bible School service that he and Penny had spent the last week preparing. There would be Bible verse recitations followed by a community potluck. Penny was both humbled and proud of their efforts while Geoff was eager to show her off and give her the credit she deserved. He'd even purchased a small gift for her from a local elder—a pair of fish skin earrings he'd purchased from a local woman.

"Get some sleep," Geoff instructed. "Tomorrow's a long day."

The cold sweat from the nightmare had receded. Geoff pulled his blanket up, tucked the edge of it around his shoulder, and punched down his already flat pillow. He missed his bed. Sleeping on the thin mattress was another sacrifice he made for the Lord. It wasn't an easy one.

Not now. Breathe. Pray. Count sheep. Whatever it takes. Go back to sleep.

It was the same thing he told himself once or twice a month when his past woke him up. A small price to pay, all things considered. He closed his eyes and begged God to dull the pain knowing full well he didn't deserve any reprieve. Geoff instructed himself to focus on the positive things that came part and parcel with servanthood. The sound of children laughing and singing praises. The moment when a sinner came and gave his life to God. The powerful peace that came over someone in the midst of life's worries when his brothers and sisters in Christ gathered together to pray.

As Geoff reined in his thoughts, a restful peace descended upon him. His muscles relaxed, and with it the tightness in his chest loosened its stern grip on him. He welcomed sleep and tuned his ears to the dull rain that fell outside.

Thank you, Jesus.

"Have you always been a servant of the Lord?" Alexie asked.

Ignore him, Geoff's brain screamed. *But what if the old man really did want to know about Christ? What if this was his moment to truly accept Jesus? Alexie could well be on the verge of salvation, altering his life once and for all, and all you want to do is sleep. How greedy and selfish.*

"Not always."

"You enjoy it. Exotic travel, meeting new people, new cultures. It must be a true joy."

The sound of a jar lid popping off preceded the smell of fish. Salmon, though Geoff couldn't distinguish if it was king or red or silver. Tinged with the smell of smoke and vinegar, the odor was strong and tart. Last summer's harvest, probably one of Alexie's last jars.

"I have fish," Alexie said. He smacked his lips as he indulged.

"No, thank you." Geoff didn't think he'd ever be able to eat fish again after helping Alexie's family cut and put away their catch. It was a bloody, messy event that the whole family participated in with sheets of cardboard spread out over the living room floor. They used every part of the salmon. Fish heads were cut off and buried to make stink heads. The eggs scooped out of the fish bellies to be used for salad. The tender flesh hung out to dry or canned in small jars that would last them for the tough winter ahead.

"Why do you do it then?" Alexie asked between bites.

"If I didn't, who would come teach you about salvation? When God calls, you don't ask why or for how long. You say, 'Send me' and He does." The words tumbled out, rote memorization of what he'd been taught in the church. Though he felt some satisfaction, even a great deal of satisfaction at times when he was ministering to the needs of others, his number one reason for working in the church was the sense of obligation. "No matter what?" "No matter what."

"You have to go? Now? When we're supposed to be planning our wedding?"

Geoff hugged Starr tight. "I'm sorry. It's important. When God calls..."

"I know. You have to go." She stepped out of his embrace, and the distance between them grew.

"Are you tired? From doing His work?" Alexie asked.

"The Bible says to not grow weary in well doing," Geoff spouted. "But yes, sometimes I'm tired."

It was a good kind of tired. The kind that made Geoff ache from a hard day's work, then lie down with a grateful heart. He had much to give thanks for out there in the tundra. A dry place to sleep, even if there was the awful fish smell and a local who wouldn't stop talking. He was thankful for Penny. She exhibited such diligence and grace in the mission field. She was kind and generous. Her love for God made him want to be a better person. She served with such fervor. He pictured her smiling face and breathed in the scent of the cherry blossom lotion that often lingered after they held hands and prayed. The way she piled her hair in a messy bun, her head thrown back in laughter when she played with the Native children. There were times he'd felt like a proud husband watching his wife with their children.

Geoff blushed at that last thought and conjured up an image of Starr seated at the rolltop desk he'd given her with her feet resting on Bridgette's backside. When Starr worked for her clients, she did so with passion. With a servant's heart.

"Why not take a break then? Rest," Alexie said.

"What if Jesus had said he was tired and needed a break?"

"Are you the Messiah?"

"We are made in His image, are we not? Called to pick up our crosses and follow Him." Sometimes Geoff was appalled at how little scripture people knew. How little their understanding of God and His kingdom. How did people like this ever manage without missionaries to teach them?

"I don't really know," Alexie said, perplexed.

"Well, you are. You were made in Christ's image in the likeness of man. You just lack His salvation. You have to come to Him like a child, willing to repent, and give your life to Him." Geoff was frustrated. *Such a fool for a wise elder.*

Alexie was mournful. "Why would any kind of God want a ruined, drunken life like mine?"

The oily strips were long gone, but the smell hung low in the air like the fog along the Bay area skyline. Geoff felt a momentary pang of homesickness clench his gut, and he willed it away. That was the last thing he wanted. A honey bucket was not as pleasant sounding as the name implied. Another inconvenience that Geoff disliked about this particular mission field.

"The good Lord uses all of His children. From the smallest to the most sinful to the most unlikely. He uses all of us." Geoff could have these conversations all day as long as the other person didn't get too close or ask anything too personal.

"Which one are you?" Alexie asked.

"What's that?"

Alexie raised his voice as if Geoff was hard of hearing. "I said, which one are you?"

"Which one what?"

"Which kind of people? Are you small or unlikely or the most vile of sinners?"

"This isn't about me or the kind of person *I* am. This is about my being here, washed in the blood. Repentant. *I'm* a child of God. *I'm* out here—away from my home and my job. Losing sleep for *you*. To make certain that you get a chance to hear the Gospel. So that you can have a chance encounter with God." He seethed. "Do you see anyone else? Is anyone else keeping you out of the VPSO's office? Your daughter isn't. She's tired of your crap—she told me so herself. You don't have a wife or parents. Your other children aren't sitting around waiting to bail you out. No nieces. No nephews to keep you company or go berry picking with. No one else to offer your fish." He was on a roll. "You have none of those things, Alexie. None."

Geoff jabbed a finger into his own chest. "You have me. Okay? Me. I'm the one that's here listening to you jabber all night. I'm the one who gave up an evening of prayer and spending time with someone special so that I could babysit you. You are the problem here. Not me. Don't worry about how I came to Christ. This is about you getting a chance—probably your last chance if you don't give up the bottle. Because you aren't promised another minute, and I'm going to be on that next plane out. Do you hear me? You don't know if someone else will be willing to come out here. You don't know that someone else will give up their modern conveniences to shit in a bucket for your wasted soul. And if no one does," he said, losing steam, "then you're facing an eternity in the pits of hell, my friend. And no one will be able to help you there. Because it'll be too late."

Geoff threw himself back against his pillow, angry and embarrassed at his tirade, but too upset to apologize. Of all the places in the world God could have sent him, He chose here. A forsaken place that provided so little activity to keep one's mind occupied. If Geoff wasn't careful, the memories would swallow him whole, and he might never recover.

"You don't know me," Alexie said. Every now and then he purposely bumped his head against the wall, savoring the noise and the contact. The sensation reminded him he was alive, that he had a problem that needed solved. He had to get past the alcohol. This wasn't the first sermon he'd heard, and Geoff wasn't the first person to remind him that his future looked grim.

When Geoff closed his eyes, sleep met him with a vengeance. With it came the nightmare he could narrate without emotion. After all, when a person has witnessed death numerous times, a person becomes numb. Unable to garner the slightest emotion. Desensitized. He knew the order of events. He'd witnessed them firsthand. It was the after effect that brought on anxiety and heart palpitations. The hourly date with guilt that nearly did him in. Thicker than honey and swarming with bees. How did a man get past the fact that he'd killed not one, but two people? How did a man lead a normal life after that?

****

Geoff was on the cusp of his eighteenth birthday the night of the crash. He had a couple of beers at a friend's house and walked home. Still in high school, he lived with his parents, the same loving couple who'd celebrated countless years of marriage. He hated them. One day he was eager to please them and enjoyed spending time with them. Then next, a bitterness and angst built up inside him like a volcano ready to erupt.

At home he ransacked the kitchen and found nothing he wanted to eat. His mother tried to placate him with an egg salad sandwich and a glass of iced tea. "Something simple," she said. Geoff knew what that meant. He would end up sitting there while his parents tried to talk some sense into him. Not a conversation he wanted to have or the kind of meal he craved. Geoff wanted fried chicken. The greasy kind from a bucket that was a five-mile drive from the house. He went straight for his father's car keys that hung from a hook by the door.

"Where are the keys?" Geoff demanded when his hand scraped the hook, and no keys materialized.

"You don't need them, Geoffrey," his mother said. "I told you. I'll make you some egg salad." Her voice shook as it often did when Geoff stormed through the house.

At six feet one inch tall, Geoff towered over his mother, Jane. She was petite and thin. She and her husband Buck had Geoff later in life, and their health had steadily declined since his birth.

"I told you I don't want egg salad." Geoff's words slurred despite his determination to sound cold and hard. He'd recently broken up with a rather nagging girlfriend who was always telling Geoff what he should wear and where he should take her. The last thing he needed was his mother doing the same—always nagging him to clean his room and stand up straight. To eat a cold sandwich when all he wanted was chicken. "I'm going out. I need the keys."

Buck came up behind Jane and put his hand on her shoulder. He was as tired of Geoff's behavior as she was. "Not tonight, son. You're in no shape to drive anywhere."

Geoff rolled his eyes. He didn't tower over his father. He matched him inch for inch and outweighed him by an easy twenty pounds. "What are you going to do to stop me?" He postured as if he wasn't above swinging a punch. A trick he'd learned in the last year. If you swaggered just enough, your opponent backed down. It was all he needed. He had no interest in a fight.

"I'll call the police. You won't treat your mother or me like this anymore."

The police. That was new. Before it had been grounding him or piling on the chores. Yelling matches most of the time. But the more resistant Geoff was, the more his parents had given in. Each day giving up a little more authority.

"Stop playing games. Give me the keys, and I'll go. You won't have to deal with me."

"I don't think so. I've already got the neighbors keeping an eye on things." Buck pulled back the shade from the window.

Across the street, a husband and wife couple raked leaves in the misty rain that had started to fall. It was an obvious ploy. Geoff didn't know them well, but they had taken a liking to his parents. The two couples often chatted over coffee and his mother's Bundt cake. The husband was good buddies with Geoff's football coach. If the coach got wind that Geoff was drinking and being a smart ass, he'd bench Geoff at the next big game. No college scouts. No free ride. No relief from his suffocating parents. Geoff needed a new plan before he lost his cool.

"Mom, come on. Don't do this. You know I love you. I'm just, you know." Geoff ran his hands through his mop of hair. "I don't know what I am. Having a tough time, I guess. Since Mandy and I broke up, I'm not myself. You know I'm not like this. You know I'm an all right kind of guy, Mom."

"I love you, too. And I know you can be a good boy, Geoffrey. So does your father. Right, Buck?"

His parents were old. That was the problem. Geoff needed discipline and boundaries. Did his parents see him giving his coach shit? No, because his coach wouldn't put up with it. Not like his aging parents whose faces were heavy with the weight of Geoff's rebellion. They couldn't cage him in, and Geoff knew it.

This was the first time Geoff had said he loved his mother in ages, and the look on Jane's face made it clear how much those precious words meant. He worried she would relent.

"Jane, honey," Buck said. He wanted this time of their lives to be over. For Geoff to grow up. When Buck turned eighteen, he was already commissioned to the Navy. Out of the house at basic training and behaving like a man. After that, he'd come home and married Jane. He was a man in every sense of the word. But, his son. Lord help him, his son was nowhere near ready to grow up or take a wife. It was a pity, too, because he'd had the potential for a good one in Mandy.

"He said he's sorry, Buck. We have to give him the benefit of the doubt," Jane said solemnly.

"See? Mom, I knew you'd understand." Geoff gave her a sheepish grin and hugged her tightly as he held out his hand for the keys.

"That's fine, son, but you're still not taking the car. I know you've been drinking," Buck said.

"Mom!"

"Buck," Jane said, holding tight to the hope that her son was apologetic. "We can go together. Like a family. Wouldn't that be nice?" She gave her son a shy smile. She wanted nothing more than for her husband and son to get along.

"Come on, Dad. A family supper? We can do that for Mom, right? The sweetest lady we know?" Geoff pecked her on the cheek.

"If that's what your mother wants," Buck said, "but I'm driving."

They trooped out to his father's Buick where Geoff made a show of opening the rear passenger door for his mother. She preferred the backseat to the front when the family was together. She said it gave her men time to bond. Geoff thought it had less to do with that and more to do with his mother feeling like she was chauffeured like a queen, but he didn't argue. There was no sense in it. He shut the door and chatted with his father about the weather, angling for a way to snag the keys.

"Getting chilly ain't it, Dad? Snow'll be flying soon." Geoff rubbed his hands together even though it was more dreary than cold.

Buck nodded and pulled his windbreaker around his middle. Aside from the graying hair and receding hairline, his age showed in the slight bulge of his waistline. Rain dotted his bifocals, and he wiped them clean, showing the age spots that decorated the backs of his hands. The aches and pains had been present for a handful of years, and the light rain made them worse. If he could get through the next few months until Geoff moved out, life would get easier.

"They're nice people, aren't they?" Geoff asked.

"Who?" Buck stood with his back to the street, his gaze drawn to Jane in the backseat. Her generosity and belief in their son had aged her as well.

"The Connors. The neighbors." Geoff smiled broadly and waved at them. The neighborhood crime watch making sure

Geoff didn't upset his parents again. He needed them off his case and back inside minding their own business. Maybe he was rebellious, but Geoff wasn't a criminal. He wasn't dangerous.

Buck turned and waved at the Connors, too. They were nice. He appreciated their kindness. Just the week before over cake and coffee, Buck shared their family's troubles about their son. The Connors had been gracious, offering to help out any way they could, and this was it. Watching from across the street, ready to call the cops if Buck or Jane gave the signal that they needed an extra hand.

With his father distracted, Geoff casually hugged Buck and snagged the keys that hung loosely in his hand. "I can drive. Hop in," Geoff said. He ran to the other side of the car where he popped open the driver door and slid behind the wheel.

Buck considered going through with it. He'd give the signal— a two-pronged approach in which he'd raise the hood and call out, "Something's wrong with the engine I think." Mrs. Connor would go inside and call the police while Mr. Connor would come across to help with the imaginary car trouble. Later, Buck would spend the evening consoling Jane, who would cry against his shoulder. Heartbroken that they'd managed to raise a son they couldn't handle. After, Buck would spend the twilight hours nursing a glass of whiskey, talking to himself about all the things he had done wrong as a father and all the things he wished he'd done right.

But he didn't. He looked again at his wife's pretty face. The woman he'd vowed to spend his life with, and his resolve crumbled. Buck could look his son in the eye and take the verbal blows while the boy was hauled off to county with his hands cuffed behind his back. It was Jane he wouldn't be able to face. The sins of the father are passed down to the son, and apparently a bad apple doesn't fall far from the tree.

Maybe this time Geoff was sorry. Maybe if they lightened up a bit, the next couple of months wouldn't be so bad. The three of them could make things work if they tried. He waved and smiled at the neighbors again. He gave his son the benefit of the doubt and climbed into the Buick.

"Looks like our boy is going to take us out for fried chicken, Jane." He patted Geoff on the shoulder.

"He's a good boy, Buck," Jane replied.

Geoff said nothing as he turned over the ignition and put the car in drive. A mile into the journey, he turned up the windshield wipers to keep up with the rain. He reached for the radio dial and turned until he found his station. When his father tried to change it, Geoff pushed his hand away.

"I'm driving. I have control of the radio," Geoff said. He was hungry and irritable. If Mandy hadn't been such a nag, he wouldn't have had to break up with her. They could be going out for supper together instead of him having to spend the evening with his parents.

Jane started up from the backseat. "Geoffrey, can you turn that down? Your father doesn't like that awful rock music."

"It's metal, Mom. Not rock," Geoff told her, his hand on the dial.

"Well, he still doesn't like it. Can you please turn it down?"

"I like it. And I'm driving. Just calm down okay? We'll be there in a minute. Geez."

His mother sounded like Mandy. *Turn the radio down so we can talk. Let's double date with Holly and her boyfriend. I don't want to go to second base, Geoff. I said no. Take your hands off me.* Women were supposed to submit, not call the shots.

"Your mother asked you nicely," his father said.

From the backseat, she started up again. Then they were both talking and trying to get their way. Geoff was sick of it. He cranked the volume up until the sound of electric guitars vibrated against his skull. He punched the accelerator as they rounded a curve.

Occasionally, when the memory visited him, sharp as a tack in the sole of his foot, he heard his mother's screams. Sharp and piercing, then fading into nothing. Just the quiet evening and the sound of falling rain, punctuated by the weight of the car landing on his lower half. His right leg, just below the knee, hot with pain, like a blow torch against the bone.

He woke up in the hospital surrounded by white. Linens.

Bandages. White capped nurses in white uniforms that hovered over him and around him with their translucent thermometers and smiles with white teeth. Under your tongue please. His arm laid stiff and useless in a white plaster cast. The call button was a small white box attached to his bed, which held him in its white bed rail arms.

Finally, a doctor in blue scrubs came in accompanied by a chaplain. They wore matching somber expressions. The doctor fidgeted. He knew how to fix broken bones, remove infections, and cut off the source of disease. Though the latter troubled him, he still felt a sense of accomplishment when it was over knowing he'd saved a life. It was death he didn't understand. Nor did he know how to console this young man who'd lost more than a leg.

"The leg will heal, son. With or without it, you'll be fine. Just fine. Hard at first—things will be hard. Have to adjust is all. When you do, you'll be okay." The doctor checked his notes. "In fact, science has come a long way. We can try a prosthetic when you're ready. Say the word, and I can make it happen. Name's Freemont, by the way. Dr. Freemont. Let me know how I can help. Okay?"

"What about my folks? They were...with me." Geoff hesitated to say he'd been driving.

"I'm sorry, son." The chaplain held his Bible against his chest, a shield against the pain.

I'm sorry. Gone. Forever. People didn't die on their way to get fried chicken. He felt the rain. He heard the music. The radio dial in his hand. Slick wet leaves that fluttered through the damp air until they landed on the slippery pavement. The guard rail. Trees. His father's arm reaching out. The sound of their screams. The weight of the car. The pain in his heart. He couldn't breathe.

The guilty sobs racked his body. The riptide pulled him in, and he could not find his way to the surface. If the car accident hadn't killed him, the grief and guilt would. Forgive me Father, for I have sinned.

"The community, your neighbors mostly, took up a collection, and they held a memorial service for your family. You've been out of it for a while now. The doctors were afraid you wouldn't make it."

"But we took good care of you," the doctor interjected. "You'll be good as new soon. Touch football maybe with a prosthetic. But no tackle. Otherwise, you can do most anything. Your girl was happy to hear that."

His girl?

"Mandy something. Blonde, curly hair. Sweet girl. She's been by every day to see you. She talks real highly of you. You're going to be okay. We made sure of it. Get a prosthetic, and you'll be fine. Just fine," the doctor said.

"Try not to be angry at your father, Geoff," the chaplain said as he put a hand on Geoff's shoulder. "Before he...passed...he told the paramedics he was sorry. He hadn't meant for anything bad to happen. His last words were how much he loved you and your mother. Let that be a peace for you. All right? He loved you. Don't let bitterness take root, Geoff. You have to accept God's will."

****

Geoff found out later that the car had flipped and ejected him. His father had been thrown into the driver's seat and then partially through the windshield. The head trauma had taken him minutes after he'd apologized, claiming fault for the accident. Jane had died instantly from a heart attack.

No one questioned Geoff. No one interrogated him or examined the angle of the car at impact against the location of its occupants. No one seemed to notice that it didn't make sense how Geoff, presumably in the passenger seat, had gotten pinned under the driver's side of the vehicle. They had simply taken Buck Stone at his word. Accepted the fact that he'd miscalculated the curvature of the road. The car had gotten away from him leaving its passengers powerless.

The Connors were the only ones who knew the truth, and he wasn't sure what they would do with the information.

As Geoff learned to walk with a walker and then with crutches, he learned a great deal of information about his parents from their lawyer. He was an only child, and though he had a maternal aunt, she was much older than Jane had been and lived in a nursing home with dementia at the time of her sister's death. No one told the woman about the accident. Geoff was left to figure out the estate plans on his own.

His parents had been financially sound. They owned a row house in San Francisco that they'd purchased during the early years of their marriage when they had traveled west for their honeymoon. Located on Steiner Street, the house was part of a collection of pastel painted homes called the Painted Ladies. Though they had returned to North Carolina to set down roots and be near Jane's sister, they dreamed of making California their retirement destination. Once, during a small blip in the market, Buck and Jane lost a good renter and suffered through a series of bad ones. To offset the loss of income, they'd contracted someone to remodel and the two-story house became two smaller units. An unexpected plan that turned out to be a good investment. By the time Geoff was thirteen, there was no debt. They continued to live well on the East Coast, and soon, when Geoff was ready for college, they'd be able to sell their family home and relocate out west.

Geoff inherited everything. An unlikely exchange for having killed his own parents and the Connors agreed. The couple came to Geoff's home on a dreary day giving Geoff a sense of déjà vu. He let them in. Mandy, who was helping him with laundry, stepped out of the room at his request.

"You doing okay?" Mr. Connor asked.

"I guess. It's hard. Them not being here," Geoff admitted.

Mr. Connor nodded. "Yes. Something like this forces a person to grow up. Be a man."

"Yes, sir," Geoff answered. He didn't know what it meant to be a man but had a feeling Mr. Connor was implying Geoff needed to take his licks and own his behavior.

"We've been talking," Mr. Connor said. "Me and my wife. And we decided." He squeezed his wife's hand and lowered his voice. "Not to say anything."

"You mean..." Geoff wasn't sure how to finish his sentence.

He looked over his shoulder for any sign of Mandy.

"That's right."

Geoff's relief was followed by the sour taste of guilt. Not only for what he'd done to his parents, but for what this lie was clearly costing the Connors. They were good people. How many times had he heard his parents say that?

"I don't know what to say," he mumbled on the verge of tears. Damn, he was always crying or almost crying these days.

"We should have done something. We could have. And now," Ms. Connor dissolved into quiet sobs.

Mr. Connor helped up his wife and led her to the front door. There wasn't much any of them could say to soothe the other. "They were good people. They didn't get a second chance. You did. Take it, son."

As soon as it seemed an appropriate time of mourning and recuperation, Geoff sold his parents' home and moved into an apartment with Mandy. They tried to make it work, but the nagging and arguments escalated. She wanted him to open up to her, and he didn't dare. After six months, Geoff told her he'd found a job in the Midwest. Something simple and sedentary, far away from the place that had ruined his life and his dreams. Mandy had no desire to join him. She was fearful of his hot temper and had no idea how to help him. She cried when he packed his belongings and drove out of town. He cried, too.

After a decade of traipsing around the Midwest, Geoff was out for a drive, exploring a new city in Indiana when he stopped for gas. He was between jobs and on the hunt for something different. A new town with new people. In a diner over a burger and fries a small town preacher sidled up to him for a friendly chat. The preacher knew someone who knew someone and something about a community mental health agency in search of a receptionist. Geoff was wary. It sounded like a woman's job, but the preacher was persuasive.

He took the chance. If it didn't work out, he could pick up and leave again. Go further west, maybe even to San Francisco. The doctor had been wrong. It wasn't the leg that needed managing. It was the guilt. As it turned out, Geoff stayed in the job for a year. He settled into a one-bedroom apartment, adopted Bridgette, and made decent friends in the agency. One friendship stood out among the rest—the one with Starr Randel.

****

By the time the sun rose to its height in Hooper Bay, Geoff's neck was stiff and sore. His eyes burned from the fitful night of sleep. He stretched and yawned, assessing every ache. As he struggled into a sitting position, he took stock of the sights and sounds rattling around in the air.

Alexie snored like a freight train. He slept propped up in the opposite bed. The salmon jar was on the floor empty. His mouth hung open, and Geoff imagined flies buzzing about the vinegary smell of brine. Alexie's daughter hadn't allowed him to go home for his toothbrush. Geoff made a mental note to order a gross and ship them to the village. It would be part of his and Penny's action plan.

Overhead, Geoff heard the drone of small planes free to travel above the delta without the nuisance of fog and rain. He hoped for a light breeze to keep the mosquitoes away. A day like that meant the tundra would come to life with folks drying out from the last few days of bum weather. Kids would be out playing in shorts and qaspeqs with rain boots in case of leftover puddles. Any uncovered skin would be puffy and itchy, proof that little boys and girls were like buffets to the droves of mosquitoes that hid in the tundra, waiting to be discovered.

"Time to get up. Day's half over." Geoff nudged Alexie with his foot. He wasn't ready for another day with his charge, but he would deal with him if it meant a shower and movement to work out the night's kinks. Then breakfast. Preferably with Penny. He'd asked her to pray for him, and the sound of her voice might soften the unruly ache in his heart.

He had so many what-if's running through his head. Was God calling him to a life in the mission field? What if God was calling him to end things with Starr? Could he do that? Did he want to? Had God finally forgiven Geoff for the deaths of his parents? If so, what he had he done to gain that forgiveness?

"Just give me a sign, God," he whispered.

Someone pounded on the door and matched the pounding in his head. "Geoff? Geoff, it's Penny. Wake up."

Geoff rubbed the sleep from his eyes. He'd slept in his prosthetic to make trips to the honey bucket easier in the night, and now he struggled to a standing position. He hoped Alexie wouldn't wake up just yet. If this was a sign from God, Geoff didn't want any interruptions. "Coming. I'm coming."

He eased the door open and stepped into the arctic entryway. His rain boots and Alexie's were tossed in one corner. Geoff's jacket hung crooked from a nail. Out here people took their shoes off before entering a house. The foyer became a landing pad for shoes, boots, outdoor gear, and small chest freezers filled with the season's harvest. Berries, salmon, moose, caribou.

One thing Geoff appreciated about Penny was her calm demeanor. Unlike Starr, Penny talked through problems and was appreciative of Geoff's offers to help. Starr fretted internally and was often inconsolable. She pushed Geoff away when he tried to intervene.

"You have to go, Geoff. Rudy just called. It's Starr. You have to. You can't stay. They can get a plane out. It'll be ready soon."

"Hey, calm down. Slow down. What do you mean Rudy called?" Geoff touched her shoulder in an effort to soothe her.

"He called the church. That's where I was. Praying. I've been feeling so bad, and I needed to get it off my chest. To talk to God and get past this. I was the only one there, and he called. It's my fault. I know it is." She flailed her hands and kept looking behind her.

"Stop. Nothing is your fault." Geoff could barely keep up. He grasped her hands in his. "Penny, slow down. I'm here. We can figure it out together. Whatever it is. Start from the beginning."

Penny took a cleansing breath. "From the beginning. Okay. I was at the church. I was praying."

Geoff rubbed her hands. "And then Rudy called?"

She yanked her hands free. "I wasn't trying to cause problems. Honest. I just thought because you were here and I'm here. That maybe there was something. I don't know. It's stupid. But you said I was like Boaz. I mean that you were like him. I didn't think. And now this."

Penny was half crying again, her hands fluttering in front of her face like psychedelic butterflies that didn't know where to land. Her gaze danced about never landing on Geoff for long. Her voice rose and fell with every half sentence until Geoff wanted to grab her by the shoulders and shake the whole story out of her head.

"What happened, Penny?" he demanded. Penny stopped talking, shut right up as if a leak had been plugged. Then she gulped a deep breath and blurted, "Starr is in the hospital. She tried   to   kill   herself."

CHAPTER SEVENTEEN

Geoff made it as far as Bethel and got weathered in. The ground fog that rolled in thick as butter didn't care that Starr needed him back home. He stumbled into a coffee shop located upstairs from Marlane Aire, the same airline that had just deposited him. He had no choice but to pray and wait for the weather to improve.

Inside the coffee hut, he sank heavily in a folding metal chair and pulled himself close to the table. It was covered in a plaid vinyl tablecloth and remnants of the last customer's order. He refused to cry. This was his punishment for his recent sins and getting caught up in some romanticized notion of a Biblical fairy tale.

"Boaz," he muttered. "More like Bozo." How could he have been so dense?

He needed a plan. Until he was sure about what was going on with Starr, he had to be prepared for anything.

No more pretending. No more hopeful fantasies that suicide and depression will go away if we brush it aside. Starr will have to accept that she needs help.

His bag was packed tight with clothes, shoes, and various items he'd collected since the trip began. He knew he had a notebook in there somewhere, and he let his hands be his guide instead of dumping his gear all over the dirty floor. In the tundra, particularly Bethel, the ground was covered with a sheen of silt in the summer. The dry weather and constant wind pushed the volcanic ash around until it coated people and vehicles. When the wind ceased, the dust settled, and people carried it around on the bottoms of their shoes and muck boots. A broom stood in the corner of the coffee shop—a lonely soldier in the war on cleanliness.

"Almost there," Geoff said to himself when he wrapped his fingers around a pen with no cap. He set the pen next to his untouched coffee and reached into the bag again for a notebook. Anything would do at this point even if he had to write on the back of a VBS booklet. He felt along the inner lining for the pockets he'd managed to forget. They were deep, and perhaps he'd shoved a notebook or two inside one of them in his haste to escape San Francisco. He wanted to cheer when his fingers grazed a hard corner wedged inside the folds of the opening. He yanked back the zipper to a get better hold.

"Finally."

Along with the treasure he'd been seeking came a small container of hazelnut coffee creamer and one of Starr's bracelets. Geoff rubbed furiously at his eyes. His nose ran, and he sniffed back the emotion as he gave his table and the one next to it a once over.

"You got any napkins?" he asked the guy behind the counter.

The worker was an older guy, race unknown. He wiped down his counter with strong arms, a vicious circular motion, and a well-used rag. His ears stuck out from his head, but his hearing didn't seem to match.

"What?" The guy cupped a large hand behind one ear.

"Napkins. You got a napkin? Something to wipe the table or my face." Geoff made a washing motion above the table and over his face. "Napkins."

"Aye. Yeah. I'm coming." He hurried behind the counter and swept the rag across the vinyl tablecloth. "Hold your horses. You want coffee?"

Geoff grabbed his items one by one and lifted them when instructed. "Sure," he replied.

The beaded bracelet had been his idea, a last-minute item he'd found in the attic in an old cigar box. To Geoff, it looked like something a novice had made, and he'd chosen it because he didn't think it had much value. If he happened to misplace it, the loss would be small. Starr's menagerie of bracelets was one of her coping mechanisms. He thought he'd be more aware of her if he had the trinket with him even while far away. He was ashamed he hadn't even pulled it from his bag.

The creamer was a three-ounce surprise. Six weeks into the trip and he'd managed to push his relationship so far onto the back burner of his mind, he hadn't even realized Starr had put the little bottle into his bag. Drop of rain fell against the coffee shop window and streaked the dirty pane. He put his hand against the dry side of the window.

"Not raining in here, but the coffee will keep you warm." The man with the ears set a Styrofoam cup of black coffee in front of Geoff and returned to his counter.

A little boy, no more than four or five, climbed into the folding chair opposite Geoff. The boy's hair was the color of ink, straight like Midwestern straw. He mimicked Geoff and put a chubby hand against the glass. "Raining, see?" he said and held out his hand for Geoff to inspect.

When Geoff didn't show any interest, the boy pulled his hand away and scrambled off the chair. He ran out the open door and down the stairs to the airline terminal. His muck boots slapped the floor as he ran. Geoff looked out the window again, unable to pray or think. His plan to form a plan was a failure. It was no surprise to him when Ian looked back at him and then sat in the chair the little boy had vacated.

"Do we have to do this now?"

"That's part of the problem," Ian said. "You're always running away."

"I didn't run from the mission field. God called, and I went, didn't I?" Geoff reminded him. He tore the wrapper from the creamer container and squirted four shots into his coffee. The cream dove below the surface and stirred up the cheap coffee. A handful of grinds floated on the surface. Geoff cupped the Styrofoam with both hands and held it to his nose. He breathed in Starr's scent, and he needed a napkin more than ever.

"You miss her," Ian said.

"If she knew who I really was—if she knew my past—she would dump me."

"So you can be forgiven by God but not by man?"

Geoff bristled. "Weren't you the one who told me she wouldn't understand? That she wouldn't be able to forgive me for what I did?" He gulped the flavored coffee, burning his tongue and tasting Starr's presence all at once.

Ian shrugged. He tore the napkins into thin pieces and piled them together like kindling. "Do you forgive her?"

"You can't be serious. I'll be lucky if she forgives me. I'm the one who failed here. I'm the one who didn't keep my promise to her."

"You can't fix her. You can't be there every minute," Ian said.

"I shouldn't have left."

Geoff's cell phone rang before Ian could remind him of his earthly limitations. The Hooper Bay church number danced across the screen. He didn't want to answer it, worried that Starr had taken a turn for the worse and they were calling to tell him he was too late. Had she found a way to end it all while under the watchful eye of medical professionals?

"Hello?"

There was the faint sound of static, and Geoff pictured the far-off village by the bay where he often felt as if he was about to float away from civilization. It had been both peaceful and unsettling as he walked along the beach, the water cold to the touch despite the sun hanging above him. That yellow ball was a deceiver.

"Waqaa, Brother Geoff."

"Alexie?" Geoff asked, surprised.

The old man said nothing, and Geoff knew he was on the other end, his eyebrows raised in a silent yes to Geoff's question.

"What can I do for you?"

"You left in a hurry," Alexie said. Geoff turned away from the dining area for privacy. Outside on the tarmac, a handful of puddle jumpers were tethered to the asphalt. The wind knocked against the planes making them look like toys being tossed about by an invisible hand. Geoff felt the same way. His mind was all over the place trying to decide what to do and how best to help Starr. Splattered with the memories of the loss of his parents, and muddied with the confusion his feelings for Penny left in the pit of his stomach.

"I have a family emergency," he said into the phone. "Sorry, I didn't say goodbye."

"You make it to Bethel?"

"Barely. Weathered in now. Hoping to fly out tonight."

"It will work out."

His eyes watered. "I hope so," Geoff answered.

"I can keep you company," Alexie said.

Geoff pulled the phone away from his ear and reeled it back in. He didn't have the time or patience for this. "That's kind of you, Alexie, but I'm afraid I'm not in any shape for conversation. Not right now."

"Maybe not conversation but company at least. You stayed with me."

Alexie's timber was strong unlike Geoff had heard it before. He was sober and clear minded through the phone line. Geoff found an unlikely comfort in his voice. "In my culture, we are qulirista. Storytellers. We believe everyone has a story inside them. A life story, a story that teaches or has morals for the younger generations. We believe elders deserve respect and have wisdom to share with their children and grandchildren, even their great grandchildren."

"Those are good values," Geoff said.

"I have many stories inside me."

Geoff knew Alexie wouldn't tell the story unless Geoff asked him to. It wasn't in the Yup'ik culture to push themselves on someone. The Yup'ik people were patient, believers in radical acceptance of whatever they encountered. Bad weather, poor hunting seasons, disease, and even death. Whatever the universe doled out, Alexie and his people didn't push back.

"Okay," Geoff said. He didn't want to be rude.

In Hooper Bay where the sun shined in contrast to the weather in Bethel, Alexie Daniels held his daughter's phone against his ear and trudged along the beach. The ocean water rolled up to the sand and eased its way out again. This was his happy place. His hair and ears were clean from his wash in the steam. He wore fresh clothes, and though they were disheveled, they made him feel both confident and humble. He was on day four of sobriety. The change refreshed him.

"In my culture," Alexie said, "we talk about where we came from. We know our roots and our ancestors. Often we are named after another, a relative who has passed away or an elder who has influenced a community. My wife would say: My name is Agausin Esther Bean Daniels. Named for my mother of Chevak and my father is Samuel "Sam" Bean of Toksook Bay. She knew her grandparents and great-grandparents. Whenever we traveled, she ran into her aunts, uncles, and cousins. She was well known by her Yup'ik name, Agausin, and her English name. People loved her dearly. My granddaughter is named for her. Other girls have been named for her, too."

"You must miss her terribly," Geoff said.

"If she were here still, I would tell her I'm sorry. I would be a better husband."

Geoff was in no mood to counsel Alexie. "I'm sure you did your best."

"I was jealous of Esther. When others praised her and spoke highly of her family heritage, I made fun. 'For a Native woman, she can't cut seal. She makes akutaq like a kass'aq—berries but no salmon.' I hurt my Esther because I was hurting."

Along the shore, Alexie stopped walking. He stood in silent remembrance of a wife he lost too soon. The memories that washed up with the shells were hard and pointed. They pricked his conscience like the shells against his bare feet. He had to tread carefully, or he would find himself at the bottom of a bottle.

"When that wasn't enough, I drank. One bottle. Two. Ten. It took away all of my misery, all my pain. But it hurt her. All because of jealousy."

Geoff waited patiently on his end of the phone. If there was an uplifting point to Alexie's story, it couldn't come soon enough. Geoff thought his guilt had reached capacity, but he found room to add more. Jealousy is a spiteful emotion when you think someone has it more or better than you do.

Alexie continued, "My wife knew who she was. Not me. My father was Carl Daniels. He was a good man from Hooper Bay. Part of Castner's Cutthroats platoon. He helped fight the Japanese in Adak. He was a warrior."

"I didn't know that," Geoff said. The historical tidbit sliced through his worries.

"I was adopted to his sister. They called her Lady. And her husband Bo. I know my adopted parents' parents, but I do not know my mother. I never knew her. She left me."

Quiet tears filtered through to Geoff's side of the phone. "Alexie?"

"It's okay. Tears are good. They're part of the healing process," Alexie said. He sniffled and breathed through the pain. He wanted a bottle. He wanted Agausin. If she were there, he would make it right. "Growing up, kids made fun of me, called me names, and teased me with the little information there was about my birth mother, a kass'aq lady from the war."

"But..." Geoff struggled to come up with a suitable finish to his sentence. *But she must have loved you. But women give their children up if they know someone else can take better care of them. But what does this have to do with me?*

"Even that didn't make it right for me to hurt my Esther. Or to cause trouble for my daughter. Did you see the picture?"

"What picture?" There was movement in the coffee shop, people picking up their carry-on luggage, disposing their trash. Geoff checked the time. He had to get to Arctic Air soon.

"The one in your coat pocket. It's my father, Carl Daniels."

Geoff held the phone with his shoulder and patted down his pockets. There, in the right one, was an old photo of a young man in military attire. His face was creased and worn from years of handling. The water was frozen behind him, and a canteen was slung over one shoulder. On the back, were the words, "Circa WWII."

"I didn't know your father was military," Geoff said.

"He wasn't. Not really. He was a rough guy. Mean and angry about what, I don't know. There were battles on Attu and Kiska. A military base was built on Adak, and Native people were driven out of the Aleutian Islands. Only Castner's Cutthroats stayed. They were a group of hard men. Some Native and some only native to Alaska. They knew how to live off the land and how to survive in the cold winters."

Geoff's own problems took a backseat to Alexie's unfolding story. "That's something to be proud of, Alexie. Did you ever get to meet your father?" He had so many questions. *Why did your father give you up for adoption? Did he die in one of those battles?*

"After the war he returned to Hooper Bay. He didn't speak of those days. As a boy, I wanted to know, but I was afraid of what he might tell me. I took the teasing from my peers. In our culture, you respect an adult's silence."

"I don't understand why people teased you. Did they disagree with your father's role in the war?"

"They teased me for who I was. For what I didn't know. Only my adopted mother told me, and even she didn't know all of the story."

"Oh," Geoff murmured, still confused.

"See the picture? The torn edge?" Alexie asked.

Geoff fingered the edge of the photo.

"The missing side shows my birth mother holding me. My adopted mother told me she was a nurse in the Navy in Adak. The picture was taken when they gave me to my parents and returned to Adak. After that my kass'aq mother tore me and her out of the picture and left the rest with my father." Alexie paused, and Geoff pictured him wiping his tired eyes the way he often did when he was upset. "You sure God can use a drunk, Brother Geoff?" The craving was intense.

"God can use any of us," Geoff reminded him.

A man with a safety vest entered the cafe, shouted, "Shuttle going to Arctic. Leaving in five minutes," and left.

"I have to go," Geoff said.

"Eee. Yes"

Neither man hung up.

"Will I hear from you again?" Alexie asked.

Geoff hesitated. "I have a lot going on right now. Family...stuff. I can't promise...anything." He would not cry. He wouldn't.

"I'll pray for you and for your family.

A kass'aq man taught me that prayer is powerful."

Geoff smiled. "Yeah, it is. Thank you, Alexie. I appreciate it." He had to get off the phone.

"Quyana."

CHAPTER EIGHTEEN

Starr knew the drill from having admitted a handful of her own clients to acute care facilities. No sharp utensils. No shoe laces. No privacy.

The emergency room sutured her wrists. Six and eight, respectively. The black threads wove tight little train tracks up each arm. Her bracelets wouldn't cover those scars. It was the loneliness that crept in and took up lodging beneath her breastbone that surprised her. No amount of deep breathing seemed to help. Sdax shut down.

"I gave in, Sdax. I finally agreed to the party you begged for, and this is how you treat me. You know what this means, don't you?" Starr asked.

Liam Bernard watched his newest client from the one-way monitor in the hallway. "Who's she talking to?" he asked the nurse on duty.

"Beats me. Do you see someone in there with her?" The nurse jotted some numbers on his patient list and walked away. "I thought you were the psychiatrist around here."

"Therapist," Liam muttered. "Counselor, if you prefer." He hated the misconception that just because he provided care to mentally ill patients that people figured he was a shrink.

A true shrink was a medical doctor, a psychologist, or a psychiatrist. All of them held a doctorate degree of some sort. Medical doctors and psychiatrists could prescribe medications to their patients. Liam was considered a mid-level provider. He carried a leather satchel, a DSM5 manual, and a master's degree in professional counseling.

"It means my master's degree is useless," Starr said to her silent wisp. "It means no job, no real quality of life. And these," She said, holding up her bandaged wrists. She scooted to the head of the bed, pulled her knees against her chest, and rested her forehead on her knees. The smaller she made herself, the less the nurse could see her. "You can't just..." She wanted to lecture Sdax and make her understand the gravity of the situation, but she had trouble finishing her thought. *Can't just what? Trick me into thinking I want to live? Pretend this wasn't your idea?* "You can't just change your mind about something like—something this serious," Starr scolded.

She couldn't bring herself to say it. Death. Dead. It was one thing to feel like a failure at love or her career, but to acknowledge she failed at death was the failure of all failures. She was puzzled about how things ended and how Sdax managed to change her mind in those final moments. Starr bit down on her thumb nail and gnawed frantically. Her cuticles were a ragged mess, and nothing had sorted itself out yet.

Starr had been at home, hiding out. The news about a suicide in a nearby community tipped the scales. Unable to fathom a way out, she'd given in to the fear.

"I can't do this anymore, Sdax. It's time." Sdax bounced on her toes.

"Yes! It will be the best party ever!"

That was enough to convince Starr. She laughed for the first time in ages and they scoured her closet for her best dress. She considered one of her favorite Bohemian skirts, but Sdax wrinkled her nose at it. "It has to be special. Like this one."

The dress was a glorious blue and short-sleeved with a trim waist. From the neck to the bodice, the fabric transitioned to the deepest shade of midnight. Along the hem were brilliant white stars. The designer label read: Shooting Stars. She never wore it, but there was something about having a dress named after her that made Starr feel special. She pulled the dress over her head and slipped a pair of nude sandals over her feet. A short-sleeved white sweater helped cover the marks on her upper arms.

"How do I look?" Starr asked.

"So pretty. Can we wear the special bracelet, too? Pretty please?" Sdax held her breath in anticipation.

"A special party definitely calls for a special piece of jewelry," Starr replied. She held out her wrist for the chunky ivory bracelet, and Sdax slid it over her hand. "Ivory covers a multitude of sins."

"Then how come we never wore it before?"

Starr shrugged. "Because people point and ask questions. They want to try it on, which means we have to take it off or risk being rude."

"And that's when they'd see?" Sdax asked.

"Yeah."

Starr clutched the photo of her grandmother holding her uncle against her chest. She imagined seeing them when she crossed over into purgatory or heaven—wherever her deed took her—and tried not to think about what her parents would say if she happened to see them. Then Starr had taken Sdax's small hand in hers, and they marched resolutely into the kitchen where they chose the sharpest knife in the holder.

Starr didn't think of their house as hers any longer. The ivory bracelet was at Geoff's, resting with the box of old letters a safe distance from whatever mess she'd made.

Sdax shimmered into view and stroked Starr's wrists. "Are you mad at me?"

"I'm nothing."

"I think you're something," Sdax said shyly.

"What do you care? Now I have nothing and no one. Neither do you." Starr turned away from her, determined to make Sdax feel as bad as she did.

"They don't have anything either. I saw them," Sdax said. She gripped Starr's fingers, desperately clinging to the woman she needed to protect her.

"Stop talking nonsense. You didn't see anything." Starr pulled the cheap pillow tight against her stomach. "Go play a game or something. I don't want to talk to you right now."

Sdax faded into the far wall at the sound of the entry buzzer. It was the therapist. He was an anomaly with his thick, wiry beard and flannel shirts that he wore untucked over a pair of stiff blue jeans.

"Hey, I figured you might be ready for some company. We have a lot to talk about."

Starr weighed her options and decided talking to him would be easier than reliving the images. She wouldn't give Sdax the satisfaction, but the images of the dead had frightened her.

"Okay," she said.

Liam set down on a folding chair and straddled it backward. His hands were empty, no notebook or pen and no laptop. Starr was struck by the memory of her first session with Morris. *"You're not writing this down?" Was a therapist truly paying attention if he wasn't taking notes?*

Liam Bernard did not look like any therapist Starr had ever known. He was stocky and plump with a bushy beard and dull green eyes. He carried a brown leather satchel over his shoulder, and when he sat, the bag hung along his right side. Her therapist owned a man's bag. Yet he had a rugged look about him, the kind that made Starr think he was used to hiking through the wilderness and foraging for his own food or creating a makeshift shelter out of fallen trees and clumps of drying mud.

"Do you hunt?" she asked. The question made her blush, but she hadn't been able to help herself. His intent and quizzical stare made her feel like prey.

"Sometimes." He wished he was hunting now. High in a tree stand, hunkered down in silence waiting for his prey. Head to toe camo, thick boots with soft soles perfect for sneaking behind an exquisite buck. When he taught clients about finding their happy place, that's where he went.

He missed Pennsylvania. He surreptitiously glanced at his watch. Had missed it for four hundred and eighty-eight days and counting. The heartache was supposed to lessen living in

California. It hadn't, though. He missed his son. Hell, he even missed Georgia though she'd poisoned their son against him.

The summer she moved out, Liam spent more time in the tree stand than at home. He bathed in the creek and cooked what he hunted over a campfire at night. The sound of a crackling fire and his radio his only company. The whiskey and memories tormented him. They called out to him, and he answered, pouring one shot after another until he was drunk on her ghost.

"You?" he asked Starr.

Starr shook her head and blinked back the tears the sound of his voice triggered. Gruff and deep, like water gurgling over a pile of gravel. Unlike Morris' and Geoff's, but it made her think of them just the same. A failed relationship and a failed opportunity to help a client. She was a disaster. "What do you do when you kill something?"

Liam sighed and waited. Therapy was like hunting in that way. The still quiet of an early morning, squinting against the bright daybreak. Listening. His ear trained to listen for the swift footfall of a deer or the lumbering steps followed by the scraping of fur against the trunk of a tree. Long before he set foot in a therapy room, Liam had listened, and it trained him well for that sudden burst of a bullet being released from its chamber, the sound of breakthrough in a client's voice.

He took a sip of water and rattled the ice cubes against the glass as he tried to conjure up the hot burn of liquor against the roof of his mouth and his throat. Smooth oil for his vocal cords would help him think and say the right words. "Depends. Are we talking about animals or people?"

She flinched, and Liam felt bad. As usual, he let his issues with Georgia make him a jerk. "When I hunt, I do it with a mission. A focus."

"Which is?" she asked.

"Sustenance. Food. The meat is how I fuel my body so that I can live."

"How can you do that? Willingly take the life of something. Don't you think it's selfish?"

"So you're a vegetarian."

Starr remembered the fried chicken she and Ms. Caulton had. She hadn't given any thought to the bird's life before breading and frying it. Just like she hadn't given Morris' life any thought the day she decided to transfer him and go out on her own. His blood was on her hands. "I don't think I can do this," she whispered.

Liam got up. "Wait right here," he said, knowing it sounded ridiculous. There was nowhere for her to go.

He returned empty-handed and dug in his satchel. There they were. "Maybe these will help," he said.

Starr didn't want to be intrigued, but the therapist in her couldn't resist. "What are they?"

"They're cards with feeling words on them. I'll hold them up, one at a time, and you let me know if it triggers anything. Or if the word describes an experience you've had. It's nothing special really. You've probably used similar things in your own practice a dozen times." He worried he was rambling and had somehow insulted her skills as a therapist.

"That's pretty good. So the client doesn't have to talk if she...isn't ready. Right?"

"Exactly. Should we give it a try?"

She shrugged.

Abused.

Bullied.

Lonely.

Scared.

Sad.

Guilty.

Ashamed.

Starr flinched. She was ashamed of her actions, for not having known better or pressed harder when Morris' disposition changed. She was a good therapist. She knew better. Or should have. Fear pressed against her sternum and threatened to choke her.

Victim.

Hurting.

Drugs.

"Maybe that's not the best one," Liam said. "I'm not suggesting you're using substances. The medics said there was no trace of alcohol or drugs in your system."

"Then why do you keep holding it up?"

"Right."

Abandoned. Starr thrust her chin upward. He hit a nerve with that one, too.

"By whom?" he asked.

"Everyone," she said, surprising them both.

"That's a lot of people. Can you name them? See if we can shorten the list?"

"My parents. My patients. Geoff." Starr couldn't decide. Was the first or the last harder to say?

"He called again today. He wants to see you."

Geoff was her emergency contact, but he wasn't on her visitor list.

"I doubt it," she responded.

"And your parents? Why did they make the list?" Liam asked.

That was easier. Starr spent years building a thick armor of numbness toward her parents' leaving her. "My father killed my mother and then himself when I was a kid. He left a note that said he was 'tired of her tears'." She waited for his silent assessment of her, for the flicker of shock followed by a forced and rushed recovery. Therapists weren't supposed to have feelings. They weren't supposed to be shocked by anything a client told them. She knew this. She'd done it. Could he pass that same test?

Liam frowned. He looked genuinely sad. "I'm sorry for your loss."

Starr snorted. "You can't be serious. I haven't showered in two days. My food is served on a tray, and I have to use a spoon to eat everything. Someone gets paid to watch my every move from a monitor in the hall."

"And?" Liam challenged.

"And I have real, present day problems. But you want to apologize for my parents' deaths?" She turned away from him. "Try again, oh, wise one."

Liam sipped from his cup and tried not to let her attitude get to him. The job never got easier. He slid something out of his bag. "Do you know who this is?"

"That's my grandmother," Starr said. "That's her son. My mom's brother. I never met him." She slid her finger along the frayed edge of the photo.

Liam put another photo in front of her. It too was frayed along the side. "And him?"

Starr examined the picture closely. The man had dark skin and a deep frown. He wore what looked like army gear and a canteen was slung over one shoulder. Behind him was a body of water. The canteen rested against his right hip and disappeared into the tattered edge of the photo. She shrugged. "No. I don't know him."

Something Starr couldn't identify lurched in her throat. An emotion, a curse, a dry heave—something. The man matched perfectly with her grandmother and uncle. She saw now how the canteen's edge rested against the bulky, dress-like parka her grandmother wore. In fact, the fur trim resembled the man's hat and mittens. The backdrop behind them also lined up—still water stretched as far as the eye could see. Was the water frozen? She turned them over trying to unsee whatever it is that rendered her speechless. But that only made it worse.

"Geoff asked me to bring these to you. He thought you might want this one of your grandmother and that you might recognize this man." Liam knew he was grasping at straws. The photos were a mysterious puzzle he wanted to rule out. If nothing came of it, no harm, no foul.

Starr smirked, and with a deadpan stare, she released the photos and let them flutter to the floor. Her energy depleted. Her eyelids weighed a thousand pounds.

"Starr?" Liam's voice sounded like he was a million miles away.

She ignored him and welcomed the emptiness. She wanted the quiet sound of death to come to her. She pictured the coffin Sdax has repeatedly begged her to see. It was white and sturdy, surrounded by flowers. She breathed in their fragrance. People milled about, murmuring and tearful. It was just like Sdax promised. They'd all come to see her and to celebrate her life. She breathed out the pain. There was a small opening in the crowd, and she stepped into it. Six feet away was her place of eternal rest.

The path was clear and inviting. It would all be over soon.

Dear Reader,

After *Soaring Alone* was released, my childhood best friend asked for Starr's story. Maybe because in my previous life, I was a mental health therapist. Or maybe because in the opening chapter of Soaring Alone, Starr Randel was in session with Rachel James, and while they talked, Starr twisted her bangle bracelets round and round her wrist. Honestly, I never gave much thought to Starr's story. Nor had I expected that scene with the bracelets to be something several readers asked, "What's the deal with the bracelets?" For a long time, even I had no idea what the deal was with those bracelets.

I believe *Shooting Sdax* is meant to be performed on stage. In the early stages of the first draft, that's how I saw it—visually from a premium seat in a dark theater. The characters were different too, linked into the story of the Jones family from my collection Sons of Steel. That story line faltered, and the characters packed up and left. I was devastated. Saying goodbye to Jack-Jack the first time was hard enough. Saying goodbye to his granddaughter Tilly felt like rejection. Though they didn't stick around, Tilly reminded me that I'd written a piece of that collection in second person point of view, which led me back to the vivid details of Carolyn Keynes' book You. If you haven't read You, know that it's graphic, that it has a way of seeping into your being like a tapeworm that won't let go. With Keynes' book on my mind and my grudging resignation to stop trying to be a playwright, I dove into Starr's story where I met Morris and later Liam. It was not an easy book to write. Partly because of the challenges the characters face and partly because I didn't want to see them hurt. In fact, the first time I told my husband about the story line, I cried as I pictured that last scene with Starr and Sdax. My heart broke for them. I knew I was onto something when my husband teared up.

Some people will tell you suicide is selfish. They will remind you of the pain the deceased leaves behind for the living. Perhaps some leave this world for selfish reasons or with vengeance in mind. Others see suicide as the last resort, the only resolution they can think of to stop whatever pain plagues them. We don't know a person's truths unless they feel safe enough to share them with us.

If nothing else, take that thought with you. Be a safe person. Be the kind of person others can talk to and others can lean on. Validate their feelings, thoughts, and ideas. See them as a unique individual. For some, a kind word or a genuine smile goes a long way. You don't have to know all the answers. You don't have to be the 'fix it' guy or gal or hold a degree in psychology to make a difference. When you see someone, say hello. Smile. Pass out compliments with sincerity. That's how we stop the stigma of mental health. That's how we change someone's day—maybe even someone's life.

Sincerely,

V. Jolene Miller

P.S. To help fight invisible diseases, consider giving to the following organizations:

American Association of Suicidology:
          https://www.suicidology.org/
American Foundation for Suicide Prevention:
          https://afsp.org/
National Alliance of Mental Illness:
          https://www.nami.org/

ABOUT THE AUTHOR

V. Jolene Miller is a writer with a LPC. She writes for and about the misfits, the misunderstood, and the underdogs of life. When she's not writing, Victoria enjoys traveling, reading, and running. She lives in the last frontier with her husband and giant puppy, Omar where Victoria works a day job in order to finance her love of pretty notebooks and running gear. She's a 2018 graduate of the University of Alaska-Anchorage where she attained her MFA and received a Jason Wenger Award for Excellence in Creative Writing for her collection, *Sons of Steel*. In January 2019 she launched a combination pop-up/online literary boutique celebrating readers, writers, and the pages between us.

You can connect with Victoria at:
www.authorsinkalaska.com
Instagram @vjolene_author
Twitter @AuthorsInkAK
Facebook @AuthorsInkAlaska